Just Jackie

My Life Is Like a Fruitcake

JENNY CUMMINGS

AN ORIGINAL WOMEN'S FICTION NOVEL

Just Jackie: My Life Is Like a Fruitcake

Copyright © 2021 by Jenny Cummings

Book layout by Amber Helt at www.RootedinWriting.com

ISBN print: 979-8-9851538-0-4

ISBN e-book: 979-8-9851538-1-1

Like my character Jackie, my wonderful, longtime friends have enriched my life.

For my dearest friends, especially my college gang: Mary Beth Kilgore, Georgia Martin, Dianne O'Dell, Kathy Pugsley, Suzi Perry, Priscilla D. Watkins, and our special angel Joan Zinante Matthews.

For Susan, Lynn, and Sylvia.

And every Jackie, Bethany, Donna, Gina, Kate, Susanna, Paula, Phyllis, and Ann I have known.

A NOTE FROM THE AUTHOR

One of the biggest laughs in my family is the A I received on a college creative writing assignment. I was staring at a blank page the night before the assignment was due. What to write? What to write? Nothing came to mind, so I chronicled my family's previous Christmas vacation. Underneath the grade, my professor wrote, "Excellent! You have a very vivid imagination."

It's easy to develop interesting characters when you have an unpredictable family and quirky friends to draw from. While this novel is fiction, I pulled bits and pieces from my personal experiences. Most of my characters are from my imagination, but some are amalgamations of people I have encountered.

In some ways, Jackie is my alter ego. In creating her, I drew from personal experiences and pictured how my life may have turned out if I had made other life choices or had a different family. My wonderful real-life mother was a career woman and an inspiration to me. But what if I had been the daughter of a stay-at-home mom? What if I had married sooner and raised a family? What if? What if?

And what if I try to list all the people who provided inspiration for my characters and plotlines? The list would be too long, and I would hate to forget mentioning someone.

So, a blanket "thank you" to my many amazing friends, family, and former coworkers. I'm blessed to still have close friends from grade school, high school, college, and my post-college career days. My fabulous cousins are also my best friends. And a heavenly "thank you" to my wonderful brother, parents, grandparents, aunts, and uncles. I miss you!

—Jenny Cummings

* * *

1

I stumble from the den to the bathroom, then back to my recliner. Shoulders drooping, feet dragging, and brain dead. If I didn't know better, I might think I died and came back as a zombie. I haven't showered for two days, so when I get a whiff of my armpits, I smell my rotting body.

Not that I know how decaying flesh smells, but I associate it with a dead squirrel I once found in my grandpa's pasture. I still remember that putrid odor and how it made me gag. Now my armpits smell the same way. I want to shower and do something with my frizzy, graying hair, but my tired sixty-nine-year-old body doesn't have the energy.

After eight heartbreaking months, I am ready for the year to end. My morning is spent wallowing in my worn brown corduroy recliner—my home for the past week. I eat, sleep, and devote my waking hours wrapped in the warmth of the chair's overstuffed arms. I still shudder at the thought of sleeping in my bedroom—too many ghosts, too many sad memories.

On an intellectual level, I know spirits aren't roaming my house. But, on an emotional level, when my forty-year-old home settles a bit or the aging plumbing moans, I am convinced spirits want my attention. I've grown used to a friendly presence, but not the sorrowful memories.

Old photo albums and scrapbooks clutter my den. Remembrances of happier days brighten my mood.

The stomach-turning ding-donging of the doorbell jolts me from my peaceful thoughts. I sit silently, hoping the person goes away. *Bang! Bang! Bang!* The pounding starts.

"Jackie, are you home?" my neighbor's grating voice asks. "It's me, Delores. I just want to say hello and be sure you are okay."

I would be okay if my snarky neighbor wasn't hammering her fist on my door. *Better answer or she might call the police.* I crack the door open and stick my head out so she doesn't see me in my pajamas and stinky bathrobe. The humidity rolls in and covers me like a wet blanket.

It is one of those balmy Houston days: midsixties, not too hot, not too cold. It's hard to anticipate December weather here. Some days are wintery and some are summery. Many times, we have winter, spring, summer, and fall all in the same week. The one thing you can count on is the moisture clinging to everything.

"Hello, Delores. I'm fine. Busy tidying up around here." *What a lie.* I haven't done much housekeeping in weeks, and my house looks like a pigsty.

She throws her head back and slaps her right hand over her chest. "Oh my goodness, Jackie. I hope you don't feel as bad as you look."

"I'm okay." Of course, I'm not, but she doesn't deserve to know.

The saccharin in her voice is nauseating. "You poor dear. You've been through so much lately. Is there anything I can do for you?"

"Thank you for your concern. I'll call if I need anything." I politely try to close the door, but she puts her hand in the way.

"I've got a brand-new bottle of Visine," she says in her pretentious la-di-da voice. "I'll be glad to bring it over."

Darn. She's seen too much of my round, bloated face and my puffy, bloodshot eyes. "I have some, but thank you for your concern."

"But your eyes . . ."

I want to slam the door in her face, but that would not be neighborly. So I thank her again and slowly close the door.

What a witch! I don't need her to tell me how I look. I know I am a hot mess—physically and mentally. And she doesn't give a rat's behind about how I am doing. I'm sure she will hustle home and immediately call all the busybodies on the block to tell them how crappy I look.

"Hi, this is Delores," I say out loud, mimicking her prissy voice. "I visited Jackie this morning. She looks like she hasn't slept in a month of Sundays. Just dreadful. Her face is all puffy and her eyes are swollen. And pee-yew, she smells to high heaven. I know the poor dear has been through the wringer lately, but she could at least take a bath. And I'm sure she's got cockroaches living in that messy hair of hers."

While I'm up, I forage for food in the kitchen. What

distinguishes me from a zombie is my craving for comfort cuisine instead of human flesh.

The downside of my not hosting Christmas this year is a lack of leftovers. I already finished the cold pizza and am down to the Christmas fruitcake, which is still unwrapped. I grew up hating fruitcake and still don't care for it.

Aunt Millie, my mother's younger sister, gave us a store-bought one every year. I think she got them on sale in January and saved them for the next Christmas. They were always dry and tasted like cardboard, and each holiday Mom forced us to eat some with our dinner. I couldn't wait to be a grown-up and never have to eat another dry, crappy fruitcake with yucky-looking green stuff in it.

Now, my dear friend Gina makes me one for Christmas. She puts a great deal of love into baking them, so I graciously tell her how delicious they are. As fruitcakes go, hers are pretty tolerable. When Gina said she soaked this year's batch in extra rum and brandy, she wasn't kidding. When I peel off the cellophane wrapper, the strong fumes give me a bit of a high. I return to the den with a generous piece before taking my first bite. The savory blend of fruit and spices explodes in my mouth, and the delicious flame of liquor tickles my taste buds. The pecans crunch as I slowly savor each bite. It is impossible to stop after one slice, so I head back to the kitchen for a second helping.

I debate bringing the entire cake with me to the den, but I keep promising myself each bite will be my last. So much for promises. I justify the repeated trips as needed exercise. By the fifth serving, my slow walk to the kitchen becomes a mad dash for "just one more" piece.

My step has a little more bounce, probably from the rum and brandy.

Lately, I've been trying to convince myself I'm still at my normal weight, despite all my recent months of stress eating. Yes, my weight would be normal if I were six feet tall instead of five-five. Tomorrow is always a good day to start a diet—or whenever I get around to it.

My favorite chair smells like me, so around five o'clock, I decide it's time to take a nice hot shower and wash the rat's nest sitting on my head. Too tired to hold the blow-dryer, I comb my hair and let it air-dry. My golden-brown hair has more silver than gold and has become more wiry than curly. If I don't use conditioner and blow it dry, I have the I-stuck-my-finger-in-a-light-socket look. *I already feel like a zombie, so why not have the hair to match?*

My hair is just long enough to ponytail it through a ball cap or pile it atop my head on bad hair days. Lately, looking presentable hasn't been a big concern, especially on a night when I'm not planning to see anyone.

I open my dresser drawer in search of clean night-clothes and find one lone pair of pajamas—a never-worn gag gift from my best friend Bethany. The tacky black-and-gold leopard-print nylon set has a pullover top with a deep V-neck that points down to black satin letters that read PARTY ANIMAL. I put them on and hee-haw inwardly as I look in the dresser mirror. The plunging neckline might look sexy on a young woman with perkier breasts, but my drooping old boobs are hanging down so low that the lettering is on my waistline and not across my chest. At least the pajamas are clean and have long sleeves and long pants. Good enough for tonight.

It's dark outside when I nestle into my recliner and

nibble on the last treasured piece of fruitcake. It melts in my mouth as I savor each scrumptious crumb.

Fortunately, Delores didn't show up while I was eating the liquor-laden fruitcake. She would have been more gossipy.

"Hi, this is Delores," I tell whatever friendly spirits roam my house. "I visited Jackie this morning. The only thing that stunk more than her smelly body was the alcohol on her breath. I guess she's been drowning her sorrows in booze."

Instead, I'm drowning them in a fruitcake that's drowned in booze.

For the first time in my life, I am all alone on New Year's Eve. But this is the way I want it. No one asking me if I'm okay or tiptoeing around me for fear I might fall apart.

Vroom. Ah-ooo-gah. "Happy New Year." *Beep, beep. Vroom. Ah-ooo-gah.* The sound of rowdy revelers cruising the neighborhood is as bad as listening to a warm-up of a heavy metal garage band. I smash a pillow over my head to muffle the outside racket, but I can't mute the noise inside my head. I begin talking back.

Jackie Jackson, time to get off your fanny and get your act together. My inner voice sounds oddly like my mother scolding me.

You're not the boss of me. I'll do it when I'm good and ready, and I'm not ready. Oh my, I would never talk back to my mother this way.

It's time to stop the pity party.

It's my pity party and I'll cry if I want to. Besides, I've been holding it together for months now. I've earned the right to take a few days off and wallow in my sorrows.

Jackie, it's time to move on.

"Not now," I yell out loud. "I'm too comfortable in my recliner."

Quit feeling sorry for yourself and be grateful for your loving family, great friends, good health—

I am grateful, so quit nagging me, I continue debating in my head.

This is just a small bump in the road of life.

"Enough with the clichés! This is no small bump. I think I hit a giant boulder."

I give up trying to sleep and turn on the TV, then quickly turn it off. I can't handle the joyful celebrations from around the world. On New Year's Eve, it is always midnight somewhere.

Meanwhile, the fruitcake is causing a war inside my body. The sugar rush makes me want to get up and dance, and the liquor makes me drowsy. I haven't slept much lately, so the booze wins the battle. If I can just get a decent night's sleep, I know I can get back to normal— or some semblance of normalcy.

An hour later, I finally feel myself drifting off to a nice, peaceful sleep.

* * *

The booming, crackling sounds of fireworks wake me from my best sleep in weeks. One ear-splitting kaboom shakes the house like a microearthquake. The howling of the neighborhood dogs forms a chorus with the whooshing and crackling explosions that echo throughout the block.

I take a moment to rejoice. "Thank you, Lord, for getting me through these challenging times," I say, clasping my hands in prayer and looking upward. Yes, I am grateful that a difficult year officially ends, and I can start a new one with a clean slate.

After a trip to the bathroom, I try to get back to sleep. The fireworks slow down to small, intermittent bursts as merrymakers drive by honking their horns and screaming, "Happy New Year!"

It's useless to think a pillow around my ears will drown out the noise. I try anyway. Again, the only sound that's louder than the outside racket is the nagging voice in my head.

Jackie—

Zip it, voice! I can't take it anymore!

I grab my purse, jump in the car, and head away from the city. I have no idea where I am headed, but I have a full tank of gas and want to go as far away as my Toyota will take me. Anywhere is better than my house. Too many depressing memories, too many ghosts.

I enter the freeway and head toward an old highway that leads to some small towns. I envision a tranquil, picturesque bed-and-breakfast where I can enjoy a good night's sleep and regroup. A misty fog surrounds the car, and the temperature is dropping. I push the heater knob but cold air blows out. The heater is either broken or I don't remember how to turn it on.

My feet grow colder by the minute. I wiggle my toes and feel a furry sensation covering my feet. Oh my gosh. I left home in my ratty red house shoes. Even worse, I look at my arms and realize I'm wearing the ridiculous nylon party-animal pajamas. *What possessed me to leave home looking like this?* I once wore mismatched shoes to work, wore mismatched dangling earrings to a party, and left home with a jumpsuit on backward, oblivious to the pocket on my back. But going out in my pajamas is a first.

Jackie, what the heck are you doing? Turn the car around and get your big fat rear end back home. Running away won't accomplish anything, especially if you take yourself with you.

Blinding lights, whizzing cars, and hazy fog are more than I can handle. My heart is doing a stomp dance in my chest, and I can barely breathe. I have to head home before I wreck my car or get arrested for indecent exposure.

Toll road? Oh bullcorn. I wasn't paying attention and now I'm on a darn toll road.

I look for an exit so I can turn around and head back home. After a mile or two of nervous driving, I find an off-ramp. A flashing sign greets me and declares I need to pay an exit toll. I grab a handful of coins from my console and toss them in the basket, then drive on the feeder road looking for an underpass where I can make a U-turn. The fog turns into a light rain.

Hopefully, music will calm me. I reach for the radio, momentarily taking my eyes off the road. When I look up, a dog runs in front of me. I hit the brakes. The car spins on the slick road and skids a few feet. Driving 101 —don't slam on the brakes. Especially when the road is damp. My heart beats faster as the stomp dancers come out for an encore. The driver behind me blasts his horn, then waves his middle finger while he passes me. How rude!

By now, I am coming unhinged, and I begin crying. A mental breakdown. Yes, I am having a mental break-down. That explains my erratic behavior. The past few months have been tumultuous, to say the least. Life slapped me to the ground, and when I got back up, I realized the picture-perfect life I had imagined for myself was likely ruined in the photo lab years ago.

Yes, it is obvious. I am having a mental breakdown. I drive a few feet, then pull to the side of the road. I stop the car, close my eyes, take some deep breaths, say a little prayer, and try to compose myself. After a few moments, I feel calmer, open my eyes, and prepare to drive back onto the access road. My foot slides off the brake and hits the gas pedal, causing me to peel out. *Darn house shoes!* More spinning on the damp road and more swerving.

Then comes the ominous *woo-woo-woo-woo* siren noise and red-and-blue flashing lights behind me. Yikes! A police car pulls me over. The stomp dancers in my chest pick up their pace to supersonic speed. I take several deep breaths as I look in the rearview mirror and watch an officer walk toward my car. I roll down my window and turn on my interior light.

He leans into my window. "Good evening, ma'am." He pauses, then corrects himself. "Ah, it's morning, so good morning."

"Good morning, Officer." My car's interior lights allow me to identify him. He is young, Black, and has a wholesome face. His name tag reads NELSON.

"I observed you swerving on the road. Did you do a little too much New Year's Eve celebrating?"

I tremble and do my best to appear composed and sober. "Officer, first a dog ran out in the road and my car skidded when I hit the brakes. Then my foot slipped off the brake and I accidentally hit the gas pedal. I promise you I haven't been drinking."

"ID please." He circles the inside of my car with his flashlight.

I grab my purse and dig through the junk, searching for my wallet. *Oh, crapola! I took it out the other day to pay for the pizza delivery and forgot to put it back!* "I'm sorry, Officer. I left my wallet at home."

He takes a step back. "Ma'am, I need you to exit the car."

I hesitate, wondering what he'll think when he sees my party animal attire.

He blinds me with his flashlight and opens the door. "Ma'am, I asked you to exit the car, so please step out." His words seem harsh, but his tone is calm. I can tell he's a nice guy trying to do his job.

I swing my feet around to make a graceful exit. Instead, I ungracefully stumble out.

"Are you sure you haven't been drinking?"

Oh dear. I hope I'm not drunk on Gina's liquored-up fruitcake.

His voice remains calm. "Please move to the back of your car."

My body shivers in the frigid dampness. I wrap my arms around myself, more to cover my plunging neckline and cold, nippy boobs than to keep myself warm.

"Sir, I promise you, I haven't been drinking. I'm just clumsy. Could I please get my raincoat out of the backseat?"

He retrieves my raincoat and hands it to me. I quickly put it on, hoping he doesn't notice the *party animal* statement on my chest, and move to stand between the two vehicles. His headlights are blinding.

"Ma'am, why are you out driving in your night-clothes?" He looks at his watch. "It's about one twenty in the morning." His tone becomes harsh. "You should be home and not out alone. Especially on New Year's."

My head droops. I nervously move from side to side, trying to keep my feet warm. *Look up, Jackie! Make eye contact so he doesn't think you have something to hide.* "I'm sorry, Officer. I've had a bad day. Well, a bunch of bad days. I went for a ride to clear my head. I got a little lost and was heading back home when you stopped me."

His furrowing eyebrows tell me he doesn't buy my story. Desperate times call for desperate measures, so I play the sympathy card. Maybe sharing my recent traumas will elicit some pity.

I give him a *Reader's Digest* version of the past three months.

"That's a lot to handle," he says compassionately.

Rain drizzles against the pavement, and a passing car splatters mud on us.

He jumps slightly when a car swerves around us. His voice sounds worried. "Ma'am, we need to get off this road and out of harm's way. I'm going to take you to our substation to sort things out."

"What about my car?"

"We're a few minutes out from the station. When we get there, I'll have another officer retrieve it for you."

He watches me closely as I turn off my car's interior light, grab my purse, and lock the car. Then he asks for my keys.

He politely opens the passenger door of his vehicle and helps me into it. While he walks around to the driver's side, I imagine the headline: ELDERLY WOMAN ARRESTED FOR INDECENT EXPOSURE AND DRIVING UNDER THE INFLUENCE OF FRUITCAKE. Getting arrested would be bad enough, but I would hate to be called elderly. These days, journalists refer to anyone over fifty as elderly.

The ride to the substation takes about ten minutes.

Ten awfully long minutes as I struggle to converse with Officer Nelson.

"I didn't get your name," he says when we stop at a red light.

"It's Jackie."

He turns to me. "Hey, my mom's a Jackie. But her real name is Jacqueline. I guess you're a Jacqueline too."

I try not to sound sarcastic. I hate when people assume Jackie is a nickname. "No. I'm just Jackie."

"Well, nice to meet you, just Jackie."

"Nice to meet you, too. I wish it were under different circumstances. Thank you for being so patient with me."

I get a good look at him before the light turns green. He has a kind face and a wide smile. He reminds me of a young Harry Belafonte.

I squirm on the car seat. "Am I being arrested?"

"You'll be detained until we can straighten matters out."

Instead of enjoying the brief lull in our conversation, I open my big mouth. "You remind me of a young Harry Belafonte."

He quickly glances my way. "Who?"

"Harry Belafonte. He's a popular singer, made some movies too. Very nice-looking man."

"What does he sing?"

I struggle to think of titles. "Uh . . . well, there's 'Day-O,' you know, the 'Banana Boat Song.'"

He shakes his head. "Sorry, I'm not familiar with that one."

"Really? It's sung at basketball games these days. Just the 'Day-O' part."

He keeps his eyes on the road. "Sorry, I haven't been to a basketball game in a while."

I talk too much when I'm nervous. My inner voice tells me to shut up, but I keep blabbering. "I'm sure you've heard 'Jump in the Line,' the song in *Beetlejuice*." I stop myself from doing a hand-to-elbow hand jive. He will think I'm drunk for sure.

"Beetle what?"

"*Beetlejuice*. It was a very popular movie. I think the 'Day-O' song is in it too."

His voice lights up in recognition. "Oh yes, I remember the movie. It was one of my grandfather's favorites. I watched it on TV with him once when I was a kid."

I'm growing older by the minute as I calculate the math in my head. Yes, I could be his grandmother. It's official. I'm elderly. We pull up to the substation before I have time to insert my slipper-clad foot any further into my big mouth.

We walk through the station door and into a large room full of desks and two side doors that lead to who knows where. I envision myself being walked through one of them and straight to a jail cell. The smell of burned coffee permeates the air, but the warmth cocooning me feels heavenly. Cold rainwater squishes between my toes. I slide my feet, hoping not to trip in my house shoes. I'm afraid to ask for a towel or something to dry off with. And I really, really have to pee.

"Where's your ladies' room?" I ask.

Officer Nelson points to a door. "We only have one. It's unisex."

No time to deal with my public bathroom phobias. I rush in and line the seat with toilet paper a second before my bladder gives out.

Officer Nelson is waiting outside the door when I

exit. "Your car is being picked up and will be here in a few minutes."

"Thank you. Will I have to pay a towing charge?"

"No. Two officers are taking care of it for you."

He leads me to a folding metal chair next to an old wooden desk. The furniture looks like it survived an air raid. As soon as I sit down, the flickering fluorescent light hanging over the desk makes me dizzy.

There are about ten desks occupied by officers processing some obvious drunks. The constant hum of sloshed men berating their captors reverberates through the room. I am the only woman, and I feel them all glaring at me and wondering why an old lady got arrested.

Officer Nelson sits behind the desk. I am relieved to have him process me. Maybe he will treat me with kid gloves—or, in my case, grandmother gloves.

"Is there anyone I can—"

Two screaming, handcuffed drunkards interrupt our conversation. Office Nelson glares at them and shakes his head.

"Sorry for the noise. It's a busy New Year's. By the way, happy New Year."

"So far my year's not off to a good start. Am I being arrested?"

"No, ma'am. You appear to be sober." He glances around the squad room and shrugs his shoulders. "We've got bigger problems to deal with. But I need to get you home safely. As I started to say, is there anyone I can call to pick you up?"

I look at the wall clock; it's almost two. Who would I dare call at this early hour? *Ba boom, ba boom, ba boom.*

My heart races at the thought of friends or family learning about my predicament.

Sheer panic runs through my veins, increasing my dizziness. The flickering light doesn't help. This must be what a panic attack feels like. A throbbing headache compounds my anguish.

"Miss Jackie, is there someone I can call?" His soothing voice pulls me back to the present.

Gulp! I choke on what little spit I have left. My mouth is as dry as Aunt Millie's fruitcake, and a hacking cough bellows out of me.

"Let me get you some water," he says, standing up and walking to the water cooler.

Meanwhile, I'm thinking how much my life's become like a fruitcake. Nutty, crummy, and full of yucky stuff that washes down better with booze.

Officer Nelson interrupts my self-deprecating thoughts when he returns with the water. "Did you think of someone to call?"

I grab the cup and chug the water to quench my thirst. "No need to call anyone. I'm okay to drive home."

"I'm sorry. I can't let you do that."

I try not to sound sarcastic. "Why not? I'm sober. You even said I appear to be sober. I promise you I can drive myself home."

He picks up a notepad. "Miss . . . I'm sorry, I never got your last name."

"Jackson."

"Miss Jackson, first, you don't have a license or any identification on you. You aren't properly clothed, and you don't seem to be in a good frame of mind. Therefore, I need to call a friend or family member. Preferably someone who can bring your driver's license or some form of identification."

The only person I can trust to help me out of this pickle is my dear friend Jimmy Taylor. "Yes, I have someone," I answer as I dig through my purse for my cell phone.

Jimmy is my best friend Bethany's ex-husband. Much to her chagrin, we remained friends after their divorce. He also lives a couple of blocks from me and has a key to my house.

"I prefer that I call him." I open my contacts to Jimmy's name, press his number, and pray he answers.

After several rings, a groggy Jimmy responds. "Hello. Who the heck is this?"

"It's me, Jackie. Please don't hang up."

"Are you okay? What's happened?"

Officer Nelson's watchful eyes make me nervous. "I'm okay. Well, yes and no. Please do not hang up. This is no joke. I've been detained by the police and need you to pick me up."

"What?" Jimmy yells. "You're with the police? What did you do?"

"We'll discuss that when you get here. I need you to come get me. But first, do you still have a key to my house?"

"Yes."

"Would you please stop by the house and get my wallet? I'm sure it's on the end of the kitchen counter. It's bright orange, so it should be easy to spot. I need my driver's license. Just bring the whole wallet."

His voice is more alert. "Where are you?"

"I'm not sure. Let me put you on the phone with the officer. He can give you directions."

A feeling of relief passes through my body as Officer Nelson gives directions to Jimmy. My knight in shining armor is coming for me. Well, at least a good friend in a shiny silver pickup truck.

Office Nelson ends the call and returns my phone, then pulls out a clipboard and some forms. "Let's get the paperwork filled out while you're waiting for your friend."

I interrupt him after a few questions. "What about my car?"

"It will be safe here until you can pick it up tomorrow. I mean later today. I'll give you a receipt for it. Now back to the paperwork."

2

"Day-O"! That darned "Banana Boat Song" keeps going through my head as I wait for Jimmy. Earlier, "Jailhouse Rock" was worming its way through my brain.

Jimmy calls about two thirty to say he stopped for gas and is about thirty minutes away. Officer Nelson graciously lets me wait in the break room. The small room is dimly lit and has a musty odor. At least I'm away from the flickering fluorescent light and rowdy drunks. The officers on duty are too busy to stop working, so I have the room to myself.

As I sit here thinking about my predicament, I grin. I did several stupid things in my youth but never got arrested or even stopped by the police. And now, at the ripe old age of sixty-nine-and-holding, I'm sitting in a police station. *Thank you, Lord, for such a sweet person as Officer Nelson!* He might have thrown the book at me—driving under the influence of a rum-and-brandy fruit-cake, reckless driving, indecent exposure! Instead, I just got a warning for "failure to display a valid driver's license."

A bellow of laughter rumbles out of my mouth while I think about the craziness of my evening. I am a short step away from hysterics when Jimmy walks into the break room.

"Gal, what's so funny?" he asks in his southern drawl.

I muffle my voice. "Pretend I'm crying and get me the heck out of here."

He looks me in the eye. "Okay now, pull yourself together. I've already shown your ID to the clerk at the front desk so we're good to go. By the way, some of the info you gave the police officer didn't match your license. Like your age. How long do you plan on being sixty-nine?"

"Forever." I throw my arms around his waist, nuzzle my face in his chest, and giggle uncontrollably. He's about six-three, so there's plenty of body room to stifle my chuckles. It takes a few moments for me to compose myself.

"Let's get the heck out of here," Jimmy says, placing his hand on my shoulder and steering me out of the room. When he opens the station door, I'm overwhelmed by a great sense of freedom—and gratefulness. *Lord, thank you for seeing me through my moment of weakness. Please see us home safely.*

Jimmy holds my hand as we walk through the parking lot. His tanned skin feels rough, but my small, pale hands enjoy the warmth of his touch.

As we approach his truck, I let go and giggle until I almost wet my pants. My endorphins have been locked up way too long. After months of stress and heartache, laughter is exactly the release I need.

A bewildered Jimmy steps back and scans me from head to toe. "What the heck? Are those your jammies under that raincoat? And you're wearing house shoes?"

"Yes, and it's a good thing I had my raincoat in the backseat, or things could be much worse." I snort and try to muffle my hee-hawing.

"I'm glad you find this funny, because you scared the bejesus out of me when you called. Can you stop cackling long enough to tell me what the heck happened?" Jimmy has an endearing Texas twang and good ole country boy mannerisms. He's a wonderful, good-hearted man whose friendship I treasure. Now in his midseventies, he is still drop-dead gorgeous, although his once jet-black hair is heavily salted with streaks of silver. An avid fisherman, he maintains his rugged, tanned look. And despite a bit of a beer belly, his butt still looks nice in a pair of jeans.

I stop bellowing long enough to answer him. "Start driving. I'll tell you the whole screwed-up story once we're on the road—and once I can stop laughing."

The fog lifts, the drizzle stops, and traffic dissipates. It's smooth sailing the rest of the way home, so there's plenty of time to talk.

As my story unfolds, Jimmy listens and shakes his head. "You really know how to start a new year."

"More fireworks than I wanted."

"Well, happy New Year, or I should say, 'happy New Year's Day.'"

"Oh noooooooooo. I forgot I'm supposed to have lunch with Bethany today. You know how she is, so there is no way I can cancel." I glance at the clock on the dashboard. It's three forty-five. "How far are we from home?"

"Fifteen minutes, give or take," Jimmy answers.

I count on my fingers. "Okay, that's five, six, seven, eight, nine, ten, eleven . . . I might get seven hours of sleep before she picks me up at noon."

Jimmy grunts. "Babs is never on time."

"Babs. It cracks me up when you call her that. She hates that nickname."

Jimmy lets out a low snort. "When you're born with a name like Bethany Ann Babinski, you should expect some teasing."

"Speaking of names, she still has your last name. Never changed it either time she remarried. I take that as a sign."

"She didn't stay married to either of those two dudes long enough to change her name." Jimmy pauses. "Hmm, when she married me, she became Bethany Ann Taylor. Her initials are B-A-T. Yep, Bat fits her. An old bat who drives like a bat out of hell."

I sigh loudly. "Yes, she does drive that way."

Jimmy is silent for a moment. "Sorry, I didn't mean to speak ill of her," he says in a serious tone. "She's not such a bad old bat. But she still irritates the heck out of me at times."

"You still love her. Admit it. That's probably why you've never remarried. And I know she still loves you. She's too stubborn to admit it."

"Stubborn as a mule and then some. Anyway, I never was good enough for her. She did her best to change me. But you know me—what you see is what you get."

I tilt my head his direction. "Remember that movie *McLintock!*?"

Jimmy focuses on the road. "Yep, one of my favorites."

"Remember when John Wayne takes Maureen O'Hara over his knee and spanks her?"

"Best part."

"That's what you should have done to Bethany years ago."

He quickly glances my direction. "Yep, but knowing her, she would've had me arrested."

I grin as I picture Jimmy tossing Bethany over his knee. Apparently, he is picturing the same thing, and we chuckle together.

Bethany and I became friends back in college. She has done many stupid things throughout the years, but the dumbest thing she did was divorce Jimmy. I don't think she genuinely appreciated him when they were married, and I have no doubt that she regrets leaving him. But she's too pigheaded to admit she still carries a torch for him.

I turn to Jimmy and shake my index finger at him. "Look, it goes without saying, she can never find out about my little escapade."

"You got that right," he answers loudly. "First, she'll want to get you committed to the funny farm. Then she'll be ticked at you for calling me and ticked at me for picking you up. And you know how she holds grudges. Just ask Lynn Ann."

When their only child, Lynn Ann, divorced, she moved in with Jimmy for a while. Bethany considered it the ultimate betrayal and called her a traitor. She was very unforgiving.

"I mean," Jimmy continues, "what did she expect our

daughter to do? Move in with her and that pompous, highfalutin new husband of hers?"

"Pompous. That's a good way to describe him. Call me a hopeless romantic, but I still have hope for you two."

Jimmy reaches over and pats my hand. "She's lucky to have you as a friend after all these years. You're one of the few people who can put up with her crap."

"So true," I say with a smirk. "I still remember that first day we met in college. I think they placed us together because we were journalism majors. No bones about it, she did not want me for a roommate, and she did everything imaginable to run me off."

"She's good at being bitchy."

"Did I ever tell you about the time she tortured me with her flute music?"

"No," Jimmy says, turning to me. "Don't recall that story."

"Every night for a week—" I grab a tissue from his console for a dainty sneeze.

Jimmy gives me a "bless you."

"Thank you. Anyway, every night for a week, right as I was settling down to study, she pulled out her darn flute and started playing the most awful sounds. She claimed she was learning to play the Polish national anthem to surprise her grandfather for his birthday. I'm sure she made up notes as she went along and deliberately played off-key to irritate me. It worked."

Jimmy pats my hand again. "And still, you stuck around and put up with her."

"Glad I did. I would have missed out on a great friendship."

Jimmy snickers and shakes his head. "You two have had some pretty wacky adventures."

"Funny thing. I've spent the past several days going through photo albums and scrapbooks and remembering those good ole days. There were times the two of us deserved to be arrested. Still can't believe that at my age I was almost incarcerated."

Jimmy chuckles. "Everything turned out okay. It could have been worse."

"Thank you for rescuing me once again. You've helped me survive the past few months."

"It's been a little rough for you lately, but you're a tough ole gal. Okay, so you went a little berserko last night, but you're going to be fine. I'm sure of it."

"Ugh," I moan. "Nothing like getting liquored up on Gina's fruitcake and going bonkers."

"Oh, Jackie, you're something else. But I'm proud of you for what you've taken on this past year. You should be proud of yourself too."

A stillness looms over the freeway during our wee hours of travel. I appreciate my time alone with Jimmy and the opportunity to express how much I value him. During all the years I've known him, we never spent much one-on-one time together.

I take a deep breath. "I already feel better. I needed a good belly laugh. But this is one story I can never tell on myself."

"Our secret," he assures me.

"I genuinely appreciate all you've done for me lately. You are a true friend."

"I'm here when you need me."

"Well, then, do you mind calling me around eleven

to be sure I'm up? I've got to be awake in time to get presentable and pick up things in my messy house."

"Glad to."

Our conversation slows as I grow groggy and struggle to stay awake. I'm relieved when we reach my driveway.

* * *

I wake up shaking from a terrible nightmare. It's almost ten thirty, so I climb out of the recliner and head to my bedroom to shower and put on makeup. Then comes my wake-up call.

"Good morning, sunshine," Jimmy says in his sweet southern voice.

"Good morning to you, too. I'm already up and moving."

"Get any sleep?"

"A little, except I had a horrible nightmare about being arrested—"

"Darlin', that was no dream," Jimmy says with a burst of laughter.

"Let's be clear. I did not get arrested last night. I was detained. There's a big difference. Anyway, in my dream, I really did get arrested. I got lost in some podunk town and hit a mailbox. Barney Fife showed up to arrest me."

"Barney Fife?"

"Yes, and he put me in some horrible jail cell," I say, walking into my closet to search for something to wear. "Then I was sent to a kangaroo court where I was charged with a federal crime because I hit a mailbox. Oh yes, Matlock was my lawyer and Howdy Doody was the judge. I woke up in a sweat right as Howdy sentenced me to ten years' hard labor."

"You need to stop watching those late-night reruns."

I cradle the phone between my head and shoulder and take a blouse and a pair of slacks off their hangers. "Yep. Anyway, thanks again for helping me out last night. We still need to pick up my car."

"Call me when you get back from lunch with Babs, and we'll take care of it."

"Will do." I toss the outfit onto my bed.

As I hang up, Bethany calls to be sure I remember our lunch plans. I assure her I haven't forgotten.

"Glad you remembered," she says. "I want to start the New Year right by taking my bestie out to lunch. By the way, I'm running a little late."

"That's okay. Why don't you honk when you arrive, and I'll come out?"

"Okay."

Anxious to get out of my bedroom, I hurriedly put on my clothes and retreat to the den to tidy up in case Bethany comes in.

She is never on time, so when she says she is running a little late, I know "noonish" could be as late as one o'clock. She arrives around twelve thirty and knocks on the back door. So much for honking.

Bethany retired from her PR job seven years ago, became bored, and started hustling real estate. She's a great self-promoter, loves putting up signs with her picture on them, and is still as high-strung and sassy as ever.

As always, she tears through the door, walks past me without saying hello, and begins one of her tirades. "I just cannot believe that jackass," she says, prancing through the kitchen.

Bethany has aged well and still dresses immaculately. She has never changed her hairstyle and continues wearing her wavy, ash-blond locks just past her shoulders—long enough to toss around. Something she loves to do. She inherited her German mother's flawless fair skin and has yet to have a wrinkle on her face. I wouldn't be surprised if she resorts to Botox injections and keeps her hair so blond with a bottle of bleach. She claims otherwise.

"Who?" I back away and stand out of her stomping path.

"That dumbass of an ex-husband." She continues through the dining room, leaving me to trail her.

I can't resist the temptation as I ask her, "Which one?"

Bethany stops and turns toward me. At five foot nine, she's intimidating when she glares down and gives me the evil eye. "Jackie Ann, that line quit being funny years ago."

When she calls me Jackie Ann, I know she's ticked. "Sorry," I reply semiapologetically.

I don't find divorce funny, but her last two marriages were comical, to say the least. Husband #2 was certainly a rebound. I was surprised she married a bald man because she has such a hair fetish. He was also short and old. The only thing he had worth looking at was his bank account. She dumped him right after their first anniversary. At least she got a nice home and divorce settlement out of it.

Husband #3 wasn't the charm she hoped for. Nor did he work out as her retirement plan, which is to marry a rich man and live happily ever after. He was wealthy when they married but lost his fortune in some bad investments. As the money dwindled, so did their love.

Bethany continues to the den. "You know which dumbass I'm talking about. The one who lives two blocks from here."

Yes, I know she's talking about Jimmy. I think he is truly the only man she has ever loved. "What has Jimmy done this time?"

She parks herself in front of the fireplace and puts a hand on her hip. "Nothing really. The usual. He's out there mowing the lawn in a muscle shirt. No muscles, of course, just a beer gut hanging out. I hope he freezes his dick off. If he has a dick."

I watch my tone, afraid to sound too defensive of Jimmy. "You're always on his case about something," I say halfheartedly.

"Oh, for criminy's sake," Bethany answers with her favorite expression. "Can I help it if I find it irritating that he's out mowing his lawn in shorts on a holiday? He should be reported to the homeowners' association for wearing those tacky shorts in the dead of winter."

I sigh under my breath. "We live in Houston. There is no real winter."

She throws an arm up in the air. "Well, at least he has the decency to wear Bermudas. At his age he can't wear short shorts or his balls will hang out. There's nothing worse than seeing an old guy with his balls hanging down to his knees—"

"I'm starving," I interrupt, knowing she will rant for thirty minutes otherwise. "Let's go. And take a different route so we won't have to drive by Jimmy's house. Or drive by if you must."

Sure enough, she drives by his house. Sometimes I think she comes to see me so she can spy on him. Jimmy smiles and waves when we pass.

"What's he grinning about?" Bethany grumbles.

"For heaven's sake, can't the poor man simply smile at us without you getting riled up?"

"Since when did you become his protector?"

I ignore her question and say little more. She's driving too fast, as usual, and isn't paying attention. We bounce in our seats when she hits a speed bump. "Slow down. We're in a neighborhood."

I laugh inwardly, remembering Jimmy's comment. She does drive like a bat out of hell.

Fortunately, the China Café is four blocks from my house, and it doesn't take long to get there. It's a small restaurant with the kitchen awfully close to the dining tables. The sweet aroma of sesame chicken hits me as soon as we enter. My last meal was Gina's fruitcake, so hunger pangs gnaw at me.

We have a lot to talk about, but I hope for some idle chitchat and none of her remember-when stories. A server rolls a cart past us with heaping plates of steaming stir-fried meals and other entrées. When a whiff of wonton soup drifts by my nostrils, I want to grab the egg rolls off the neighboring table. I am starving!

The waitress brings our menus, quickly followed by glasses of water. She trips a bit as she walks away, prompting Bethany to ask, "Remember when we worked as cocktail waitresses at that nightclub?"

I groan. "I'm still trying to forget."

Desperate to supplement our incomes, cocktail wait-ressing seemed like a good idea. We quit after two nights of gagging smoke and putting up with drunk customers. Plus, the work was much harder than we expected, and we were lousy at it. I forgot some of the orders, couldn't read my handwriting when I wrote an order, and had trouble making change. Math was never my strong point. Oh yes, and we tripped several times.

Awkward silence descends while we stare at our menus. I wait for Bethany to start the conversation, but maybe she is waiting for me. My growling stomach wants to order one of everything. We end up with our usual—sweet-and-sour pork for me, kung pao chicken for Bethany.

I clear my throat, trying to force words out of my mouth. "I'm sorry I haven't been in touch with everyone the last few weeks, but—"

"You don't need to explain." Bethany interrupts, twirling her hair, a habit she has never broken. "I could barely make it through the funeral. I can't imagine how hard it was on you."

My tense shoulders relax, and the knot in my stomach eases. She usually tries to pry things out of me. *I am lucky to have such good friends.*

"I talked to Kate last week," Bethany says, switching to a happier topic. "She'll be in town next week and wants to get together."

"That would be great."

Kate is one of our close friends from our college dorm days. She and her husband, Tom, moved to Dallas several years ago.

"I've already talked to the rest of the girls," Bethany says, referring to our other college friends. "Their calendars are open, so we need a date from you. Real estate is slow this time of year, so I'm flexible."

"My calendar is open, so you all pick a date." I lift my glass.

Bethany picks up her water, and we clink our glasses. "Here's to a great new year," she says.

"Yes, here's to a happy new year," I answer.

"It will be great for all of us to get together," she says. "I'll plan something at my house."

I feel a big smile spreading. "It's amazing we've all remained such good friends since our college days. That says a lot about us."

Bethany grins. "Yes, it says we're not very good at making new friends."

My smile turns to laughter.

As we eat, Bethany raves about a new condo community where she has some listings. "I've been thinking about selling my house and moving there. I could easily get into the condo lifestyle. They have lots of amenities, like an exercise room. Oh, and a heated pool. No lawn to maintain. They have a section that is all adult . . ."

I tune her out. This is her indirect way of hinting that I should sell my home and move on with my life. I'm not sure if she has my best interests at heart or wants the listing on my house and another commission for selling me a new home.

* * *

Lunch is the break I need, but I am ready to go back home for some solitude.

I climb into Bethany's big SUV, looking down as I put my foot on the running board. A shiny penny glistens on the ground. Aha! A penny from heaven, and I know who sent it.

I pick it up and clutch it to my heart. My special angel is signaling she is watching over me and things will be okay.

Bethany drops me off, and I retreat to my den. The shiny penny remains clutched in my hand. I hold it to my heart once again before putting it on the end table. Now it's time to call Jimmy so I can get my car back home.

Two hours later I'm back home and resting in the solace of my favorite chair. I know I should spend the rest of New Year's Day looking forward. Instead, I reflect on the past, especially the night I met Rick. A seemingly chance encounter with this mysterious man became a defining moment in my life. At age twenty-seven, the experience challenged my entire belief system and, in many ways, changed the course of my life. Every detail of that evening and the weeks that followed are etched in my memory.

3

I nudged my way through the crowded, smoky room with my small purse clutched in one hand and a drink in the other. It was my monthly travel club mixer held at a hotel party room. I glanced around looking for familiar faces, not paying attention to the people in front of me. As I turned to move forward, I bumped into the most gorgeous and mysterious-looking man I had ever encountered. A pendant light dangled above his head, giving him a halo.

He stood an inch or two taller than me. We were eye-to-eye and, in my mind, heart-to-heart. The overhead light shimmered across his tanned skin, making him look like a bronzed statue of a Greek god. I felt the heat rising from my heart to my head as all my senses unfurled. The rest of the world seemed to stand still around us. The swirling thoughts in my head sounded like words off the pages of a cheesy romance novel.

He had the most entrancing, bewitching, devil-may-care air about him. My first thought was *wow, look at this ruggedly handsome bad boy*. Then I blinked, looked at him again, and thought, *wow, this guy has the aura of an angel and the face to match.* I was intrigued. *Is this what love at first sight feels like?*

When I say I bumped into him, I mean I almost knocked him over and spilled my scotch and soda on his shirt. Thank goodness I wasn't drinking red wine.

"So sorry. I'm such a klutz," I said, putting my purse under my arm and starting to wipe his shirt with my cocktail napkin.

He took the napkin and blotted his shirt. "No need to worry," he said in a strong, suave voice. "This is a fast-drying shirt."

"Hi. My name is Jackie."

"Hello, Jackie. My name is Rick."

As I looked at him, I sensed we had met before. "Do I know you? You look familiar."

"I get that often. I think I have one of those ordinary faces."

There was *nothing* ordinary about Rick, and I knew we had met before. But how could I forget meeting him? He had the arm muscles of a bodybuilder. His eyes said, "I may look bad to the bone on the outside, but I'm all sweetness on the inside." He was movie-star dreamy—part James Dean, part Robert Redford. I was under his spell.

I spotted a couple getting ready to leave a table at the end of the room. "It's pretty crowded. Let's grab that table before someone else gets it."

We headed to the table. He pulled a chair out and seated me. A true gentleman. I hoped through our conversation I would figure out where our paths had crossed. Since we were at a travel club mixer, I started off with some small talk about the organization.

"I have always wanted to travel," I told him. "The club has some affordable trips. So far I've only been on two of the weekend excursions."

What a lie. Saying I joined to find a rich husband to travel with might run him off. With my luck, he was there looking for a wealthy woman to take him places.

I quickly moved to more meaningful conversation. The journalist in me was ready to get down to the *who, what, when, where,* and *why.* Oh yes, and *how*! Yes, *how* could I get this devilishly handsome man interested in me?

"Where are you from?" I asked. "I can't place your accent."

"I am an Air Force brat, so I grew up all over. Germany, Japan, different parts of the States. And you?"

"I've always lived in Texas. Mostly the Houston area. It sounds like you've already done a lot of traveling."

"I do like to travel, but I joined the club mainly to make new acquaintances. I moved to Houston two months ago and want to meet new people."

Rats. So maybe I hadn't met him before. "What brings you to Houston?"

"Work. I'm a longshoreman."

A longshoreman was not what I hoped for. I wanted a lawyer or banker type. Still, there was something extraordinary about Rick, and it seemed snobbish of me to think I was too good for a longshoreman. I needed to act interested and not let my disappointment show.

A waiter interrupted our conversation. "Can I get you anything to drink?"

Rick gave me a go-ahead look, signaling me to order first.

"I'll have another scotch and soda," I answered.

"Nothing for me," Rick replied.

I felt like a lush. "On second thought, could I please have just the soda?"

"I worked in Mobile, Alabama, for four years," he continued once the waiter left. "I recently took a job at the Port of Houston."

Alabama. Never been there. Why did he seem so familiar?

"Where did you live before Alabama?" I asked.

"California. I rode with Hells Angels for a few years."

Hells Angels? How was I supposed to respond to that comment?

He looked at his watch. "I did not notice how late it is. I must be at work early in the morning, so I need to call it a night. Very nice meeting you."

"Likewise."

And then he vanished. He didn't even ask for my last name or my phone number. Did I do or say something to spook him? Maybe he didn't want to discuss his time with Hells Angels, or maybe he was married and had to go home to his wife.

My heart quickly sank to my knees when he walked off so abruptly. I expected him to turn and wave back at me as he headed for the door. Instead, he disappeared in a flash. Disappointment set in because I had high hopes of getting to know him better.

* * *

For thirty long days, I eagerly anticipated the next travel club meeting, longing to run into Rick again. I couldn't get him out of my mind. There was something exceptional about him. I just wasn't sure what it was, and I still couldn't remember where we had met.

The day of the next meeting was a Friday—payday—and I lived from paycheck to paycheck. This was back in the days of my first job working as an entertainment writer for a publishing company. We usually got our checks before noon and cashed them during lunch hour. I was down to eight dollars in my purse and didn't have much more in my bank account. Around three o'clock some guy we'd never seen came in to tell us we wouldn't get our checks until Monday. Such a crappy boss—he sent someone else to do his dirty work.

Loud groans rumbled throughout the office. Mine was the loudest. I sensed smoke coming out of my ears and felt my head readying to explode. I needed my paycheck! When five o'clock came, I rushed out the door and stomped across the parking lot to my car. It's a wonder I didn't shatter the window when I slammed the car door.

I sat in the car contemplating my choices: go home and cry or go to the club mixer in hopes of seeing Rick. Fantasies of a romantic encounter with this gorgeous man quieted my anger and motivated me to go home, dress up, and head for the mixer. I scoured my apartment for loose change and stashed dollar bills—enough money for a drink or two. Fortunately, this month's gathering was at a once-popular nightclub that enticed our group with half-price drinks and free hors d'oeuvres.

I arrived and immediately scanned the crowd for Rick. Ah, there he was, standing by himself. Two women came up to him, so I turned away and pretended not to see him. I grabbed a scotch and mingled with some members I had met on one of the weekend excursions. I hated scotch, but it seemed like a sophisticated drink.

The disco music and flashing lights were annoying, and the one scotch I drank was going straight to my head. I wove my way to the bar and switched to soda. Much of the crowd had moved to the dance floor, giving me a clear view of Rick. The two women walked away, and he stood alone. I turned my head as not to appear to be staring at him. A woman I knew stopped to say hello. While we talked, I caught a glimpse of him looking at me. No way I was going to walk over and talk to him. He would have to come to me.

My work dilemma kept playing over in my head. I was tired and cranky and wanted to go home. If Rick had any interest in me, he would have asked me for my phone number the night we met. And now, he wasn't making any effort to talk to me. My hopes for a sizzling romance with Mr. Gorgeous were fading, so I decided to go home and call it a day.

As I neared the exit, Rick caught up with me and called my name before tapping my shoulder.

"Oh, hi, Rick. Didn't notice you were here." I was such a liar.

"I hope I am not being too forward, but you look like you might need a ride home."

"No. I've got my own car. And no, I haven't had too much to drink. I've been sipping on soda sans the scotch."

"I did not mean to offend you. I merely want to make sure you are okay to drive." He shrugged his shoulders as he held out his hands with his palms up. "Can I at least follow you to make sure you arrive safely?"

"That's okay. I'll be fine."

His brow furrowed. "It is dangerous for you to be out alone in the city. I want to make certain you arrive home safely."

I looked into his sparkling, sweet eyes. My heart melted faster than Blue Bell ice cream on a hot tin Texas roof.

"That's gentlemanly of you. Sure. I don't live far from here."

He walked me to my car. "That dark blue truck over there is mine," he said, pointing to a nearby vehicle.

"Okay. I'll pull out and wait for you," I answered, climbing in my car.

I backed out of my parking space, drove forward a few feet, and waited for him to drive behind me.

One of my internal arguments heated up as I drove home.

Should I ask him to come into my apartment?

Heck no. For all you know, he could be an ax murderer.

But I want to get to know him.

You want to get to know an ax murderer?

But he's so handsome!

Yes, but he could be a handsome ax murderer.

I desperately wanted to get to know him better but decided to play it safe. It was already stupid of me to let some stranger follow me home. But I didn't think of him as a stranger.

He pulled into the spot beside my car when we arrived at my apartment. He knocked on the passenger window as I started to open my door.

"May I talk to you in your car?" he asked.

I wasn't smart enough to think he might murder me or steal my car. So I let him in. At least he didn't ask to come up to my apartment.

He sat quietly, looking straight ahead. I couldn't stand the awkward silence. I've never learned to keep my big mouth shut.

"I'm still trying to remember where we've met," I said.

He turned toward me. "We have never met, not in the traditional sense. However, I have been watching over you for a long time."

"Spying on me?" My voice grew louder. "You've been spying on me?" *Maybe I should worry.*

He shook his head. "No. Merely watching from afar."

From afar? What the heck does that mean? From across the street? From outer space?

I momentarily flashed back to a dream where I was abducted by aliens. It was such a life-like experience, and I was never sure if was real or just a delusional nightmare. Maybe it did happen, and now one of them was back to visit me.

I gave him a questioning look. "Are you a space alien?"

"No, I am not from space." He looked forward, then after a brief pause, turned his head back toward me. "However, in a sense, I do come from another dimension."

I shook my head and raised my voice. "This is getting too weird for me. Please get out of my car."

His tone became formal and preacher-like. "Fear not, Jackie. I have not come to harm you." He sounded more like a man of the cloth than a man of the ship docks.

He twisted his head and shoulders toward me as far as he could on the bench seat of my '76 Ford Escort. "I know this may be difficult for you to understand. But the time has come for me to tell you who I am and why I seem so familiar. I'm a spirit who has been watching over you."

I threw my head back. "What? You're some kind of a guardian angel?"

"We do not call ourselves that, but yes, I am akin to a guardian angel, if that is the language you prefer to use."

I mentally slapped my face. "Wake up, Jackie," I said under my breath, "you're having one of your absurd dreams."

He tilted his head. "What?"

"Nothing. Just thinking out loud. Look, Rick, or whoever you are, I've heard a lot of ridiculous lines in my life, but I've never had a man claim to be my guardian angel."

"Jackie, I speak the truth. I need you to accept what I have to say."

I pulled back. "First, I don't believe in angels, so I don't believe in you. I was brought up to believe that there's no such thing as life after death. When you're dead, you're dead. That's the end of it. And there is no such thing as heaven because you live your heaven and hell right here on earth. If there isn't a heaven, then there aren't angels, so there is no way I could have a guardian angel or some kind of spirit watching over me."

A half smile played across his face, and he spoke softly. "I understand why you feel this way. You took everything Granny Louise said as gospel. However, she wasn't always right."

Granny Louise was my dad's mom, and I took everything she said as fact.

My mouth dropped open. "How do you know her name?"

"I know everything about you," Rick said matter-of-factly.

I wasn't sure if I should laugh or jump out of the car and start running. Instead, I became numb and couldn't move. I listened carefully while he recounted some of the most difficult times in my life. He said he had been there, watching over me each time.

How did Rick know the details of my horrific family tragedy and how it affected me? It was something I rarely discussed and would never have brought up with any of my travel club friends. And so many other trying times in my life. How did he know so much about me?

I was positive I was wide awake and not dreaming, so this had to be some elaborate joke. There was only one logical explanation. He had to work for the FBI, they had a massive file on me, and he was using that information to screw with my head. Yes, he had to be a psychopath who got his kicks out of telling women he's their guardian angel.

He continued talking about my problems at work and said my job would soon come to an end.

"What? I'm going to be fired?"

"No, it will merely end. Do not become distressed when it happens. You will find a better position with more stability and the flexibility you will need in future years."

Cars pulling in and out of the parking lot of my apartment complex distracted me. A sense of anger came over me—anger at my noisy neighbors and at Rick for suggesting I would lose my job.

"Are you okay?" Rick asked.

"No, I'm not! I don't know who you are or what kind of game you're playing. Please get out of my car."

He placed his hands out and moved his palms downward. "Please be calm, Jackie. In time, you will grow to understand what I have been telling you. Your life has a purpose, and you have many wonderful experiences ahead. You need to have patience. Make the right choices—"

"Wait a minute," I interrupted. "I remember where I've seen you! The wreck I was in last year. When I got rear-ended by a truck and the firemen came. You were one of the firemen, weren't you?"

"Yes, but—"

"So, you're a fireman, not a longshoreman?"

"I am neither—"

"So, you weren't with Hells Angels, either?"

He shrugged. "I was—that part is true."

"Where are your tattoos?"

"I said I rode with them. I did not say I was one of them."

I slapped my hand on the steering wheel. "Now I get the joke. You were one of Hells Angels' angels."

"So to speak."

"Could they see you?"

"No."

"Then why can I see you?"

"You do not always see me. And you are not supposed to see me. In reality, you are seeing a vision of how your mind imagines me."

"In reality?" I asked as I attempted to throw my hands up in disgust. I held in a big *ouch* when my left hand hit the steering wheel. It was hard to quell the anger. "*Nothing* about this conversation has anything to do with reality. Please stop the crap and get out of my car!"

"I assure you I speak the truth. Please be calm and listen to what I have to say." Rick's comforting voice somehow put me at ease.

I relaxed in my seat. "Back to this vision of you. I'm not actually seeing you, but I think I'm seeing you?"

"Correct. You are seeing a vision of what you think I resemble."

"So, this is all a hallucination?"

He shook his head. "No, I exist."

"What happens if someone walks by and sees me talking to you?"

He grinned. "They may consider you are talking to yourself. Do not worry, for I will not let that happen. I will distract them with something else."

"What about tonight? I saw you talking to two women. I guess they could see you, right?"

"Yes, but because I wanted you to see me and hopefully come my way."

I looked at Rick and rolled my eyes. "You are so full of it. What about the mixer the night I met you? I didn't just see you. I spilled a drink on you. I sat and talked to you."

"I intentionally let you see me that night. For two reasons. First, I needed to prevent you from meeting a man who was headed toward you. He was an unsavory and dangerous individual. I also wanted to create a rapport with you. I have known for some time that you were conscious of my presence. When you had your car accident last year, I sensed you were able to see me."

"Why were you there?"

He clasped his fingers together as if he was going to pray. "The truck driver fell asleep behind the wheel. I had to wake him in time to keep the accident from being catastrophic. I remained until I was certain you were safe. You were not meant to see me or remember me. That is a special ability most humans do not have. I knew it was a matter of time before you started remembering happenings you should not remember, so I thought it best to talk to you now. To save you some confusion in the future."

I shook my head and narrowed my eyes. "I could never be more confused than I am right now."

"That is understandable," he said.

His soft voice calmed me. I twisted toward him as much as I could on the bench seat of my car. He took my shaky hand and gave me what I can only relate to as a palm reading. He showed me the triangle in my palm and told me what it meant. It sounded like a bunch of mumbo jumbo and was too esoteric for me. I didn't remember anything he told me about the significance.

"A spiritual awakening is in your future," Rick said, releasing my hand. "One that will put you on a path to enlightenment."

"Now you're talking gibberish."

"Jackie, it is important you listen to me. I need you to be prepared for this new spiritual path. You will encounter some strange phenomenas, and I do not want you to be fearful when they happen. You need to be receptive to the new experiences that will unfold in your life."

I glared at him. "I've never been much of a religious person, so I find this spiritual path stuff to be a little ridiculous."

"There is a difference between religion and spirituality. Although you were not educated in any particular religious doctrine, your upbringing was in a spiritual environment. Your grandfather Will had a profound influence on you."

I stilled, though I shouldn't have been surprised. "How do you know about Grandpa Will?"

"I told you. I know everything about you. Do you remember the college philosophy course you took?"

"Yes," I said warily.

"I was there when your classmates debated the existence of God. At the time, you sided with those who did not believe God existed. I knew you had your doubts, but I also knew that, in time, you would quit doubting his existence." Rick paused. "Your spiritual awakening is coming. As I stated, you need to be receptive to new experiences that will take place in your life."

"When is this going to happen?"

"When the time is right."

"I don't get it." I didn't know what to think. The rational part of me knew this had to be a joke. There are no such things as guardian angels. I also realized I was not dreaming. This was really happening.

"This has to be a joke. A well-thought-out, cruel joke," I said in the harshest voice I could muster. "Do you work for the FBI? Who are you? Really, who are you?"

He tilted his head, his eyes seeming to peer into my soul. "I am a spirit who watches over you."

"Cut the bull. I can see you. You are a person, not a spirit."

"Your mind's eye has created a vision of what you believe I resemble."

I reached over and poked him with my finger, but I couldn't feel his body. My heart pounded, my hands shook, and a big lump caught in my throat. Sheer terror coursed through my body. I was ready to jump out of the car and call for help. Ready to commit myself to the nearest loony bin.

"In time, you will understand the importance of our conversation. For now, I do not need to watch over you. However, I will return when you need me. At times, if you see or sense me, do not be frightened."

He opened the car door. "Wait, Rick—or is that your real name?"

He paused and twisted to look at me. "I have no name, but you may call me Rick."

"So, all I have to do is call out for you, and you'll be there?"

"It does not work that way. I will know when you truly need me. Most of the time, I leave you to make your own mistakes. There may be occasions when I must step down and help you. Such as the time you slipped out of your grandmother's house and headed down to the river by yourself—"

"The time I got spanked for sneaking out?"

"Yes. I had to awaken your grandmother from her nap so she would notice you were gone. If she had not been calling your name, you would have kept walking, slipped, and fallen into the water."

"You saved me from drowning?"

"No, you weren't going to drown. However, your grandmother would have been seriously injured going after you. You would have suffered from immense guilt."

I froze, stunned he knew about the incident. Not even the FBI would know about it. I was six years old at the time but remembered it so vividly. Granny Louise cried as she spanked me. It was a light pat on the behind, but it hurt because I had upset her. I remembered her saying, "Please don't ever sneak out again. What would I have done if you fell into the river and drowned?"

Granny and I never told anyone about it, so how did this Rick character know?

"You have kept me busy over the years," Rick continued. "Most of the time, you do an admirable job of managing your life. You have a wonderful life ahead of you if you make the right choices. Always act from your heart *and* your head. More importantly, know that I am real and God is real."

He stepped out of my car, made a tumbling hand gesture—as if he were bidding me adieu. Then he gradually faded away. Even his truck vanished. I've often questioned my sanity, but never as much as I did that night.

* * *

The next morning, I woke up with a giant headache. I sat at my kitchen counter and sipped my first cup of coffee. *Did that actually happen? Is Rick my guardian angel? Did someone drop LSD in my soda? Do I have a brain tumor that's making me hallucinate?*

I started recalling what I believed happened, the things I remembered Rick saying to me. Yes, he had to be some diabolical madman who played one heck of a joke on me. Guardian angels do not exist.

I had almost convinced myself that I was the victim of an elaborate hoax. Then I noticed something on my kitchen counter next to my purse—a white feather. I couldn't imagine where I had picked up a white feather or what it meant. So, I headed to the library for some Saturday morning research.

There were numerous books and articles on guardian angels—enough information to suggest it wasn't so far-fetched to believe I could have one. But nothing I found in the card catalog helped when it came to the meaning of white feathers.

"Do you need assistance?" one of the library staff asked.

"I'm researching the symbolic meaning of finding a white feather."

She tapped her index finger on her chin. "Offhand, I don't recall any such books, but I have always heard that when a feather appears, an angel is near."

The back of my head tingled, and an ice-cold shiver raced through my body. No further research was necessary. Maybe my encounter with Rick was real. My rational side also kept peppering me with everything it could remember about brain tumors and LSD.

I decided not to tell anyone about Rick. Who would believe me?

Little by little, the things he foretold unfolded in my life. I also developed a better understanding of a childhood trauma that had haunted me for years.

A few years later, I became aware of another angel, or spirit, who watched over me. The one who sent those pennies from heaven.

4

"She's here," Mom shouted from the front door.

My stomach knotted and my entire body quaked when I joined Mom on the porch. The day of reckoning had arrived. The Wicked Witch of the West had landed in the driveway of our shabby, one-story Fayetteville farmhouse. Her broomstick was one of those early fifties cars with long fins. It was solid black.

I watched in terror as mean old Miss Moore stepped out of her car. My life flashed before my eyes—all eight years of it. My horrible third-grade teacher was making a home visit, and my short life was coming to a catastrophic end.

The first day in her classroom had been the most terrifying day of my young life. My first- and second-grade teachers had been sweet, kind, and pretty. But not Miss Moore. She hadn't even cracked a smile when we walked into the classroom. She was tall and skinny and wore a long black skirt with a plain black blouse. Her straggly black hair came down to her shoulders. I gawked at her long pointy nose and chin as she stood in front of her desk with her arms folded.

I flashed back to that scary movie *The Wizard of Oz*. When Miss Moore looked down her ugly nose with her frosty, steely eyes, there was no doubt in my childish, impressionable mind. My new teacher was a genuine witch. A witch with very white skin instead of green flesh. Still, I knew she was a witch.

She was also a grouch who spoke in a harsh and demeaning tone. I crouched like a frightened bunny each time she looked at me. And now the wicked witch was in my driveway. I trembled more with each step she took.

A winding stone sidewalk led from our gravel driveway to the front porch of our wooden farmhouse. I clung close to Mom's side as we watched the evil woman make her way toward us. My thoughts turned to my bad classroom experiences. Would today be worse?

Miss Moore had constantly berated me in school. She had also insisted on calling me Jacqueline instead of Jackie. I didn't have the nerve to correct her. "Jacqueline, sit up straight. Jacqueline, you are not sitting in a lady-like manner. Jacqueline, quit hunching over. Jacqueline, you have terrible penmanship."

One day, she'd sent me home with a note that read, "Please teach Jacqueline to be more ladylike and sit with her legs together. She also needs to work on her posture."

Mom had thought I had some other girl's note.

"No," I'd said. "Miss Moore always calls me Jacqueline. I don't know why she does that."

"Maybe she thinks Jackie is a nickname and your real name is Jacqueline."

I did not understand what Mom meant by a nick-name. My dad was a Jack and named me Jackie. Until then, I had never questioned my name. I hold that ghastly Miss Moore responsible for creating my dislike of my name. It wasn't even good enough for a teacher to use.

Hopefully, today she'll call me Jacqueline and Mom will correct her.

Annual teacher home visits were a tradition in my small Central Texas school. Mom was determined to make a good impression on Miss Moore. She had sent my brother, Carl, two years younger than me, to play in the barn because she didn't trust him to behave. I was glad he took his cat, Pussy, with him. I was afraid the witch might steal the black feline to be her familiar.

Carl should have taken our cocker spaniel too. Penny came barking around the corner of the house and headed for Miss Moore, who was now halfway up the sidewalk.

"Shoo," Miss Moore said as she swatted her purse at the dog. "Shoo. Go away."

"Uh-oh," I told Mom. "I don't think she likes dogs."

Penny did an about-face and ran in the opposite direction. She must have known a witch when she saw one.

"I thought you said she was old," Mom whispered. Miss Moore was probably in her early thirties, which to me was old.

She carried a notebook under her arm and wore a brightly colored skirt and jacket instead of her trade-mark dark clothes. *Hmm, she's wearing her Sunday-go-to-meeting clothes.*

Mom was radiant that day in her blue seersucker

shirtwaist dress. She had let her hair down, which meant untying the bandanna she usually wrapped around her head and unpinning her reddish-brown curls. She had soft porcelain skin and never wore makeup. She had dressed me in last year's yellow Easter outfit, brushed my golden-brown curls, and pulled them back with hair barrettes. We were determined to make a good impression.

Miss Moore inched closer to the front door. I feared flying monkeys would swoop in behind her. The moment of reckoning arrived once she stepped onto the porch. Mom opened our squeaky screen door and ushered Miss Moore inside. I walked sheepishly behind them.

The aroma of freshly brewed tea and Mom's batch of warm sugar cookies made our small living area feel inviting. Mom escorted Miss Moore to the couch, but the old witch said she would prefer the armchair.

After some idle chitchat and the obligatory serving of tea and cookies, Mom and I sat on the couch. The coffee table divided the small space between us and Miss Moore. I wished we had a bigger living area so I didn't have to be so close to the witch. I kept reminding myself to sit up straight and keep my legs together.

An awkward silence descended as my teacher scanned the living room with her disapproving eyes. "Oh my," she said, looking toward the front door. "Mrs. Johnson, is that a rifle on the wall?"

"It's a shotgun," Mom answered.

Country women in Texas had to be good with a gun, and my mom was no exception. Dad had taught her to use a 12-gauge shotgun, and she could kill a rattlesnake thirty yards away with the first shot. That had happened a time or two.

Miss Moore raised her shoulders like a cat on its haunches. "Oh my," she said, shaking her head in disapproval. "One would think it would be dangerous to have a gun in the house. Particularly when you have children."

Mom let out a low sigh, then tossed her head back indignantly. "Not as dangerous as having a rattlesnake in the front yard."

I expected things to go downhill from there. And they did.

"Is your husband home?" Miss Moore asked. "I would like to meet him."

Mom squirmed on the couch. "No, he works out of town."

"Oh my," said Miss Moore. She seemed to say *oh my* and *oh* a lot. I knew she meant it in disapproving way. "What line of work is he in?"

"He's a roughneck."

"Oh," the witch replied, looking down her nose at us. "He works in the oil fields?"

"Yes," Mom said softly.

I could hear it in Miss Moore's voice as she gave us the you-are-oil-field-trash look. I was used to being called that by some snotty, mean girls in my class.

Miss Moore opened her notebook. "I'm sure you want to know about Jacqueline's progress in school."

Mom, please correct her. My name is not Jacqueline.

Mom did not correct her. She must have been afraid of her too.

Carl interrupted our conversation as he barreled into

the room, carrying his cat in one hand and a tow sack in the other.

"Look what Pussy can do," Carl said, setting the cat down and letting a mouse out of the burlap bag.

Pussy pounced on the mouse and turned it into his afternoon snack. That was when I learned how the expression *toss your cookies* originated. I tossed mine all over the coffee table.

Mom's expression said it all as she pursed her lips, narrowed her eyes, and glared at Carl. It was her mad-momma look. Miss Moore left abruptly about five minutes later.

* * *

Sometimes I wanted to strangle my little brother, especially that day—it's a wonder I passed the third grade. But most of the time, we got along exceptionally well. Carl was the good-looking one in the family and could have easily been a child model. He inherited my dad's dark brown hair, hazel eyes, and perfect V-shaped face. He looked like a young Rock Hudson.

Living in the country, he was my only friend, except for my imaginary ones. Our small house had two bedrooms, so Carl and I had to share a room. Many nights, I waited for him to fall asleep, then quietly unlatched our bedroom window screen and crawled out. Penny would join me while I sat in the backyard and gazed at the stars.

My imagination ran wild with visions of Peter Pan swooping me away to Neverland. I was in love with Peter and looked forward to our evenings together. I also enjoyed talking to my friend George. To me, George was real, but my mother insisted he was imaginary.

There was a time I loved telling Mom about my conversations with George. I also told her Peter Pan was going to take me to Neverland, where I would grow up to become a famous ballerina and marry a handsome prince.

One day, she looked at me, shook her head sideways, and said, "Jackie Ann, George isn't any more real than Peter Pan. And you are howling at the moon if you think you'll grow up to be a famous ballerina. Quit living in your fantasy world and go clean up the mess in your bedroom."

I knew I was imagining Peter Pan. But George was real. And who was she to squash my dreams of becoming a famous ballerina? I refused to let her crush my aspirations and continued to live in my fantasy world. I just quit talking to her about it.

5

"Sweet sixteen and never been kissed," Carl taunted.

"How do you know?" I said, turning on the television in the living room. "Maybe I have, maybe I haven't."

"Who would kiss your ugly face?"

At that moment, little did I realize that approaching sixteen and never having been kissed would be the least of my worries. Nothing could have prepared me for the hours ahead.

"I have had it with y'all's arguing," Mom said as she walked into the room.

Friday, August 20, 1965. Our tempers flared with the sweltering Texas sun. I kept my cool by looking at the calendar. Three more days until my big birthday.

Five years earlier, Dad had moved us to a rural community about twenty miles west of Houston. We now lived in a frame house with three bedrooms and two baths—a vast improvement over the old farmhouse. The small window air conditioner in the living room became our salvation on scorching days like this one. At night, we turned off the "too darned expensive" unit and slept with the windows open. Fans helped circulate the air.

"Have y'all packed your things?" Mom asked. "We're leaving early in the morning, and you know how your father is. He'll leave you behind if you're not ready to go."

Dad was taking Monday off so we could spend a long weekend with Granny Louise—a last hurrah before school started. Grandpa Ned died when I was five, so I didn't have many memories of him. Granny continued living alone on their farm outside of San Antonio. She had always looked old, even when she was young. I guess because of the hard, rural life she led. She had gray hair for as long as I could remember, was short and a little heavyset. She obviously enjoyed her own cooking and loved to feed us.

There was a big pond on her property where Carl and I fished from the bank and went swimming. We also had horses to ride. Mom would drop us off there for the first two weeks of summer. This weekend would be our only family summer vacation: three fun-filled days with Granny Louise.

I salivated at the thought of the two-layered German chocolate cake she promised to bake for my birthday. She lathered her velvety chocolate creations with coconut and fresh pecans from her trees. The only thing better than her cakes was her crunchy fried chicken. And no meal at her house was complete without the buttered mashed potatoes she served with to-die-for gravy.

Hunger set in as I thought about Granny's great cooking. "Mom, can we eat our sandwiches now? It's already six thirty."

"I guess," she said. "Looks like your father is running late."

Mom had expected him to be home by six o'clock, but by nine, he still hadn't arrived. Carl and I watched TV while Mom paced back and forth from the kitchen to the front window. A loose floor plank in the middle of the living room squeaked when she stepped on it. She kept wringing her hands and sighing beneath her breath.

"I think she's mad," Carl whispered to me.

"Seems worried," I answered. "Worried and mad."

"That damn Jack," she said as she looked out the window for the umpteenth time. "He's probably in a bar somewhere with the rest of the roughnecks."

I leaned toward Carl's ear. "Yes, he's probably out drinking."

I remembered a big fight I had overheard between them. Mom said we wouldn't be so poor if he didn't drink his paycheck before he got it home.

Around ten o'clock, I heard a car drive up, expecting it to be Dad.

"Say good night to your father when he comes in," Mom said. "Then get to bed."

We had a specific order for welcoming him home: Mom would hug and kiss him as Carl and I waited for our turns. Carl and I followed Mom to the door, but before she could open it, there was a loud knock. The three of us stepped back. Dad wouldn't have knocked, so who was at the door?

Mom moved to the window and peeked through the blinds to see who it was, then turned to us. Her look frightened me. She cradled her chin in her hands and lowered her head and paused before looking up again.

"Something is wrong." Her tone was as frightening as her look.

Another knock sounded. Mom opened the door. I grew more terrified when two uniformed men entered the room. They introduced themselves as being from the sheriff's department.

Mom fell to the floor and sobbed as we learned Dad had died in an oil rig accident. That was the first and only time I ever saw her cry. Mom was warm and caring but guarded her emotions. She considered crying to be a sign of weakness, so I realized she had to be hurting as she knelt on the floor weeping.

It was Rick's graphic description of that night and the days that followed that led me to accept that he might be a special spirit who looked over me. I genuinely hoped he had been there to help my dad "cross over." I was in a state of shock when Rick described my father's death and didn't ask questions. Years later, I wished I knew more about how Rick helped my father transition from life to death.

Rick did say that my father's death marked the turning point in my life and that of my family. And it did.

The settlement Mom got from Dad's oil company changed many things. She never said how much she received, but it was enough for her to buy us a brick home ten miles closer to our northwest Houston high school. The rented wood-frame house we'd been living in wasn't much to look at, and the long bus trip home kept me from participating in after-school activities. Now I could walk to school and had a nice home so I could invite friends over.

After an exhaustive day of unpacking, Mom and I sat at the kitchen table to enjoy some cold sweet tea. "Have you thought about what you want to do after you graduate?" she asked. "You never talk about wanting to go to college."

I wiped my sweaty brow with a napkin, contemplating my answer. In the past, I hadn't considered it as an option. My parents had made it clear that they could only afford to send Carl to college because, after all, he was a boy.

"You can go to business school and become a secretary," Dad had said.

"I would love go to college," I answered Mom. "I've been thinking about becoming a home economics teacher."

Mom's eyes sparkled as a gentle smile spread across her lips. "If you want to go, you can. We can afford it now."

Yes, I wanted to go to college. My fantasy of earning a bachelor's degree was the cornerstone of my master plan—the checklist I had created for becoming the perfect wife and mother.

My childhood had been okay, but with Dad gone most of the time, my life had lacked a deep connection to him. I'd dreaded Girl Scout father-daughter banquets. The one time Dad promised to make it, he had showed up too late and had been drinking. I'd cried in my room all night. As much as I loved my mother, I sometimes had blamed her for picking a husband who had spent most of his days living in an oil field bunkhouse. He had spent weekends resting but occasionally had taken us on quick trips to visit relatives.

Having a perfect life with a perfect husband and perfect children became my dream. Along with a nice brick home with a white picket fence. My kids would not be ashamed of me because of my lack of education and social graces. I wanted to be a well-educated woman they would be proud to call their mother.

Decorum and etiquette were foreign to Mom, and she mispronounced most of her words. Aunt Millie had attended college for a year. "She's such a smarty pants," Mom would say of her younger sister. "If I could buy her for what's she's worth and sell her for what she thinks she's worth, I could buy a new car." Or she'd be able to buy a new washing machine, or whatever was on her current wish list.

Aunt Millie constantly corrected Mom's grammar and how she pronounced words such as *worsh* instead of *wash*. On one of Aunt Millie's visits, Mom asked me to put the silverware on the table.

"It's flatware, Ann! It's flatware," Aunt Millie said.

Until then, I'd believed we owned real silver. Thanks to Aunt Millie, I would never be embarrassed by making that faux pas. And I would *wash* my clothes and hope to someday visit Washington instead of *Worshington*. And go to the library and not the *liberry*.

Yes, I was going to attend college, learn social graces, and become the perfect wife and mother for my perfect family!

What could go wrong with that plan?

6

Day One of interviews at the palace of Prince Charming.

The dashing royal sits behind his desk of gold. He stands as Cinderella enters the room. She sheepishly walks toward him. Her clothing? Tattered. Her hair? Disheveled. She's a hot mess.

"Cinderella? I hardly recognized you," says Charming. "Please be seated."

Cinderella hands him her résumé, curtsies, and sits.

"I see the glass slipper fits you perfectly." Charming glances at her credentials. "Enlighten me about your formal education. What are your qualifications to become my princess?"

"My handsome prince," she says, "I have many years of experience toiling as a slave to my ugly stepsisters."

"But no formal education?"

"No," she says. "Just on-the-job training."

"Sorry, you do not meet my requirements." Charming leaps to his feet, points to the door, and bursts into song. "Get along home, Cindy, Cindy. Get along home, Cindy, Cindy. Get along home, Cindy, Cindy. We'll never marry, so go away!"

Cinderella rushes out in tears. Where is her fairy godmother when she needs her the most?

The prince sits back down. "Next."

The door opens. Trumpeters herald my arrival. I enter, donned in my elegant white ballgown. My coiled golden-brown locks trickle to my shoulders. I am beauty personified as I sashay to his desk of gold. He stands. I hand him my résumé and curtsy before him.

"Jacqueline Annabel?" he asks.

"Yes," I reply, knowing I am starting off the interview with a big lie. Somehow Jackie Ann doesn't seem royal enough. He asks me to be seated. I sit. He sits.

"I see that the glass slipper does not begin to fit on your foot. My, what big feet you have. Natheless, I understand you have other qualifications that make you the perfect wife to bear my perfect children. And, as a prince, well, I am the perfect man. What is your formal education?"

"Your Royal Highness, I have a degree in home economics."

"Wow, you *are* the perfect woman. Marry me and we will live happily ever after!"

* * *

Step one of my master plan: earn a degree in home economics. Every man on campus would want me, and I would land my perfect husband by the time I graduated.

That was my goal throughout my junior year in high school. During my senior year, I became interested in journalism. My work on the school newspaper and some writing awards led to a work-study scholarship at a nearby college, an opportunity I could not turn down. The scholarship covered my tuition and was payment for serving as assistant features editor of the college's student newspaper. Minor change in plans—major in journalism and minor in home economics.

Mom and I were seated at the kitchen table when I told her. "Isn't that a silly combination?" she said. "Gonna write cookbooks?"

I handed her pages torn from the college catalog with my subjects circled in red. "No. I'm taking classes in consumer finance, child development, etiquette, nutrition, household management—"

"No cooking or sewing?"

"No, I already learned that stuff earlier in high school."

"And why these classes?" she asked as she handed back the pages.

"To make me a better—" I stopped short of saying *a better wife and mother*. That might hurt her feelings. "A better person. More well-rounded."

Mom shook her head. "Hmm, if I know you, you'll change your mind a dozen times. I'll be happy if you earn a degree that gets you a job. But do it in four years, because that's all we can afford."

* * *

My senior year was coming to an end, and no prom date was anywhere in sight. When it came to dating or being a part of the "cool" social circles, I considered myself an outcast. The newspaper staff became my clique. Beyond that, I was one of the school's "nobodies."

A life-changing moment came from a conversation with a classmate named Mattie. I admired her poise, self-confidence, and beauty. Our junior class had voted her Most Popular, and our senior class selected her as Most Beautiful.

Mattie shared with me that her self-confidence came from telling herself she was beautiful. "You can't be beautiful," she said, "unless you believe you are. You must believe in yourself."

Lack of self-confidence. That was my problem. Sure, I did well in journalism, but that was talent. If I had confidence in that setting, why not have it in other aspects of my life? I needed to believe in myself. Such a simple concept. Why didn't I learn this sooner?

Senior assembly was scheduled two weeks before the prom. Time to put myself to the test. I stood in front of the mirror, smiled, and gave a queenly wave as I mentally listened to the roaring crowd applaud me. The day had arrived. The chubby country bumpkin from the oil field patch was now a lovely, confident young woman. I kept smiling as I looked in the mirror and told myself I was beautiful.

"My, don't you look nice today," Mom said when I pranced out of my bedroom holding a brush and hairpins.

"Thanks." I beamed, handing her the brush. "Would you please put my hair up in a bun?" My favorite childhood memories were of Mom fixing my hair. I could do it myself, but I loved having her brush and style it.

"There," she said once she finished. "You look so pretty."

I hugged her. "Thank you."

"Let me drop y'all off this morning," she volunteered. "Don't want you to get your hair and makeup all messed up."

During the short ride to school, I reminded myself over and over, *Jackie, you are beautiful.*

Pretend you are Mattie. I entered the auditorium. *Shoulders back, stomach in. Hold your head up high. Let a smile dance on your lips. Glide across the floor as if you own the place. Keep your cool, Jackie. You can do this.*

The lively noise of chatting students filled the auditorium. Everyone applauded when the class officers rolled out a CLASS OF 1967 banner and taped it in front of the stage. I scanned the crowded room for a place to sit. Ah! There was an empty seat next to my latest heartthrob. I raced to take it before another girl beat me to it.

He was the vice president of our writers guild. I had a crush on him but was afraid to look at him during club meetings. I considered him semicool and out of my league.

"Is this seat taken?" I asked.

He looked up and grinned. "It is now."

Thump, thump, thump. My heart galloped. *Don't be nervous. Smile and carry on a conversation. Keep smiling.*

It worked. Two days later, he stopped me in the hallway and invited me to the prom.

I survived prom and graduation. Then on to bigger and better things—college! Time to put my master plan into action.

7

I anxiously opened the big manila envelope, ignoring the buzzing noise of other excited college freshmen. The information inside would be life-altering—every-thing I needed to know about campus life. Maps, brochures, and mimeographed sets of rules were on top. Finally, the most important sheet.

Roommate:
Bethany Ann Babinski
Sophomore
Katy, Texas
Journalism Major

My insides got all giggly when I read the information. We shared the same middle name, lived a few miles apart, and were both journalism majors. Visions of a new best friend floated in my head when I headed out of the student union with my registration packet.

I was like a shaken bottle of Dr Pepper ready to explode when the cap was removed. I needed to keep a lid on my excitement and not embarrass myself in front of the line of students waiting for their own packets. Yet, I could not help but do a little foot shuffle as I envisioned dorm life. Bethany and I would be instant friends. No doubt about it.

I entered my dorm room and surveyed my living quarters for the next year. Apparently, Bethany had arrived before me and claimed her space—the bed by the window. Clothes and boxes cluttered the bed. Taped above her headboard was a giant poster of Elvis from his *G.I. Blues* movie days. Ah, we both liked Elvis. *I cannot wait to meet her.*

The compact room had twin beds, built-in desks, bookshelves, and barely enough room to turn around. But the cool breeze from the central air conditioning and the scent of lilac air freshener won me over. A small piece of paradise!

Bethany had struck again. She had claimed her closet space, so I took the other side. And she had also marked her territory in the bathroom medicine cabinet.

As I arranged my toiletries, the adjoining suite door opened and revealed one of my suitemates.

"Hi, I'm Angela. Angela Bernardi," she said with a sweet, bubbly smile.

"Hi, I'm Jackie." I finished putting away my items.

A redhead popped in behind her. "Hey, I'm Gina. Want to come into our room for a visit?"

I scanned their room, which, except for the decor, mirrored mine. It was decorated with posters of Galveston, and their matching bedspreads had a seashell motif. "Let me guess," I said. "You're from Galveston."

"You guessed it," said Gina as she sat on one of the beds.

Angela pointed to the desk chair. "Have a seat." She plopped down on the other bed.

Angela was about five foot one and wore her dark brown hair in a short bob with a side part. Her light olive skin complemented her greenish-brown eyes. From her name, complexion, and the way she moved her hands as she talked, I pegged her as being of Italian descent.

Gina was of medium height with fair skin and freckles. With her bright red hair and updo, she reminded me of a young Lucille Ball.

"So where are you from? Gina asked.

"Houston. By the way, I like the way you've decorated your room. Apparently, you two knew each other before arriving on campus."

"Been best friends since parochial school," Gina said.

"I'm Italian Catholic. She's Irish Catholic," Angela interjected with a grin.

I knew little about religion and assumed all Catholics were the same. *Must be an inside joke.*

The slamming of the bathroom door interrupted our conversation.

"Sounds like someone is pissed," Gina said. "Must be your roommate. Guess we're making too much noise."

"Have you met her yet?" Angela asked.

"No. I'd better go introduce myself."

I should have stayed in the comfort of Angela and Gina's room. A tall, green-eyed monster was waiting for me in mine.

Bethany was hanging clothes in the closet when I entered the room. "Hi, I'm Jackie. You must be Bethany."

She ignored me and kept arranging her closet. When

she finished, she turned to me with her hands on her hips.

"Look, I'm sure you're a nice person and all, but if I could have my way, I would not have a roommate. So please don't bother me with any stupid chitchat or your petty problems."

My high hopes for a new best friend faded quickly. Bethany was a belligerent, quick-tempered, cantankerous witch—with a capital *B*. Oh yes, and vain too. She flipped her long ash-blond hair around as she laid the ground rules, occasionally twirling a piece with her finger.

I quivered with fear as the tall monster continued listing her demands. "And whatever you do, do not touch any of my stuff. Do you understand?"

Her mean look and cruel tone took me back to the third grade. It was Miss Moore all over again. My shoulders drooped and I cowered like a frightened bunny. "Yes," I muttered. "I understand."

She shook her scolding index finger at me. "Remember, don't touch any of my stuff. And stay out of my way."

My first night of college life, and I already wanted to quit and go back home. I cried myself to sleep—very silently, so the witch didn't hear me.

* * *

Day two came. One more day before classes started. I walked to the cafeteria for breakfast and stood in line with two girls named Donna and Susanna. At first, I thought they were twins. They looked almost identical with their beige skin, medium statures, and shoulder-length brown hair.

I was surprised to learn they were roommates who met the day before. I envied how they talked like long-time friends. Both were history buffs who wanted to become history teachers and had much in common.

We ate breakfast and planned our day.

"Last night we decided we want to join a sorority," Susanna said. "Want to come with us to the rush orientation? It starts at ten."

Sorority life had not been a consideration, but, desperate to make new friends, I said I would be happy to go with them. The presentations from each sorority and the friendliness of the girls in attendance piqued my interest. Maybe this wasn't such a bad idea. A sorority might increase my chances of finding my dream man.

"Let's go for it," Donna said when the event ended.

"I'm game," Susanna chimed in.

"I'll think about it," I said.

And I thought and thought about it. This would be the ultimate test for me—I could shed my self-abasing oil-field-trash complex. On the other hand, rejection could scar my fragile ego beyond repair.

That night I made a collect call from the pay phone in the dorm hallway. "Hi, Mom, I'm thinking about joining a sorority."

"You? A sorority?" she asked.

"I'm not sure I can get in, and it is a little expensive."

"How much?"

I explained the costs.

"Well, if you get accepted, I'll foot the bill." Her words sounded supportive, but her tone said, "You don't have a snowball's chance in hell of getting in, so I don't have to worry."

As I filled out the application, I, too, didn't think I stood a chance. I had three high school clubs to list, but no leadership roles. At least I had some journalism awards.The biggest feather in my cap was the whole assistant-features-editor thing for the college newspaper, a worthy accomplishment. And, of course, I had my winning personality and good looks. *Think like Mattie. You are just as pretty and smart as the rest of those girls, so put on your big girl britches and go for it.*

* * *

Cafeteria lines were a great place to meet other coeds. That night I stood next to Kate, one of the nicest people I had ever met. She was about five-three and had long, silky, dark brown hair with bangs. She had a medium complexion that was tanned by, as she put it, lots of sunbathing. Besides her good looks, she had the grace, charm, and manners of a true southern belle. I liked her instantly.

"Let's hang together," she said at the dinner table. "My roommate has a boyfriend. I don't think she is going to be around much."

"My roommate is a witch, so sure, let's stick together."

Sorority rush activities filled the first weekend. Then came the wait for an invitation to be delivered. Or a rejection letter.

Yippee! Donna, Susanna, and I were invited to join the same sorority. We hugged each other in the dorm lobby and jumped up and down like schoolgirls. Then Bethany entered the building. I stepped aside.

"Greek bitches," she said when she passed us.

I was starting to hate her!

The following Tuesday, Bethany and I walked together to our news writing class. "I may have been a little harsh on you when we first met," she said. "I had a bad roommate experience last year and tried to get a private room this year but couldn't afford it."

"Sorry you had a bad experience," I replied. "I'll do my best to be a good roommate." I stopped to open the door to the building.

Bethany turned and smiled at me for the first time. "I think I'll be able to tolerate you."

The rest of the school year went smoothly, and we formed a nice friendship, despite me spending much of my time at the sorority house.

The following school year, Donna, Susanna, and I moved into the sorority house. We stayed in touch with our dorm friends, and Bethany and I occasionally talked to each other in the journalism building.

Little did I realize back then the important role my dorm gang would later play in my life.

8

When I looked into John's sweet, puppy-dog eyes, I heard my mom singing one of her favorite songs. Some of the words perfectly described how I felt at that exact moment. I was bewitched, bothered, and bewildered.

Modern translation—I was in love and I was all shook up!

It was the beginning of my junior year in college, and I wondered if my master plan would make it off the drawing board. In other words, I had a lackluster love life and no perfect husband prospects in sight. Not even a decent boyfriend prospect. I did have big expectations at the end of my freshman year. But he didn't make his grades and was drafted. The Vietnam War tore apart many college relationships.

This magical moment happened as Donna and I walked across campus. She spotted her boyfriend, Max, with his fraternity brother John and waved them over to us. We were all headed to the student union for a snack, so we walked together.

I was downright awestruck by John. He wasn't what I would call dreamboat handsome, but he had adorable honeycombed dimples when he smiled. It was one of those boyish, half-grin smirks that seemed to start at his heart and flow out to his sweet, luscious lips. I wanted to jump across the table and kiss those juicy, sugary lips. Right after I ran my fingers through his thick, wavy, dark blond hair and pinched his adorable cheeks.

John, a business major, was the son of a commercial real estate developer in Sugar Land, a fast-growing city about twenty miles southwest of Houston. He planned to join the family business when he graduated. Ah! A nice-looking, college-educated man from a well-to-do family. Check! Check! Check! I mentally filled in the boxes for my perfect man. Within our first fifteen minutes at the student union, I was already envisioning my life with him.

Now, my master plan was to live in Sugar Land with my sugar, John. In my spare time from being the perfect wife and mother, I would write for the local newspaper and win a Pulitzer Prize. Hey, if I was going to dream, I was going to dream big.

And John was my big dream.

Max and Donna had been dating for eight months, but this was my first opportunity to spend time with Max. He reminded me of a dark-haired version of a Ken doll—suave, good-looking, and clean-cut. The way they fawned over each other was almost nauseating, but I was happy Donna had such a great relationship going for her.

It was a perfect fall day. The autumn leaves were falling all around us as the men walked us from the student union to our sorority house. Each gentle breeze sent a whiff of John's manly Old Spice cologne my way. Oh, he smelled so good.

Conversation became awkward when we reached the steps of the sorority house. If I had kept gazing into John's endearing eyes, I might have tackled him to the ground and been all over him. Oh, how I wanted to pinch those adorable cheeks—front and back. I glanced at Donna and Max. When he kissed her goodbye, I glanced back at John, who was standing in front of me. Wow, he was tall and husky. I felt so petite next to him. You can't put a price on feeling petite. Plus, his feet were bigger than mine.

"I enjoyed meeting you, Jackie," he said. "Maybe I will see you around campus again."

He remembered my name! I was so choked up I couldn't think of a suitable reply. "Maybe so," I finally uttered.

Maybe so? What kind of dumb answer was that? But it was all I could muster because I could barely speak. Yes, I was all shook up!

"I want that man!" I told Donna as we walked upstairs to our rooms.

She grinned and shook her head. "You and half the women on this campus."

I would just have to compete. I had to have him.

Donna did a bit of matchmaking and arranged our next "chance encounter." We were inseparable after that.

Our first date was to an off-campus fraternity party —a double date with Donna and Max. I felt like the belle of the ball standing next to him. When I looked at his luscious lips, I salivated as though they were one of Granny Louise's mouthwatering chocolate cakes. Antici-pating our first kiss made me dizzy.

And then it came. The magical moment to end all magical moments. My toes curled when he kissed me. I thought that only happened in movies, but I felt them crimping. Before I knew it, I was standing on one foot with the other kicked up behind me. I got all giddy inside and turned to mush.

He kissed me like I had never been kissed before. Which wasn't saying much, because until I met John, I hadn't had many kisses—good or bad. Certainly, none with the passion he put into it. When he pulled me close, my heart skipped a beat. Or maybe it was heartburn. I wasn't sure. His tongue waltzed across my lips and into my mouth. Before I knew it, our tongues were doing a tango. Oh wow—juicy tongue action. *So this is what a French kiss feels like.*

I was in love for the first time. Peter Pan didn't count, nor did that little freckle-faced boy I had developed a desperate crush on in the fourth grade. I had chased him around the school bus shouting, "I love you, James." It had devastated me when his family moved away, and I had been sure I would never find true love again.

John was all I had ever hoped for in a man. He was my first true love. My first everything. Life was good.

Four months after we started dating, we rode out to the state park one evening and sat on a blanket as we gazed at the clear Texas sky. Stars filled the heavens, but the brightest stars were those in my eyes. I sensed them twinkling all the way from my eye sockets down to my toes—those toes that still curled when he kissed me.

We both saw it at the same time. "Look! A shooting star."

"Quick! Make a wish," John said.

I closed my eyes—I knew what my heart wanted. *I wish John will be mine for eternity.*

Moments later my wish was coming true.

John leaned toward me, took my hand, and looked adoringly into my eyes.

"You are everything I could wish for," he whispered. "I love you."

It's a good thing I was sitting on a blanket, or I might have fallen over. "I love you too," I said softly.

He stood, extended his hand, and pulled me up. He held me tightly, then stepped back. "Jackie, will you do me the honor of wearing my fraternity pin?"

Would I? Oh, would I! It's a wonder I didn't rip the pin off his shirt.

We were hot and heavy when our junior year ended. Oh, what a summer of love we had before fall classes. Our pinning ceremony took place at the beginning of the semester. His fraternity brothers gathered on the front steps of the sorority house alongside my sorority sisters. Donna and Max, who were pinned the previous spring, stood beside us. The candlelight ceremony symbolized John's commitment to me and our commitment to each other as a couple.

My master plan was falling into place. First, graduation, then trading a fraternity pin for an engagement ring. Next would be my perfect wedding, then raising my perfect children, and living in bliss in my perfect home with my perfect husband. My plan was in motion and my perfect life was ahead.

* * *

Two months before graduation, John called me on a Saturday morning and asked if I would like to drive out to the state park with him. He said he had something important to talk to me about. We already had a date planned for that night, so I wondered what it could be.

Is he going to break up with me? He had seemed a little preoccupied the past week, but when I asked if anything was wrong, he said he was concerned about final exams. He had ended each evening's conversation by telling me how much he loved me, so I nixed the fear of him dumping me.

There was only one logical explanation for his strange behavior. Oh my gosh. This was it. He was going to propose. How romantic of him to pick the spot where he first told me he loved me and gave me his fraternity pin.

John was quiet on the way to the park. I assumed he was mulling over his proposal. When we arrived, he stopped the car, looked away from me, and sat silently for a few seconds. When he turned to me, his eyes were watery.

"Jackie, I want you to know how much . . . how much I love you. I could never . . . I could never love another woman as much as I love you."

From the emotion in his voice, I knew I was in for one heck of a romantic proposal. But how was he going to get down on one knee if we were still in the car?

"I did something very stupid," he continued. I'm not sure of his exact words after that.

John told me he had been unfaithful six weeks back when he went home for the weekend to celebrate his grandmother's birthday. He partied with some high school friends, got drunk, ran into an old girlfriend, and had a fling with her.

My head swirled as his confession unfolded. How could he have done this to me? Could I forgive him? Yes, I could. This wasn't so bad. At least he was being honest with me. Why did he have to tell me about it? I would have been happier not knowing.

But his confession grew worse. The ex-girlfriend was pregnant, and he was going to marry her. Their families were close friends, and he saw no way out of it.

I was crushed. It felt as if a big Mack truck carrying heavy oil field equipment ran over me. Crushing every bone in my body and smashing me to smithereens.

All I could do was sob when John told me he was sorry.

"Once the baby is born, I can leave her. Then I'll come back to you."

What the heck? Dump me for his knocked-up ex-girlfriend, then dump her to come back to me? I shook my head, tossing my angry thoughts around, then took a deep breath and turned to him. "Go to hell, you lousy bastard! Take me home." As I shouted at him, I sensed my broken shards of bones pulling back together to make me whole again.

What a horrible jerk. And to think I wanted to marry him.

Time for a new master plan. No more immature college boys. I would graduate, become a successful businesswoman, and marry a bank president. Or a doctor, or a lawyer, or an Indian chief. Yes, an Indian chief, as long as he had a big tribe that lived on oil-rich land.

9

My palms started to sweat as I tightly gripped my bouquet. In a few minutes, a church full of people would be staring at me. But first, a quick hug for the maid of honor, who was radiant in a long, lime-green satin gown. The adorable flower girl held her basket of white rose petals in one hand. She smiled and blew me a kiss.

I barely had time to compose myself before it was my turn to walk down the aisle. *Walk with confidence. Head high, stomach in, and for heaven's sake, don't trip.* My pointed-toe high heels were killing my feet, and I ached with each step. Dozens of butterfly cocoons were hatching in my stomach and fluttering around. *Please, Lord, don't let me throw up or trip.*

There at the altar stood John, more handsome than ever in his tuxedo. I glanced toward Max, who was standing next to him. I knew I would become a blubbering idiot if my eyes locked with John's.

Dumm dumm da dumm. Dumm dumm da dumm. The wedding march echoed throughout the church as everyone stood. Donna was exquisite in her stunning white bridal gown. Max was the dashing Ken doll groom. Susanna, the maid of honor, stood across from John, the best man. As a bridesmaid, I was paired with Donna's Cousin Itt. The family had hoped he'd shave and get a haircut for the wedding, but he didn't.

Having to dance with Cousin Itt at the reception made me cringe. Seeing John sitting with his very pregnant wife was even more cringeworthy.

* * *

The summer of 1971 was the beginning of my new station in life. Always a bridesmaid, never the bride.

It was also the beginning of life after college. I moved home for the summer and began my job search. One of my journalism professors recommended me for a reporter's slot at the *Houston Chronicle*. I was ready to become a real-life Brenda Starr until I discovered it paid minimum wage—$1.60 an hour. The salary belonged on the funny pages along with Brenda Starr. So much for wanting to be a news reporter.

"You have to begin somewhere," Mom scolded when I told her I turned down the offer.

Yes, I did, but I didn't believe in starting at the bottom. There had to be better opportunities, and I wasn't in a rush to find them. I worked for a temp agency as I continued weighing my options.

Donna and Max began their married life in Humble, Texas, about twenty miles northeast of Houston. Angela, an English major, and Gina, a science major, landed teaching jobs in the Houston area and moved into a large apartment community in the southwest part of the city. Kate was poised to become a retail buyer and lived at home while she completed a trainee program at Neiman Marcus. Susanna was hired as a history teacher in the Houston neighborhood of Spring Branch and moved into an apartment near the campus.

Our college gang had picked up a new member when Bethany had moved off campus her junior year to live with her high school friend Paula. They had graduated a year before us and rented a small house in the southwest Houston suburb of Bellaire, which was near their jobs. Bethany worked in the public relations office of a major oil company, and Paula was an art teacher.

Paula was the quiet type and loved classical music and opera. Bethany was outgoing and loved rock and roll. And then there was the huge Elvis poster Bethany tacked up in their living room. It clashed with Paula's Monet reproductions. The only things they had in common were their long blond hair and fair complexions. Yet, they were remarkably close friends.

Waiting paid off and I finally landed a fun-filled job. I became a writer for *Houston HighLife*, a monthly entertainment magazine that catered to the elite. Content for the publication focused on the city's attractions, special events, and movers and shakers. Plus, I got great perks such as free tickets to plays and concerts and opportunities to meet influential people as well as celebrities.

The job paid $110 a week with a promise of a $7 weekly raise after six months—so much better than minimum wage. I was rich! More importantly, I could afford to move out of Mom's house in northwest Houston, which was a long drive to work and away from all the action in the city.

I found an efficiency apartment in the west-central

Houston neighborhood of Montrose. The area had a "hipster" reputation and was home to art galleries, antique shops, quaint cafés, and exciting night life.

Mom loaned me her car for my temp jobs, but once I secured full-time employment, she gave me the down payment for a used 1969 Ford Falcon. Life was good! I was a professional writer with my own car and my own itsy-bitsy, teeny-weeny garage apartment. I loved every inch of that two-hundred-forty square foot, one-room efficiency.

My landlords were a middle-aged couple who had converted half of their two-car garage into a furnished rental property. It came with a fold-down Murphy twin bed, a small dinette table with two chairs, an armoire for my clothes, a comfortable wingback chair, and an end table. An old black-and-white portable television with rabbit ears sat on top of a small chest of drawers. The bathroom was so tiny that I could have easily showered while sitting on the toilet. The kitchenette had a two-burner countertop stove, a small sink, and the tiniest refrigerator I had ever seen. The apartment was drafty, musty, and not well insulated. The window air conditioning unit clanged if you turned it any higher than the low setting. The television reception was as poor as the water pressure.

I was living in paradise and had money to burn! That is, until I got my first paycheck, minus the taxes, and paid my rent, car payment, and phone bill. Reality hit me like a Mack truck careening off the expressway. Still, I was living a glorious life as a single professional woman in an exciting city. Prince Charming had to be nearby.

In January 1972, Paula got engaged. She and her

fiancé rushed their marriage plans so they could wed on Valentine's Day—his birthday. Bethany cornered me in the kitchen during the bridal shower, which was held at the home of Paula's cousin.

"Paula is moving out tomorrow and has paid her rent through February," Bethany said. "But I can't afford to live in that house by myself."

I gulped, fearing what was coming next. *There is no way I'm going to live with Bethany again. I love my private piece of paradise.*

"We can be roommates again," she said. "And splitting expenses will save you money and give you more space. Come over for dinner on Wednesday so we can talk about it."

Gina interrupted. "I didn't mean to eavesdrop, but if you two are thinking about moving, why not come to our apartment complex?" She picked up a plate of cookies. "Just a thought," she added as she headed to the living room.

"I don't think we can afford that place," Bethany whispered. "Besides, my house is bigger than most of those apartments. So, see you Wednesday?"

It was impossible to say no to Bethany, so I agreed to stop by and discuss it. My office was halfway between her home and my Montrose apartment, so the location wasn't an issue. And it would be a much nicer place to live.

When I walked into her house on Wednesday evening, I was mortified to see that Paula's Monet replicas had been replaced with *Dogs Playing Poker*. Wondering if a *Velvet Elvis* might be next, I was even more reluctant to move in with her. But as we munched our chicken salad sandwiches, she did a good job of laying out the expenses and showing me how much I could save. My six-month lease was up for renewal at the end of February so I had to make a quick decision.

"But before we decide, maybe we should check out the apartments where Angela and Gina live," I said as I grabbed a potato chip. "It might be more affordable than we think."

She sighed, shrugged her shoulders, and twitched her nose. I could see the wheels turning. "They do have something I don't have—central air and heat."

My wheels were turning too. "And a swimming pool and private nightclub for residents."

Bethany dumped more chips on her plate. "We do love to party at The Cantina. And if we lived there, we could party longer and crawl home if we had to."

"Let's check it out!" we shouted in unison.

On Saturday morning we were at the leasing office waiting for it to open. The large two-bedroom, two-bath units were out of our budget. But there was a smaller third-floor two-bedroom, one-bath apartment that was smaller and sixty dollars less. Remembering our dorm experience, I wondered if I could ever survive sharing a bathroom with Bethany again.

"It's a corner unit and overlooks the pool," the leasing agent said while she walked us across the property.

A well-built, tall, dark, and extremely good-looking man dove into the pool as we were passing. Bethany and I looked at each other with our inner smiles and raised eyebrows.

We fell in love with the apartment and couldn't sign the lease fast enough. But first, I made her agree we could decorate our own bedrooms any way we wanted, but we would keep crap art out of the living room. Unfortunately, we had distinctively different views on defining *crap art*.

* * *

If Angela and I were together, we were quiet and somewhat sensible. Add Bethany and Gina to the mix, and we were hell on wheels. Those wheels were Bethany's new, dark green 1972 GTO convertible named Jezebel. Yes, we named our cars. Mine was Franny. I wanted to own a Mustang and name it Sally, but my white 1969 Ford Falcon was all I could afford.

We thought we were hot stuff when we cruised around in Jezebel with the top down. Living in the seventies also meant hot pants and go-go boots. We loved them!

My favorite *I Love Lucy* episodes were those where Lucy and Ethel chased Hollywood stars. Scads of celebrities visited Houston, and we were like Lucy and Ethel times two when the four of us got anywhere near a big star. Today, we would be known as stalkers.

I remembered wanting to become famous so I could write my memoirs. A great chapter title would be "How I Fell for Steve McQueen." Yes, literally. We were chasing after him in a gravel parking lot. I slipped and fell on my ass right in front of him. He helped me up and was exceptionally gracious and gave us autographed pictures.

The greatest chapter would be "College Friends Meet Elvis." That was our crowning achievement—a long story worthy of an entire book, not just a chapter.

I had to get over being starstruck when it came to my

job. My no-nonsense boss expected me to be the ultimate professional. Mr. Nash was a short, brash New Yorker who fancied himself as a ladies' man. Thrice divorced, he never attended an evening event without a young woman on his arm. He loved to stroke his silly Salvador Dali mustache and usually had a smelly cigar dangling from his mouth. The stench floated throughout the office building.

When I was assigned to attend a press junket with George Peppard, I panicked. My knees weakened thinking about it. Would I be able to ask him questions, or would I stare into his sexy bright blue eyes and freeze?

"He's just a man." Mr. Nash scowled. "He puts his pants on one leg at a time, just like the rest of us."

That was a picture I couldn't get out of my mind as I sat across from George Peppard, one of the most gorgeous hunks I'd ever met. It was hard to interview him when I kept picturing him putting on his pants— one leg at a time. Very, very slowly, one leg at a time.

10

Bethany and I pitched our tent and opened our cots, debating what danger lurked around us in the African jungle. Strange, frightening sounds fluttered through my ears. The chattering of monkeys and terrifying growls of vicious animals. Deadly vines coming to life as nightfall descended, ready to creep along the ground and strangle us. Would this small tent with its flimsy zipper be able to protect us from the perils that prowled in the dark African night?

Frightening scenarios played through my mind as Bethany and I practiced setting up a tent. We had decided we would do anything to work in Paris, even if it meant surviving a month in a remote part of Africa. So remote that no one would find our bodies if we died there.

The previous week, Bethany had seen an ad in the Sunday newspaper that grabbed her attention:

Writers and Cameramen Needed for Documentary Film Expedition.

"I think I've found us our dream job," she'd shouted.

I'd glanced up from the comics, consciously trying not to roll my eyes. She was always looking for a better job.

"It's for a documentary film expedition to Africa. We might qualify for the writing positions. If we get the job, we'll travel to Africa for a month. And after the filming, we get to spend three months in Paris writing and editing the documentary."

Paris. The magic word got my attention. "Wow. Maybe we *should* apply!"

Monday evening, we met with a man called Mr. Haldar, or something like that. He was a diminutive, dark-haired man from India with a difficult-to-understand accent. He looked over our résumés, nodding his head up and down as if saying yes to himself. Maybe our journalism degrees and photography classes would pay off.

Elation ensued when he said we qualified, but we would first have to complete some training. At the end of the training, he would decide which applicants would be accepted for the expedition crew.

"If I get picked and you don't, don't worry," I told Bethany. "I won't go without you."

"Screw that. I'm going with or without you. So you'd better make the cut."

Determination drove me to make the team. I had taken two years of French in college with hopes of someday visiting France. It would come in handy when I met Jules. Or Pierre. Or Jean Claude. Or some other rich, debonair Frenchman. Finally, I could get my mom to quit complaining that I wasted two years taking French instead of Spanish.

The training comprised ten evening sessions. Bethany and I eagerly anticipated the first night, hoping there would be some nice-looking men in the group. We had recently watched *King Solomon's Mines* on late-night TV starring Stewart Granger, his generation's Harrison Ford. Bethany imagined we would meet men who were as good-looking and adventuresome.

Much to our dismay, we found ourselves among some dorks and obnoxious know-it-alls. The women weren't much better.

Mr. Haldar held the training sessions in his apartment. Five women and seven men crammed into his small living room. A love seat and one chair were his only furnishings, so we sat on the floor while he spoke. A strange aroma drifted through the room—my first introduction to incense. I despised the odor, and it made my nose itch and my eyes water.

The first night included a geography lesson explaining our travel routes, followed by instructions on how to pitch a tent, set up cots, and make a campfire. That's when Bethany and I grasped we would spend our nights in a jungle, not the Ritz.

A comedy of errors ensued as Bethany and I took our turn setting up a tent in one of Mr. Haldar's unfurnished bedrooms. We somehow managed to complete the task.

"Not too bad," Bethany said on the way home. "I think we can ace this thing."

"Paris, here we come," I answered.

Night two focused on recognizing deadly insects and poisonous snakes. Night three didn't happen! It was far more adventure than we could handle.

"Fame and fortune will have to wait," I told Bethany when we dropped out of the program.

"Oh criminy. I guess we'll figure out another way to make extra money," she said.

The next week we took cocktail waitressing jobs. Another disaster.

The expense of post-college life had dragged us down. Our caviar tastes on peanut butter budgets kept us living from payday to payday. And we always seemed to be down to our last roll of toilet paper.

We ate well on Wednesday evenings, thanks to ladies' night at The Cantina, the private club at our apartment complex. We enjoyed half-price drinks and free hors d'oeuvres, and the place was always packed with men. On Sundays, we scoured the newspaper for free events or cheap entertainment.

Those daffy days of poverty were some of the best times of my life.

11

Rugged cowboys lined the smoky saloon bars. Real cowgirls and country wannabes flirted with them and coaxed them to the dance floor. We loved to watch, and after a few beers Angela, Gina, Bethany, and I would get up the nerve to bat our eyelashes at hunky hillbillies and enjoy some Texas two-step or do-si-do to some Cotton-Eyed Joe.

It was 1973 and freely yelling *bulls**t* was considered acceptable female behavior during a Cotton-Eyed Joe. I loved the opportunity to holler out the profanity—something I would never do otherwise. Shouting it out on a Friday night after a workweek full of bull made it more fun. Most of the time, I said *bullcorn*. The taste of bitter, burning soap still lingered from when my mom used to wash my mouth with it. Carl and I had picked up some colorful language when we accompanied Dad to the oil rigs.

Fridays became our apartment gang's country and western nights, thanks to the two cowboys who lived across the courtyard from us. We enjoyed their friendship but weren't any more romantically interested in them than they were in us. They were country. We were rock and roll. But we were glad to accept their invites to go dancing at the saloons and nightclubs in nearby Pasadena. Once there, we would part ways with the guys. Our girl gang could groove all we wanted, knowing we had a designated driver to get us back home.

We partied at Gilley's Club long before the movie *Urban Cowboy* made it popular. One night, the four of us sat at a table near the stage. We scoped out the crowd, hoping to find a weekend cowboy to our liking. That's the term we used for male versions of ourselves—professional office workers by weekday, wannabe cowboys seeking romance and adventure on the weekends.

"Look at that guy's butt," Bethany said as she pointed to two men standing with their backs to us.

"Which one?" I yelled to be heard over the loud twanging music.

"The tall one with the dark hair. Look how he fills out those tight jeans. Whoa, come to momma."

Gina glared at Bethany and shook her head. "You and your butt fetish."

"What if he has an ugly face to go with the cute butt?" I asked before taking the last swig of my beer.

"Let's find out," Bethany answered. She dug through her purse and took out a small notepad and a pencil. "Watch our purses," she told Angela and Gina when she stood up and motioned to me. "Let's go. Follow my lead."

Oh heavens. Taking Bethany's lead usually meant trailing her down a pothole-filled road and into a rabbit hole with a big tar pit at the end. The notepad and pencil meant she was going to pull her reporter routine —her favorite ploy for extracting information from a man.

Thankfully, the band quit playing as we approached the men. My voice was already hoarse from talking over the music.

"Okay," Bethany said, "I get the tall guy and you get the other one."

"Oh yuck," I said as we got closer. "You're sticking me with a guy with a burr haircut. Who wears a burr these days? Sorry, not interested."

Bethany tapped six-foot-something Butt Guy on the shoulder. "Hi."

Right as she greeted him, the overhead lights came on, signaling a band break. One of the fixtures shined on him when he turned to her, putting a spotlight on his handsome face.

"Well, hi to you too, darlin'," he said in a sultry southern drawl.

His friend, Burr Haircut, turned around but didn't speak. He looked as dull as his stupid short brown fuzz.

Dead silence. I turned to Bethany, waiting for her to say something. Her eyes widened and her jaw dropped. She was turning to mush faster than Granny Louise's homemade ice cream on a Texas afternoon.

No wonder she was so captivated. Butt Guy had the whole John Wayne thing going for him, and a face that was more alluring than his rear end. He was about six-three and towered over Bethany, something most men couldn't do. His eyes looked lake blue under the overhead light, and his oval-shaped face had a high forehead and a distinctive chiseled jawline. His tanned skin hinted he was an outdoorsman. I gawked as much as Bethany.

Yes, he fit the bill for Bethany's perfect tall, dark, and handsome man. Except, of course, the cowboy part. She usually preferred the suit-and-tie type, and unless he was a rich cowboy, I didn't think he stood a chance.

It was unusual for Bethany to be speechless. She cleared her throat and tried to talk but tripped over her own words.

"Uh, I, uh—" She cleared her throat again. "Uh, well, hi, I'm Bethany Babinski with the *Houston Times* magazine. This is my friend Jackie. I was, uh, I am writing—yes, I'm writing an article about Gilley's and I'm interviewing patrons for my story."

"Let me guess," he said. "You want to interview me."

"Well, yes, if ya don't mind," she answered in a put-on southern twang.

He looked at her and raised an eyebrow. "*Houston Times*, you say. Not familiar with it."

"It's new. We're still working on the first issue."

I stood next to not-so-tall Burr Haircut as we watched Bethany masterfully extract information out of poor, unsuspecting Jimmy Taylor. He managed the sales department of a major truck dealership and had dropped out of college to go to Vietnam. He liked to hunt, fish, country dance, and barbecue. She finally got around to questioning him as to why he frequented Gilley's.

Jimmy looked down at her. "For the purdy cowgirls. Like you."

Bethany gushed like a smitten schoolgirl. I had never seen her so enamored with a man, but who could blame her? He was one gorgeous hunk.

At one point, his friend introduced himself as Bruce something or another, but I didn't pay any attention. These men looked like authentic cowboys. Two-stepping with a cowpoke was one thing, but marrying one did not fit into my master plan, so why waste my time?

A different band came out and began setting up. "Looks like Mickey Gilley is getting ready to perform," Jimmy said when the lights dimmed.

Bethany took that as a cue to wind down her phony interview.

She wrote her name and phone number on the notepad, tore the page out, and handed it to Jimmy. She gave him the goo-goo-eyed, come-hither look she liked to use on men. "Here's my number in case you remember something you'd like to add to your comments."

A mischievous grin spread across Jimmy's face. "Oh, I'm sure I'll come up with something to add."

She handed him her notepad and pencil. "And give me your number in case I think of something else I'd like to ask."

Bethany was a smooth operator. I could tell she was not going to let this one get away.

Bruce and I looked at each other and rolled our eyes. I'm sure our minds were on the same track. *Get a room, you two.*

The crowd cheered when Mickey Gilley walked on stage, interrupting the lovebirds' conversation. A photographer was setting up to take pictures, most likely for publicity purposes.

When the star began singing, the photographer started snapping. That's when Bethany handed me her notepad and pencil and waltzed toward the stage. *Oh no, here it comes. Where is the nearest hole I can crawl into?*

Yes, she jumped on stage, stood beside Mickey Gilley as he played the piano, put her hand on her hip, and gave a model pose for the photographer. Mickey didn't miss a note and kept on singing.

"Your friend is something else," Jimmy said.

"You got that right." I was embarrassed to be seen with her.

Bethany deserves credit for inventing photobombing. Any time she would see someone taking a picture, she managed to get herself into the background—or foreground, whenever possible! It was common practice back then for a photographer to walk around events with a Polaroid camera and sell the patrons the instant pictures. I cringed when Bethany would grab a photographer and say, "Follow me." Something asinine was about to happen.

The previous Friday, Bethany had hopped on stage at a western joint and posed with the singer. A month earlier we had attended a beer fest where she jumped on stage with Myron Floren, the accordion player from *The Laurence Welk Show*. No one was safe from her photo shenanigans.

> *Now, what you say—Bullcorn!*
> *Y'all say what—Bullcorn!*
> *Still can't hear you—Bullcorn!*
> *—Cotton-eyed Joe!*

* * *

Jimmy, Jimmy, Jimmy. That's all I heard Saturday morning. Bethany's infatuation with him surprised me. She always talked about finding a rich, successful husband, and was drawn to the professional types. Somehow a college dropout who hawked trucks for a living didn't mesh with her fantasies. But I had to admit, that guy nicely filled out a pair of jeans, and his rear view would make any woman swoon.

She paced around the apartment that morning, occasionally stopping to stare at the telephone.

I tried to calm her anxiety. "He probably went fishing this weekend. And if he's like most men, he'll want to play hard to get and wait a day or two to call."

"*If* he calls," she said as she walked into the kitchen for her third cup of coffee. "Darned men!"

She stomped to her bedroom and slammed the door.

A few minutes later she came back into the living room and uttered those five horrific words that always sent frenzied waves of fear coursing through my body.

"I have a great idea." She took the phone book out of the end table's drawer. "You and I are going fishing tomorrow. That way, when Jimmy finally calls me, I will work it into the conversation that you and I went fishing. That should impress him."

"If you live to tell about it. You don't know the first darned thing about fishing, and I've only fished in a pond with a cane pole." My words were useless. Before I knew it, she had us booked on a Sunday morning charter out of Kemah, a bay area about forty-five minutes away.

"We're booked on the *African Queen*," she said, bopping around the room. "And they provide our fishing gear and bait. We only have to bring food and drinks."

Words escaped me.

"Quit that," Bethany said.

"Quit what?"

"That eye roll of yours. You're always such a party pooper."

I sighed, still speechless.

"I promise you this is going to be one of our best adventures ever. Imagine a ruggedly handsome Humphrey Bogart showing us how to fish. Wrapping his masculine arms around us, teaching us to cast or whatever you call it."

I rolled my eyes and sighed again.

"Imagine us on a luxurious boat full of good-looking men. All of them eager to help bait our hooks and reel in those big fish we're going to catch."

Why, Lord, why do I let her talk me into these schemes of hers? This has disaster written all over it.

Bethany's imagination always got the best of her. It had been several years since we watched the movie *The African Queen*. She forgot Bogart played a crusty, drunken captain on a less-than-luxurious riverboat.

Dawn came way too early. As usual, I was ready on time and had the food and drinks packed. We ran late because Bethany kept primping.

"Don't worry, there won't be much traffic on the road, and Jezebel will get us there on time. And I think I know a shortcut."

We got lost and arrived too late—our ship had sailed. We looked at each other in horror as we watched the *African Queen* slowly puttering away from the dock. The ratty old vessel looked like it might fall apart and sink before getting out of the harbor. It was loaded with equally ratty men who whistled and waved at us as they drifted out to the bay.

We were glad we missed the boat!

But the day wasn't a total loss. We found another charter docked close by named *Sea Thriller*. It was getting ready to depart, so we hopped aboard and had a rather challenging and fun day of fishing, even though each of us only caught two fish that were too small to keep.

Bethany would have two tall tales to share with Jimmy—the boat we missed and the one we caught.

* * *

We were exhausted when we returned to the apartment. The phone was ringing when Bethany opened the door. It's a wonder she didn't break her neck racing for it.

She took a deep breath before answering. "Hello," she said in her sexiest voice. "Oh hi, Jimmy." She beamed. She shuffled her feet with some heel-to-toe dance action and got caught up in the telephone cord. I covered my mouth to muffle my snickers.

She mouthed *shush* at me before returning to her conversation with Jimmy. "Just putting fishing stuff away. Jackie and I got back a little while ago. We've been down at Kemah."

I listened as she piled on the bullcorn.

"Oh, you went fishing too. Catch anything?" Her fake southern accent grew more phony by the minute.

Evidently, he was telling her of his catches.

"Well, my word," she said. "You did much better

than us. We brought home three trout. I caught two of 'em."

I looked around. Where were these fish she spoke of? Were we on the same trip?

She sat down on the sofa. "I'm going to fry 'em up for dinner tonight."

A snort bellowed out of my nose. The closest Bethany had been to cooking fish was sitting at the counter of Freddie's Fish & Chips while someone else fried them.

And so, the torrid love affair began.

Y'all say what—Bullcorn!
Say it a little louder—Bullcorn!

12

The funky, disgusting stench of horse manure caused me to gag as we tiptoed down the dark trail. At any moment, I could step on a big, squishy pile of poop and ruin my white sneakers. There we were, around midnight, at the Sheriff's Posse Arena with a shoebox, a kid-size shovel, and a small flashlight. All because Bethany was mad at Jimmy and wanted to get even with him for a wrong that he probably hadn't committed.

In the early stage of their relationship, it was obvious Bethany was schoolgirl-crush-crazy about Jimmy. However, he wasn't as overtly enamored with her as she was with him, which infuriated her. She was convinced he had lied to her about going out of town for a weekend of hunting with his friend Bruce, aka Burr Haircut. So she dragged me on a "spy mission" to see if his truck was at home. It was. She became convinced he had lied to her and never left town.

She pulled into the A&W to get a soda and contemplate her next move. "Oh, for criminy's sake. He probably has some girl staying with him," she ranted while twirling her hair.

I tried to be the voice of reason. "You don't know that. Maybe they took Bruce's truck or maybe they came back early."

"Why are you taking his side?"

"I'm not. I'm merely pointing out—"

"Men lie all the time, and I'm sure he lied to me," she interrupted.

Then she uttered those five cringeworthy words.

"I have a great idea."

I turned, looked at her, and rolled my eyes.

Bethany took a big slurp of her root beer before continuing. "Let's get some horse manure, shovel it into a shoebox, and wrap it with some nice paper. Then we'll leave it at his front door. Boy, will he be surprised when he opens the gift."

And there by the light of the silvery moon, we tiptoed around horse hooey while praying we didn't get caught stealing manure from the Sheriff's Department. If we got caught, I suggested we say we wanted it for our plants.

"What if they ask us why we're out at night instead of coming during the day?" Bethany said.

"We'll tell them we work all day and didn't have the time."

Bethany made me carry the box and shovel while she walked ahead of me with the dinky flashlight. There were plenty of piles, but she kept looking for the perfect one.

My patience was wearing thin. "For heaven's sake, pick one so we can get out of here before we're caught."

Bethany finally found one that satisfied her. We

successfully delivered the package, and I thought for sure this would be the end of their relationship. But it wasn't. Jimmy accused Bethany of doing it. She denied it. They argued, which wasn't unusual for them. He accused her of not trusting him as he explained Bruce got into some poison ivy and they came back early. Bethany said he should have called her when he returned. He said he had called, but she didn't answer.

Then, in some strange turn of events, Bethany owned up to the prank and Jimmy thought it was hilarious. That's when I knew they deserved each other.

* * *

It was one wedding after another our first few years out of college. Donna and Paula were our first brides, followed by Kate, Gina, and Susanna. Bethany chased Jimmy for a year until he finally quit running and married her.

By the midseventies, Angela and I were the last unwed members of our college gang. After Gina married and moved to Texas City, Angela rented an efficiency apartment six miles from our complex.

When Bethany got engaged, we threw an announcement party at our apartment. I had planned to approach Angela that evening and cleverly ask, "Will you do me the honor of being my roommate?" But before I could get the words out, she had a witty proposal of her own. "Will you please roommate me?" she asked. "I hate where I'm living and would love to move back here and live with you."

Angela and I lived a more subdued lifestyle without our wacky friends Bethany and Gina around. Hoping for a job advancement, I concentrated on my work at the magazine. Angela enjoyed accompanying me to the weekend and evening special events I covered. Instead of hanging out at The Cantina, we expanded our horizons through cultural experiences and were content with our lives as single career women.

Bethany continually tried to hook me up with Jimmy's friend Bruce. I had no interest in him the night we met at Gilley's and still wasn't interested. He owned a small auto mechanic shop, was polite, and not bad on the eyes. Unfortunately, I couldn't get past thinking of him as a grease monkey. A cowboy grease money with a burr haircut. He didn't fit into my darned master plan— the plan that still wasn't falling into place.

13

He had a body like the Greek Adonis. I couldn't stop staring as he slowly unbuttoned his shirt, revealing more and more of his magnificent hairy chest. When he reached the last button, he gradually peeled off his shirt and tossed it on the sofa. I couldn't believe this gorgeous man was taking his clothes off in my living room. His long, silky, dark blond hair now draped his muscular shoulders.

I gasped when he began unzipping his pants. I almost fainted when he slowly peeled off his jeans and revealed the top of his hip-hugging, tight-fitting, red knit briefs. At this point in my life, I hadn't seen a man in anything but basic white boxers.

My blood vessels were going on a rampage, and I felt my face turning beet red. I was mortified. He seductively lowered his pants down to his thighs. That's when I started to sweat and hoped I wouldn't pass out.

"Take it off, honey," Gina shouted.

"Take it all off," Susanna echoed.

"Come to momma," Bethany said.

Kate blushed. "Oh my! Don't tell Tom about this."

Angela covered her eyes and bowed her head. "I can't believe this."

Paula shook her head and grinned.

Donna couldn't help herself. She had to jump up and dance with him.

Yes, a male stripper was taking it all off as my friends and I egged him on. He gyrated around the living room to music by the Rolling Stones with movements that could have put Mick Jagger *and* Elvis to shame.

This might be the last bridal shower I would ever plan, so I wanted to make it a doozy. It had to be something extraordinary and memorable. So big that planning it would keep me distracted from being glum because my friends were off to new lives and leaving me behind.

The year after Angela and I became roommates, she attended the wedding of a high school friend. She reconnected with Mike, one of the groomsmen, and five months later they were engaged. That left me planning one more bridal shower and picking out one more bridesmaid's dress. Yes, my lot in life had become "always a bridesmaid, never the bride."

Angela deserved happiness, and Mike was a super nice, well-mannered, well-groomed, salt-of-the-earth type of guy. He worked for the Oklahoma City branch of a Houston-based oil company and planned to relocate to Houston once the company had an opening. He was the kind of man every mother would want her daughter to marry. More importantly, he treated her like a queen.

I had wanted Angela's bridal shower to be unconventional and outlandish. Something my dear friend would never forget. I had made it clear that this was a girls-only party—no aunts, moms, or in-laws allowed.

After the stripper left, I removed a large framed print from the living room wall and replaced it with a hanging corkboard. "Okay, girls, close your eyes and don't peek," I said as I unrolled a large cartoonish drawing of a nude man and tacked it on the board. "Now open your eyes."

"Oh, for crying out loud," Donna shouted. "Where did you get that—and where is his thing?"

I choked on my words as I tried to answer. "There's a caricature artist at Market Square who drew it for me."

"Nice mustache," Paula said, gawking at the drawing. "I like the hairy chest too."

Bethany raised her glass of champagne punch. "I'll drink to that."

Gina moved closer to the board and eyed the drawing. "But he's not anatomically correct! Something is definitely missing."

Cackling and crude comments rippled through the room. *Maybe I should have left the booze out of the punch bowl.*

I retrieved an open box from under the serving table. "Okay, calm down, girls. Let me explain the game we're going to play. We're going to forgo the customary bridal games. Instead, we're going to play Pin the Dick on the Dude."

Quiet, sweet Angela gasped. "You've got to be kidding!"

"Me first," Bethany said, looking into the box and grabbing the blindfold that was on top.

I put the box on the coffee table and took the blindfold from her. "You'll have to wait your turn. Angela is the honoree, so she goes first."

My inside smile was as big as the one sprawling across my face as I watched my friends take their turns. The fun was nonstop. Without a doubt, it was the bridal shower to end all showers.

"Why didn't you throw me this kind of party?" Bethany whispered while we were mixing a fresh batch of punch, this time minus the champagne.

I could tell she was a little miffed. And she was still ticked off at me for snickering during her wedding ceremony. As her maid of honor, I stood across from Bruce, Jimmy's best man. I had looked at him and thought, *Better to be stuck with Burr Haircut than Cousin Itt*. I had choked as I muffled my giggles.

Bethany kept stirring the punch. I wondered what devious thoughts were going through her mind. She stopped stirring, laid down the ladle, and walked toward the center of the room.

I cringed as the words rolled out of her mouth. "I have a great idea," Bethany said, clapping her hands to get the group's attention. "I'd like to host a groomal shower for Mike. That way our husbands and friends can get to know him before the wedding."

For once, she did have a good idea, and one that wouldn't likely end in pandemonium. But knowing her, I was sure her ulterior motive was to top my party for Angela.

"A groomal shower? I love the idea," Angela said. "Mike will be flattered."

Donna stood up from her chair. "Yes, this will be a great way to welcome him into our circle. Kind of 'meet the family' because, after all, we are one big happy family."

"Yes, we are a family," Kate chimed in.

"Let's make it like a coed bachelor party," Susanna said as she headed to the punch bowl.

"Pin the Boobs on the Broad, that's what we'll play," Bethany said. "And I'll order a boob cake."

We spent the remainder of the evening planning Mike's party and enjoying sandwiches. The only date that fit into Mike's schedule was the Wednesday night before the wedding weekend, just eleven days away.

Darn it. One more couples' event where I would have to go solo. At age twenty-six, I was an old maid with no prospects in sight.

* * *

The eve before Mike's party, I was home packing my belongings. With Angela moving to Oklahoma, I was relocating to a one-bedroom apartment around the corner and six doors down from our unit. She took a break from packing to join Mike and her future in-laws for dinner.

As I separated my souvenirs from Angela's, I reminisced over the stories behind each matchbook, shot glass, and coffee mug. I never thought looking at a Gilley's Club matchbook would bring me to tears.

A knock on the door interrupted my melancholy thoughts.

I looked through the peephole and thought I must be seeing things. Maybe the fish-eye lens was distorting the view. Surely it wasn't him. Could it be him? John, the man who ripped out my heart, stabbed it a thousand times, then stomped it into the ground?

Five years had passed since the day he had destroyed my master plan with his infidelity. But the wounds were still fresh, and the crushing feelings of humiliation and heartbreak still lingered.

I was hesitant to open the door, but he had obviously seen me peering through the peephole. I took a deep breath, ran my fingers through my hair to fluff it up, composed myself, and opened the door.

John's marriage was over, and he was ready to come back to me, ready for us to reconcile.

We talked for almost an hour, mostly catching up on our professional lives after college. I kept hoping Angela would be back soon so I wouldn't have to be alone with him.

After some casual conversation, John told me he still loved me and wanted another chance.

"When I told you I would come back to you, I meant it. But it took me longer to get out of my marriage than I thought it would."

"So you're divorced?"

He wrung his hands and squirmed on the sofa. "As of last week."

What a lousy weasel. Freshly divorced and already out on the prowl.

He became teary-eyed. "I know I made a big mistake."

"Big? You cheated on me and knocked up your ex-girlfriend. I call that a colossal mistake."

"One that I will regret for the rest of my life. I've never stopped loving you. I just hope you can forgive me and give me a second chance."

There was a time when I had secretly hoped for this moment, especially on lonely nights when I had lain in bed thinking about what might have been. I never got over John. When I had longed for him, I reminded myself of the unrelenting heartache and deep pain he'd caused me. That helped get him off my mind.

I was about to ask him to leave and never come back when an idea popped into my head. *Invite him to Mike's party and strut through the door with him on my arm.* My friends would be shocked—except for Donna and Max, who had given him my address. Everyone would see that John had come back to me. I would be vindicated and could regain some of the dignity I had lost when he disgraced me in college.

Yes, I would take John to the party and have a wonderful time with him. Remind him of what he lost when he cheated on me and make him fall in love with me all over again. That wouldn't be too hard because he was sitting in my living room, professing his undying love for me.

Yes, I would invite him to the party and be charming and wonderful. Let him keep professing his love for me. Then I would dump him.

And that's exactly what I did.

14

The cusp of my twenty-seventh birthday loomed over me like buzzards ready to pounce on a dead deer. At any moment, I expected Father Time to swoop down, finish me off with his scythe, and gobble up what little youth I still had. If the buzzards didn't get me first.

Woe is me! I was so far down in the dumps that I didn't think I could ever climb out. It was also the week after Angela's wedding, and my moving day had arrived. Drizzling rain and dark skies added to the dreariness of the humid July morning. *Thank goodness the thirty-first fell on a Saturday so I can move on a weekend!*

The rain slowed long enough for the custodians to move my belongings into my one-bedroom apartment—where I was doomed to spend eternity as an old maid. I unpacked my stereo and albums, put on some music, dusted off my blue suede shoes, and commenced the daunting task of unpacking. I was rocking around and getting a lot accomplished until Elvis asked if I was lonesome tonight.

Yes, darn it, I was lonesome. And it didn't help that I

had a nagging voice in my head saying, *You wouldn't be all alone if you hadn't dumped John. Maybe you shouldn't have let him get away.*

I was tempted to call and tell him I had changed my mind. But I had to be strong and keep convincing myself that he was in my past. I didn't want to be someone's second wife, especially if he was paying child support. He cheated on me once; could I ever trust him again?

Time to listen to the Four Seasons because big girls don't cry. I was a big girl, and I wasn't going to let myself cry.

* * *

Living by myself wasn't as bad as I expected. My job kept me busy during the day. But at night, in the dark stillness of my apartment, I felt all alone.

One of my coworkers told me I needed a dog, and she happened to have a litter of Lhasa Apso–Poodle mixes she was giving away. I went by her house after work to see them, still unsure if a puppy in an apartment was a good idea.

Her young daughter, Jillian, greeted me at the door. I loved that little girl's name. As soon as I heard it, I decided if I ever had a daughter, I would name her Jillian.

Jillian was holding the most adorable white ball of fur. The sweet puppy looked at me with her endearing eyes and floppy ears and wagged her bushy tail. Before I knew it, I was home playing with my new roommate. One that would greet me at the door when I came home. One that would never get married and move away. One that would love me unconditionally and never cheat on me or break my heart. One that would probably chew up my shoes and piddle on my floor.

The only name that seemed to fit my darling little puppy was Jillian. After a few weeks, it occurred to me that if I were to marry soon and have a daughter, there would be two *Jillians* in the house. So I decided to reserve that perfect name for my future perfect daughter and began calling my dog Jill. Besides, it would be cute to sign our Christmas cards from "Jackie and Jill."

* * *

Time crawls slowly when you're not having fun, and it seemed like 1976 would never end. When the new year rolled around, my inner voice was yelling at me louder than the Texas Cyclone at Astroworld. *There's more to life than work and wallowing in your apartment. Get out there and make new friends!*

My master plan was a complete failure, and at age twenty-seven, I was still single with no prospects in sight.

"You're too picky," Mom said as we ate lunch one Sunday afternoon. "You know, it's almost Valentine's Day and you don't have a valentine."

I sighed, rolled my eyes, and took a bite of the scrumptious meatloaf she had prepared. *Why are moms so intent on seeing their daughters get married?*

"Instead of waiting around for Mr. Right, maybe you should find a Mr. Right Now," she said in her displeased mother voice.

I choked on my food as I hee-hawed. "That's a good one, Mom. If I'm lucky, Mr. Right Now might introduce me to a suitable friend."

Mom had a point. Not about me being too picky, because I had no intentions of settling for just any man. But socializing and dating could be a way to meet the perfect man I was so intent on finding.

The bar scene wasn't a good option, and work hadn't resulted in any satisfactory encounters. Yes, I had met several rich and powerful men, but they got that way by being absolute assholes. *So, where can I meet a decent man?*

The answer came a few weeks later when an advertising brochure arrived in the mail.

Introductory Offer!
Six Months Free Membership
to the New Houston Travel Adventures Club
Make New Friends . . . Venture Far and Near

It listed inexpensive weekend bus trips to New Orleans, group charters, and seating for sporting events, and an entire array of other affordable excursions. Plus, social mixers and group rates on trips to Hawaii, Jamaica, and other intriguing destinations. *This could be a good way to make new friends—more specifically, men!*

Also included were dates and locations for upcoming mixers scheduled at various restaurants, hotels, and nightclubs throughout the city. The next one in my area was the third Friday in March, only two weeks away. Not enough time to lose twenty pounds, but it was enough motivation to crash diet and drop some extra weight.

When it came to business, I was outgoing. However, in social settings with a bunch of strangers, I was more of an introvert. Fresh out of single friends, I forced myself to go alone and psyched myself up by turning it into a legitimate writing assignment. There was no need to pull a Bethany and make up a fictitious publication to worm my way into a conversation. After all, I was a writer for *HighLife* magazine, and attending the mixer as a reporter would make it much easier for me to interact with strangers.

The banquet party room at a popular restaurant was the site for the mixer. The invitation promised free hors d'oeuvres and tickets for two complimentary cocktails— a good enticement for attending. While I walked through the restaurant to the banquet room, I reminded myself to treat this as a journalistic endeavor. Wearing my favorite navy-blue business suit bolstered my professional-like approach.

Shoulders back, stomach in. Keep your cool, Jackie. You can do this. And for heaven's sake, smile and don't trip!

The roar of people talking and laughing grew louder as I neared the banquet room, signaling a fun group awaited. A tall, debonair-looking man in a three-piece suit stood at the doorway. "Welcome. I'm Gerald Wilson, executive director of the Travel Adventures Club." I graciously shook his hand and introduced myself.

He attempted to herd me through the door until I handed him my business card. "I'm with *HighLife* magazine," I said. "Your new club may be of interest to our readers."

"Thank you," he said, taking my card. "Let me introduce you to our owners." He led me around the room to meet the three owners and several influential guests.

Before the night ended, I met numerous single people, predominately women, and enjoyed stimulating conversations. They were impressed with my work at the magazine, and I became the belle of the ball. Or at least the belle of the banquet room. *This reporter stuff works. I should have brought a camera—and a notepad!*

I signed up for a forthcoming Saturday bus adventure to a nearby festival, as well as a day at the horse races in Louisiana. Baby steps, but at least I was getting out of my apartment and meeting new people. Single people like me who were using the guise of a travel club as a hookup ruse.

Next came a weekend in New Orleans, where I roomed with an amiable woman I had met at the horse races. We spent most of the weekend in the company of two brothers who were new to the group. No lasting relationships were formed, but at least I was not sitting at home.

My feature article on the club garnered some great publicity for them, which made Gerald happy. It also made Mr. Nash happy when the club bought advertising.

My first four months with the club were socially gratifying and enjoyable. Then came my encounter with Rick. Yes, just when I thought I had met a terrific man, he turned out to be some guy who may or may not have been my guardian angel. After that experience, I took a break from attending mixers and weekend excursions.

One Friday afternoon in mid-December, Mr. Nash called the staff in for an unscheduled meeting. He stood there in his usual slouchy stance and held a half-smoked cigar. He bluntly told us the magazine was folding, and we were to pack up our belongings and get out. "I've had it with this magazine and you people," he said. "I'm taking a job in New York and getting out of this hell-hole." No "thanks for the hard work you put in." And no severance pay. *I guess I can kiss my Christmas bonus goodbye, too!*

He might as well have hit me in the gut with a sledgehammer. That's how much it hurt. It was my dream job, and I was crushed at the thought of having to give it up. I had met so many interesting people, not just celebrities but fascinating individuals who had great stories to tell. And I had loved telling their stories. My ego also loved the prestige that came with the job.

It was hard to hold back the tears, but I wasn't going to let that SOB see me cry. I had to accept that I was out of a job. A job I had wanted to have for the rest of my life. Or until something better came along.

On the way home, I recalled what Rick had told me six months earlier. He had warned that my job would end, and I shouldn't be alarmed. A better position was in my future. He was right about so many other things. Maybe worrying was useless and I needed to have faith that a better job was ahead.

The hunt was on for a new job *and* a new man.

* * *

Ring! Ring! Ring! Ah, someone was calling me. I had wondered if my telephone worked.

"Hello," I answered.

"Jackie?"

"Yes, this is Jackie." *I hope she's not trying to sell me something.*

"This is Eloise with the Travel Adventures Club. We

haven't seen you in a while and want to make sure you're receiving our newsletter."

"Yes, I've been getting it. I've been busy lately with a new job." *I'm sure they don't miss me; they're probably concerned that I let my membership lapse.*

"Well, congratulations," Eloise says in a cordial southern tone. "What's your new job?"

"I'm working for *Metro Magazine* as their real estate editor." I had landed the job seven months earlier, but it still excited me to tell someone.

"Well, sweetie, I hope you can find time to come back to the club. Summer's here, and we have lots of fun things lined up."

"Thank you, Eloise. I'll check my schedule and see if I can make one of the next events." Check my schedule? Besides going to work, my calendar was empty. *Perhaps I should get back to the club.*

A few weeks after losing my job at *HighLife*, a prestigious, well-established business magazine had hired me. It lacked the glamour of entertainment writing, but it provided financial security, excellent benefits, and much better pay. The nine-to-five stress-free position was ideal at that point in my life. It seemed to be what Rick foretold—a job with the stability and the flexibility I would need in future years.

A travel club mixer was scheduled for the second Friday in July, but I was hesitant to attend. Would I still be popular now that I wasn't writing for *HighLife*? There was one way to find out. Time to hold my head up high, suck in my stomach, and get back to the social scene.

"Jackie, so glad to see you," Gerald said as he put out his hand and welcomed me. "We've missed you."

I stepped to his side to get out of the way of others

who were coming through the door. "I've been busy with a new job, but I'm glad to be back."

"Yes, I read about your new position at *Metro*. Congratulations."

"Thank you," I replied. My self-esteem needed that boost.

"If you've got a minute, there's a new member I'd like you to meet." He didn't give me time to answer. "Follow me."

We walked a few feet and stopped in front of a man who was chatting with one of the travel club's partners. Gerald interrupted their conversation and introduced me to Andrew Jones. His physical features were as common as his last name. Medium height, build, and complexion, and an average-looking oval face.

After making the introduction, Gerald left to resume his welcoming duties.

"I see an empty table over there," Andrew said, pointing to the corner of the room. "Would you like to join me?"

And so began my relationship with Andrew, a widower whose wife and son had died in a car accident five years earlier. Although he wasn't particularly good-looking, his charm made up for his lack of good looks. He was a well-connected vice president for a large bank and held an MBA from Stanford. Ten years his junior, I was a cute young thing in his eyes. Another plus. He also had lush, thick brown hair, which was important to me because I didn't want my future son to inherit a balding gene.

The more I learned about Andrew, the more mental checks I put on my master plan list. He doted on me and showered me with gifts and took me to expensive restaurants and extravagant social gatherings. We made the society pages twice when we were photographed at charity events sponsored by his bank. My revised master plan: become the wife of an affluent banker, be a society matron, raise my perfect children, and enjoy my perfect life.

By Christmas, I was staying in Andrew's big, fancy home more than in my own dinky apartment. He hated it when I brought Jill with me. He didn't like having a dog on his furniture or in his house.

"We're a package deal," I told him. "Love me, love my dog."

He had a way of sighing when he didn't agree with someone. One of those deep breaths followed by an exhale. "I'm not fond of dogs, but I'm fond of you. We'll have to reach some compromises."

In the spring of 1979, I moved out of my apartment and into his elegant, traditional two-story home. When Andrew wasn't around, I would prance through the fancy foyer and dance up and down the winding stairs shouting, "Look at me, world!" Then I would pour a glass of wine at the wet bar in the fabulous gourmet kitchen. My perfect man. Prince Charming had swept me away to his castle.

When Angela called to say she was moving back, I jumped at the opportunity to throw a party for her. Mike was being transferred to Houston in a few months, and she was coming to visit his parents and do some house hunting. I delighted in showing off my man and our lavish home. Andrew charmed my friends and they loved him. Life was good. Or so I thought.

Little by little, red flags popped up. Red flags that I would swat down and convince myself were slightly pink, not red-hot. I was so blinded by love I couldn't see the giant flaming fire-colored flags waving right in front of me.

That April, Andrew and I flew to Hawaii with the travel club. It was such a momentous time for me because it was the biggest trip I had ever taken. The first two days were romantic and wonderful. The third day included the Don Ho show. Gerald arranged for me and three other women in our group to be in Don Ho's harem and dance the hula with him on stage. I was having the time of my life. Andrew was livid, especially after the show when I was invited to a party in Don Ho's dressing room for photos and autographs. Andrew wasn't allowed, so I left him behind momentarily.

He pouted for the next two days and put a damper on what should have been a magical time. It's a good thing he hadn't been allowed in the dressing room, or he would have done much more than pout. Aunt Millie had told me if I met Don Ho to give him a big kiss for her. So I had planted a big, juicy one on him. There was a little tongue on his part. I should have stayed away from the mai tais!

Andrew wasn't warming up to my dog, which caused more conflict. And he let it be known he never wanted to have another child, dashing my hopes for a perfect family. He wasn't turning out to be the charming, happy man I had thought he was. He had bouts of depression, probably stemming from the tragic loss of his wife and son. But when he came out of one of his moody spells, he was apologetic and would win me over again with his charm and sweetness. Expensive gifts and flowers helped; I was easily bought!

When it came to housekeeping, he was downright anal.

"See this?" he asked one day, pointing to the kitchen counter.

"What?

"This spot you missed when you wiped the countertop."

He must have had bionic eyes because I could never see what he was talking about. He also complained if I didn't immediately pick up after myself.

Then came Friday, July 13, 1979, the beginning of the worst weekend of my life. The time I knew I could not spend the rest of my life with this man.

We invited Angela to dinner and a Friday night baseball game, but she called to say she had flu-like symptoms and had to cancel.

Andrew was upset. "How rude of her to cancel at the last minute. Now I'm stuck with an extra twenty-dollar ticket and no one to give it to."

His attitude was exasperating. "She sounded terrible on the phone, and here you are, griping about a darned ticket."

It was hard to enjoy the game sitting next to Scrooge. The Astros lost and his mood worsened. We barely spoke on the way home. *I can't put up with this man much longer.*

Saturday morning, I had to drive to the north part of Houston to interview a real estate developer and take photos of his new subdivision. Andrew complained about me working on the weekend and made some snide and hurtful remarks. He even alluded that I had a thing for the developer since I was willing to give up a Saturday morning. I was glad for an excuse to be out of the house but worried about Jill being left alone with Mr. Grouch.

I met with the developer for almost an hour and had plenty of notes and photos for my story. This was before cell phones, so I stopped at a service station pay phone to let Andrew know I was heading home.

It was a humid, windy day. Perspiration dripped down my forehead as I stood by the pay phone outside of the service station. After telling Andrew I was on my way home, he blurted out, "Angela's sister-in-law called. Angela died."

There was a lot of noise from passing cars, so I thought I misunderstood. "What did you say about Angela?"

"I said Angela died. She died sometime late last night."

Shock waves coursed through me. The only thing holding me up was the pay phone. This couldn't be true. Angela couldn't be dead. And what kind of a horrible reprobate would blurt out something like this to me? He could have waited until I got home and compassionately given me the horrible news, comforting me as I cried.

My heart was broken. One of my dearest friends was dead at age thirty. And a man I thought I loved was cruel enough to bluntly give me the devastating news while I was miles away from home.

I struggled to speak. "What happened? How can Angela be dead?

"I'm not sure. Call Angela's family when you get home."

What a callous jerk. I hung up the phone and walked to my car, climbed in, and sobbed. I didn't know I could cry so much. But my mother wasn't around to tell me to stop, so I sat in my car and cried my heart out.

This had to be a mistake. We had lunch together two days earlier, and she'd seemed fine. What kind of cruel joke was God playing on me? My dear friend couldn't be dead.

I never truly understood the meaning of heartbreak until that moment. There was a deep, physical, crushing pain in my chest. I could hardly breathe and was gasping for air. My heart hurt. I sobbed so hard I almost choked.

There was no way I could get on the freeway and drive home. Susanna lived about five miles away, so I drove to her house and hoped she was home. I was relieved when she answered the door. I could hardly speak as I told her about Angela. We held each other and wept.

Andrew wasn't the least bit compassionate when I called to tell him where I was and that I wouldn't be home for a while. Especially when I asked him to let Jill out to potty.

"Hurry up and get home." That's all he said before slamming down the phone.

After a couple of hours at Susanna's house, I felt composed enough to head home. I drove for two blocks before stopping in a parking lot.

"Rick," I called out, hoping my guardian angel would hear me. "I need you to help me get home safely. I need you to help me survive this."

Perhaps I was expecting something miraculous to happen, like Rick ascending from the heavens to drive me home. But he didn't come for me, and I had to pull myself together and get home on my own. I made it there safely, so maybe he was watching over me.

* * *

It was a tense, miserable weekend. When I wasn't crying about Angela, I was fretting over how much I despised Andrew. Sunday afternoon I swallowed my pride and called Mom to see if I could move back home for a while.

Andrew seemed unfazed by my moving out. We didn't discuss it, nor did he try to talk me into staying.

There wasn't much to pack because most of my belongings were in storage. I loaded the car, picked up my dog, and left.

Andrew didn't say a word when I walked out the door. His look said it all: Don't let the door hit you on the way out, and be sure to take your damn dog with you.

I expected a lecture when I got to Mom's house. She liked Andrew but wasn't happy with our living arrangement. She couldn't accept that her daughter was "living in sin."

Before I'd moved in with him, Mom and I had had every clichéd argument imaginable.

"Why should he buy the cow when he can get the milk for free?" she'd once asked.

"Would you want me to buy a car without test-driving it first?" I'd responded.

Thank goodness for the test-drive or I would have been stuck with a real lemon!

Fortunately, there was no lecture. Instead, she was understanding and comforting. She was also sad about

Angela. After Angela's mom had died, my mother became a second mom to her.

Carl still lived at home, still being the man of the house. Mom was perfectly capable of taking care of herself, but Carl considered her his responsibility. He didn't date much, and his only friends were his coworkers at the credit card processing center where he worked. He had been distant with me for the past couple of years. I wondered if he was annoyed with me for living my life while he stayed home to take care of our mother.

* * *

"She looks so peaceful," Gina said as we peered over Angela's opened casket. I grabbed Gina's hand in a tight squeeze. "Like an angel," she continued, her voice quavering. "She was such an angel in life. No wonder she was named Angela. And now . . . now . . . I can't imagine life without my best friend."

Gina and I had arrived at the Galveston funeral home around three o'clock and sneaked in through a side door. We knew it was going to be an emotional time, and we wanted to say our goodbyes before family and friends arrived. I wanted to respond to Gina, but the lump in my throat was the size of a lemon.

Looking down at Angela's lifeless body evoked the most daunting feeling I had ever experienced. My dad had had a closed casket, and until Granny Louise's death, I had not seen a dead body. I was a sophomore in college when Granny died and mature enough to handle viewing her. Yes, I was heartbroken and shaken by the experience, but she had lived a good life, had been ill, and was ready to meet her Maker. But Angela, at age thirty, had her whole life ahead of her. As I looked at her angelic face, I realized the true importance of best friends.

Gina let go of my hand, wrapped her arms around me, and wept on my shoulder. "It seems so unfair. She was the best person I've ever known." She continued sobbing.

"The best person—" I had held back my tears until I was nearly choking on them.

"Ahem, ahem." The sound of a man loudly clearing his throat interrupted our cryfest. We turned to see a funeral home employee holding a box of tissues. "I apologize for interrupting your moment of grief, but I thought you would want to know some of the family is congregating in the lobby. They will soon enter the chapel to grieve together and set up for the visitation starting at five o'clock."

We took that as our cue to grab some tissues and make a hasty retreat through the side door. Gina had invited me to spend the night at her home in Texas City, which was about fifteen miles from Galveston. We knew it would be a late evening between the visitation and the rosary service, and I didn't want to drive at night back to Mom's house in northwest Houston. Nor did I want to deal with the Gulf Freeway traffic for the funeral Mass the next morning at the Catholic church.

Gina and I returned to her house to compose ourselves. Her husband would be home after five, and once he cleaned up, he would drive us to the visitation.

"We still don't have any real answers to how she died," Gina said as we sat at her kitchen table drinking iced tea. "I talked to one of her cousins this morning. She heard that Angela developed pneumonia and something went wrong with her heart."

"Her heart?" I asked.

"That makes some sense." Gina stirred her tea. "Her dad was about thirty when he died from a heart attack."

"That's right. I'd forgotten about that."

Gina put down her teaspoon and wiped her eyes. "I guess it doesn't matter how she died. She's dead, and she took a big part of our hearts with her."

* * *

Mom's house was a welcoming place to regroup. I was still grieving for Angela and trying to get over my broken relationship with Andrew. I wasn't mourning the loss of Andrew. I had dodged machine gun–sized bullets and was glad I hadn't done something stupid like marrying him. I mourned the loss of the illusion of Andrew.

Yes, it was an illusion of a man I thought was perfect for me. An illusion of a love that wasn't real. I thought he was my prince charming who swept me away to his castle. Instead, I ended up with the prince of darkness who swept me away to a cold dungeon where my dog wasn't welcomed. A beautiful dungeon. However, there was much more to life and relationships than a nice home and my name in the society pages.

One evening when Mom was playing cards, Carl and I had a heart-to-heart conversation.

"I'm perfectly happy living with Mom," he said. "And who are you to talk to me about getting out there and living my own life? Doesn't look like you've had much luck, and now you're back home."

He had a point.

The twenty-mile round-trip commute from Mom's house to work was a nightmare in Houston traffic. By October, I was ready to move out and get back to living my life.

15

No pets allowed
Two months' deposit for pets
Pets only in ground-floor apartments
No first-floor vacancies

The apartment market was tight, and I was ready to give up. Luckily, my work friend Sylvia Garza came to my rescue and alerted me to a vacancy where she lived. It was perfect—a one-bedroom apartment on the ground floor with a private patio. The thirty-unit complex was small by Houston standards, and a swimming pool was the only amenity. But the rent was affordable, pets were allowed, and its central location inside the loop was convenient to our office.

Sylvia, the account manager at *Metro*, was an interesting character.

"I'm a Jewish Mexican," she had said the first day we met. "I inherited my mother's lighter skin. Fortunately, I didn't inherit her big schnoz."

"Her what?" I'd asked.

She had chuckled as she touched her face. "Her big nose. My good looks and hot temper come from the Garza side of the family. I was born in Dallas, so my accent is pure Tex-Mex."

Sylvia was about five-four and had silky brown hair and big brown eyes. Although she was twenty-four, our six-year age gap didn't seem important.

Her parents had met and married in New York. Her dad was born in Mexico City and was a naturalized citizen. He came from a devout Catholic family. Her mom was born in New York to Jewish parents.

"Their mothers disowned them when they married outside their faiths," Sylvia said. "They eventually got over it when my brother and I were born. Except for the religious part, Mexican Catholics and New York Jews are much alike, especially the mothers and grandmothers. They take great pleasure in feeding you, dote on their children, long for grandchildren, and manipulate you with guilt. The stereotypes are all true."

Sylvia had a repertoire of jokes and stories about matzo—unleavened bread—versus flour tortillas, making sangria with Manischewitz wine, the art of making tacos with kosher meat dishes, and celebrating holidays Jewish-Mexican style.

Her eyes opened wide when she told stories, as if someone had goosed her. She flailed her arms and switched accents as she lovingly joked about her family. She had the qualities of a stand-up comedian and kept me in stitches.

I envied how much she knew about her family heritage. I knew little about mine except that my mom's side was Welsh and English. Granny Louise said Dad's side descended from a bunch of barbarians.

* * *

My apartment was ready for me to move in by the first of November, but I had to wait until that Saturday so Carl could help me. Sylvia came by to assist us with unloading the U-Haul and served us sandwiches when we broke for lunch. By three o'clock, everything was unpacked and put away. Later that night Sylvia stopped by with a bottle of wine as a housewarming gift.

"I joke a lot about my family, but I genuinely love them," she said as we enjoyed the wine. "There's a great advantage to respecting two religions. Nevertheless, I don't fully embrace either of them. What is your religion?"

I took a sip of wine and cleared my throat. "None, really. I just consider myself a Christian. I spent part of my summers with Granny Louise. She signed me up for whatever Sunday School camp was taking place. Everything from Baptist to Presbyterian to Methodist."

Sylvia topped off our wine glasses. "Last week I discovered a New Age church that I enjoyed. It's nondenominational and embraces all religions. If you're interested, you can join me tomorrow."

I was unsure about going to any church, much less something New Age. My relationship with God hadn't been particularly good since Angela's death. But a voice inside me pushed me to go with Sylvia. Since I hadn't done well with the "old age" religion, maybe I should try something new. Besides, I was enjoying my budding friendship with Sylvia, so I accepted the invitation.

The title of that Sunday's lesson, as it was referred to in the bulletin, was LET GO AND LET GOD. I tried to pay attention, but, as usual, my mind talk was the only thing I was paying attention to.

Let go and let God? Does that mean to turn my life over to God? This is nonsense. What am I doing here? Angela was a devout Catholic who attended Mass almost every week. A lot of good that did her.

I tried to ignore the gremlins in my head and pay attention to the service. My brain finally focused in time to hear the minister's last words.

"Remember, everything happens for a reason."

For an instant, I found myself thinking what a crock that statement was. While I was lost in my thoughts, something bizarre happened. A chill tingled through my body as I sensed someone's hand touching my shoulder. We were seated in the back row, so I turned to see who was behind me.

No one was there.

I sat silently as the collection plate was passed around, and I almost drifted off listening to the choir sing. Then a voice whispered in my ear, "You are on your way."

I was so startled I almost jumped out of my seat. The masculine voice spoke once again, even louder this time. I turned, hoping I would see an actual earthly figure behind me. But, once again, no one was there.

On my way where? What the heck is going on? First the chill, followed by an invisible person touching me on the shoulder. And now I am hearing voices.

Oh my gosh. It finally happened. I had genuinely lost my mind.

Sylvia and I stayed for fellowship afterward. The people were courteous and seemed normal. What was I expecting? Witches and warlocks?

That night, as I lay in bed, my mind drifted back to the church experience. The voice was a familiar voice; one I had heard before. Oh no! It sounded like Rick.

"Okay, Rick," I said loudly, as if I were trying to summon him.

Jill jumped up and barked at the foot of the bed. I sat up to calm her, but she kept barking as if she saw something I couldn't see.

And then I saw it. There at the foot of my bed was a fuzzy vision of Rick and Angela side by side. The vision lasted a few seconds before they drifted away.

Seeing Rick wasn't such a surprise. I had gotten used to his presence. But seeing Angela was unsettling. Maybe this was one of those moments Rick had prepared me for. My initial shock eased into an overwhelming sensation of joy.

A strong scent of roses filled the room. The sweet smell took me back to my last lunch with Angela. She had talked about how much she had enjoyed living in Oklahoma and being "just a housewife." Rose bushes had lined the front of her and Mike's rental house. I clearly remembered her saying, "Not only did I have roses, but I also had plenty of time to stop and smell them."

That was the last face-to-face conversation I had with my dear friend. The tears rolled as I thought about how much I missed her.

Did I have an encounter with my guardian angel and my sweet, wonderful friend? Was this her way of saying goodbye to me, leaving the smell of roses to let me know it was her? Had Rick helped her to "the other side" as he said he had done for my dad?

My head fell to my pillow as I sobbed. The small

lamp on my nightstand was the only thing between me and total darkness. I wasn't brave enough to turn it off. Maybe the light would keep the ghosts away. Could I expect more visitors that night?

Jill licked the salty tears off my face, then cuddled up next to me, looking at me with those adoring eyes. It was as if she was saying, "I saw them too, Mommy. Angela is happy now and everything is okay."

I remembered Rick telling me about being receptive to new experiences and not to be frightened. My tears of sorrow turned to tears of acceptance. Angela was gone from this planet but not from my life—or my heart.

After that night, during difficult times, I would find a shiny penny on the ground. I called them my pennies from heaven and, somehow, I knew they came from Angela. It was her way of signaling to me she was nearby and things would be okay.

16

Granny Louise had said I was flighty and didn't know how to sit still. My homeroom teacher in grade school had told me I needed to learn to concentrate. Aunt Millie had said I had the attention span of a gnat. Dad had often told me I needed to learn to sit still, keep quiet, and listen. Mom had told me I never finished things I started.

Apparently, I was born with attention deficit disorder. So "being present in the now" and learning to meditate were big challenges for me at church services.

I enjoyed the lessons but had a hard time with the guided meditation that took place before the minister's talk. I found it hard to turn off my brain and focus as one of the church members "guided" us into the meditation.

Sylvia and I began taking some church seminars for kicks. Those kicks turned into big kicks in the rear as both of us contemplated the lives we had created for ourselves. I also realized what "let go and let God" meant. At least what it meant to me.

My darned master plan kept getting in the way of

my ability to live life as it happened. I sought men who fit my expectations of an ideal husband and put pressure on myself to excel. I never let life just happen.

Maybe the time had come to let go and let God take over the driver's seat. If there was a God. I still vacillated between agnosticism and Christianity.

The first seminar we attended was on past lives. We made fun of ourselves on the way to the church because it seemed like a silly idea. But we wanted to broaden our horizons and be open to new ideas.

"I can't believe I let you talk me into this," I told Sylvia. "Suppose I learn I was Lizzie Borden or Bonnie Parker?"

"I hope I wasn't a painted lady."

"A house in San Francisco?"

"What? No, not that kind of painted lady," Sylvia snapped. "A working girl in the Wild West. You know, a hooker."

Our silly conversation went downhill from there. We quit our giggling once we arrived at the church.

The seminar was led by a man named William. Just William, like Cher or Madonna. He was a short bald Englishman who wore a long white robe. I was glad he allowed us to tape the seminar so I wouldn't have to struggle taking notes.

As usual, I had trouble concentrating on what he was saying. My mind talk was going at warp speed. *Past lives? What a load of bullcorn. Or is it?* And on and on.

When he finished his presentation, he asked for questions from the audience.

For some strange reason, I had the need to ask if children's imaginary friends could be real. I'm not sure why

I asked such a dumb question, one that seemed to be off topic. But it popped out of my big mouth.

"That's a good question and perhaps one that falls into the realm of past lives," he answered. "Some theologians theorize children are still closely connected to their previous lives and hear or see things adults do not. Children's souls are still pure. They are closer to the spiritual realm and are still receptive to these visitors from the other side, whether they are deceased loved ones, spiritual guides, or, perhaps, guardian angels."

William was trying to wind down the seminar and didn't ask for any more questions. But I had one more I had to ask.

"So guardian angels are real?" I questioned loudly, waving my hand to be sure he noticed.

"That's a deep topic for another seminar." He closed his notebook, signaling our time was up. "But, to briefly answer your question, yes, I believe they are real. Perhaps they are deceased beings who watch over us. Or, as some scholars suggest, a specific being that is assigned to you. Ultimately, the interpretation of guardian angels is a matter of one's faith."

And with that, he bid us farewell, turned, and swaggered away with his long white robe flowing grandly behind him.

Sylvia and I went for drinks afterward and talked mostly about work-related subjects. I wasn't willing to admit William's words had left a deep impression on me. Instead, I mocked his robe and British accent.

Deep down I was developing a sense of validation. Maybe I wasn't insane after all. Hearing William say he believed in guardian angels helped erase my lingering doubts about Rick. Maybe my childhood friend George wasn't imaginary and had been an angel who liked to visit me. Maybe I did see Angela's spirit. And maybe now she's a deceased being who watches over me.

These were a lot of *maybe*s to consider, but things I once questioned had become more conceivable.

17

Owooooo . . . owooooo . . . owooooo!

The howling of dozens of wolves echoed around me as I sat under the full moon, shivering from the cool evening breeze.

It wasn't wolves making the noise. It was a bunch of howling women, and I was one of them.

Sylvia and I registered for a "Howling at the Moon" event at the church. It was led by a psychic named Karen Hornblower. Again, we poked fun at ourselves on the way there. We had progressed from studying past lives to wailing at the moon with a psychic with a comical last name. I wondered if that was her real name and if she was related to Horatio Hornblower. Then I remembered he was a fictional character, so I was glad I didn't ask.

I was relieved Karen looked like a normal person. She was of average height with medium-length brown hair and a fair complexion. She wore slacks with a white peasant blouse—no long flowing robe or weird accent.

The program began inside the church, lasted about ninety minutes, and was attended only by women.

Perhaps the men had sense enough to stay away. First, Karen told us the meaning of the expression "howling at the moon." It meant chasing after fantasies instead of living in the now. Wasting time and energy pursuing things that were unattainable, unrealistic, or not meant to be.

I guess mothers do know best. As a kid, when I fantasized about being a famous ballerina or marrying a handsome prince, Mom would tell me I was howling at the moon.

Karen gave an example that caught my attention. "As when you ladies keep looking for the perfect man. Ladies, he simply does not exist. Or if you are seeking the perfect job. You are merely howling or, as some say, baying at the moon."

Boy, did that resonate with me.

She handed out half sheets of paper and asked us to write down the unrealistic dreams we were wasting our time pursuing, as well as things we'd like to release or change about our lives. Things that no longer served us, such as bad relationships and stressful, unfulfilling jobs.

I needed a notebook, not a small sheet of paper. I proceeded to write down three simple words: *My master plan.*

That covered all the bases. It was time to let go of it, quit reediting it, and scrap it completely. It no longer served me.

After we finished writing, we walked out to the parking lot behind the church and formed a circle around a large metal bowl that sat on a wrought iron stand. While Karen lit a fire in the bowl, she gave some type of incantation asking the spirits to help us purge ourselves of things that were holding us back.

We were instructed to put our lists in the burning bowl and say "begone" as we watched the paper burn.

Sylvia and I looked at each other and had to hold back our snickers. This concept was so foreign to us. One by one, we took turns walking up to the bowl and tossing in our lists. Shouts of "begone" bellowed throughout the parking lot.

Following the bowl burnings, Karen and two of the attendees spread blankets on the ground of the parking lot.

"Please gather around and be seated," Karen said. It took a couple of minutes for everyone to get situated. She sat on the ground in a lotus position and continued her instructions. "Close your eyes and take a deep breath . . . now exhale . . . again a deep breath . . . exhale. Clear your minds and prepare to open yourselves to new life experiences."

I felt my mind opening when I exhaled. It was exhilarating.

"Now look up at the full moon and begin to howl," Karen continued.

Yes, there we were, baying at the moon. Once I started howling, my inner wolf came out. I howled until I was almost hoarse. It was so liberating, as though a ton of cinder blocks had been lifted off my shoulders. Great big, heavy bricks that had been holding me down for years. I felt as light as a feather and wanted to drift away in whatever direction the wind would take me.

When we went back inside to get our purses, Karen stood at the front door to say goodbye to the attendees when they exited. Sylvia and I were the last to leave because we had howled the longest. As we approached her, she reached out and laid her hands on our shoulders. She briefly closed her eyes, as if she were in a trance.

When she opened them, she looked straight at us and spoke with words that flowed poetically off her lips. "My sisters, it is so wonderful to see you together again on this earthly plane. I am thankful you found each other and are experiencing your spiritual awakening together."

She dropped her hands from our shoulders, turned around, and walked toward the back of the room.

I stood there frozen like a statue, too stunned to react. But I knew I had to say something.

"Wait! What are you talking about?"

She turned and spoke softly. "You were sisters in another life. You have found each other again." Then she continued toward the back of the room.

Sylvia and I walked to my car without saying a word. We got in and looked at each other with blank stares.

Sylvia giggled. "What the heck was that all about?"

Her hilarity was contagious. "I have no earthly or unearthly idea. This is too much."

We laughed until we almost cried. It was one of those laughing-out-loud, peeing-in-your-pants moments. Yes, I did pee a little in my pants. So instead of going out for a drink, we made wisecracks on the drive home. We found it easier to make light of the evening than to have a serious discussion about any past life possibilities. I sensed we were kindred spirits, but a karmic or cosmic connection seemed absurd.

All the howling wore me out. I climbed into bed with my sidekick Jill and smiled as I pictured myself wailing at the moon. After a few minutes, I settled down and turned off the lamp.

Lying there in the quiet darkness of the night, I reflected on Karen's remarks about being open to new life experiences. She also mentioned a spiritual awakening.

Maybe this was what Rick meant. I vividly remembered him telling me that when the time was right, I would experience a spiritual awakening. He also said I needed to be receptive to the new experiences that would be unfolding in my life. The time must have finally been right.

18

MONDAY: *Haircut, 5:45 p.m.*
TUESDAY: *Guided meditation workshop, 7:00 p.m.*
WEDNESDAY: *Builders Assn. meeting, 6:30 p.m.*
THURSDAY: *Magazine copy due at noon*
FRIDAY: *Dinner at Bethany's house, 6:00 p.m., pick up cake*
SATURDAY: *Sorority alumnae luncheon, noon*
SUNDAY: *After-church luncheon, bring covered dish*

A quick look at my calendar revealed how complex my life had become. I was living a double life, if not a triple one.

Sylvia and I joined the church's singles group and made new friends. The people we met were mostly young professionals. There were a few eccentrics who provided a little diversity to the group, such as the kinky-haired astrologer and a spooky-looking guy who claimed to be the illegitimate son of Lon Chaney Jr. He looked a bit like the actor, so maybe he was his son. Or not.

After Angela's death the previous year, our college gang had become closer than ever. We had a greater appreciation for life and recognized how important we were to each other.

Susanna and Donna got me involved with our sorority's local alumnae association. As the journalist in the group, I found myself volunteering as publicity chair.

Then there was my work persona as the ultimate professional. Sylvia and I were careful not to express our philosophical views with our coworkers for fear of—well, for fear of them thinking we were weird. We were still having days when we poked fun at ourselves and wondered if maybe we were slightly nuts. If we were, I assured Sylvia, we were pricey macadamias, not cheap peanuts.

Sylvia's eyes widened as she raised her eyebrows. "I think we're pistachios. We're slightly cracked and take longer to mature."

When I was with my college friends, I never talked about my church activities. Bethany was my best friend, but I wasn't sure how she would react to me howling at the moon or studying past lives. As long as we had known each other, we had never discussed spirituality. We had plenty of other things to talk about.

Bethany's Friday gathering was a going-away party for Kate and her husband, Tom. I brought dessert—a "bon voyage" cake I picked up at the bakery. Tom received a job promotion and was being transferred to Dallas. They would be three hours away, so it wasn't as though they were moving to California. Besides, he was a Houston boy and would be coming home to visit his parents, and Kate's family lived north of the city.

After we finished pigging out on Jimmy's great barbecue, we gathered to say our goodbyes to Tom and Kate. After all the toasts, Bethany made a surprise announcement.

"Since you are all here, Jimmy and I thought it would be the perfect time to let you know that we're pregnant again!"

Oh, crapola. Bethany was going to have another child. Not in my wildest dreams did I see this coming. Lynn Ann was barely eighteen months old, and when she was born, Bethany had said she would never go through childbirth again.

Everyone hugged her and congratulated her, except me. Instead of joining in, I stood stoic while selfish thoughts floated through my head.

I was the last single one of the group, and I'd be the last to have children. Bethany was already on her second child, and I *still* didn't have any prospects in sight.

I finally mustered enough fake enthusiasm to give her a hug and tell her how happy I was for her.

Yes, wench, I'm happy for you. And I'm ticked you didn't tell me first.

I was supposed to be her best friend, and she didn't tell me first. She must have had her reasons. But who was I to judge? I was hiding a whole new life from her.

I stayed to clean the kitchen. Everyone else had babysitters waiting for them at home, except for Donna, who was six months pregnant.

Oh, bullcorn! All my friends were married and having babies, and I was doomed to be an old spinster. My biological clock was ticking at supersonic speed, and I thought my ovaries were going to explode. I took a deep breath and told myself to suck it up and make it through the rest of the evening. *Jackie, be happy for Bethany instead of acting like a green-eyed monster.*

As we were finishing up, Jimmy's friend Bruce dropped by for some leftover barbecue. The guys visited in the den while I helped Bethany in the kitchen.

"Bruce and his girlfriend broke up," she whispered. "Now's your chance."

My chance? I didn't even know Bruce had had a girl-friend, and I couldn't care less about his love life. I wished Bethany would quit trying to fix us up. He was a nice enough guy. I just didn't feel any chemistry. He was clean-cut, average build, and tallish, about five-ten. He and Jimmy became close friends when they served together in Vietnam. Looking at Bruce with his burr hair-cut, one would think he was still in the military.

As he was leaving, Bruce casually mentioned he was cooking out on Sunday for the late afternoon football game and invited me to come. I said I would try to make it, knowing darn well I wouldn't. That was my church day, and I planned to attend the singles group game party.

On the way to church that Sunday, I told Sylvia about Bruce's invitation.

"Maybe you shouldn't blow him off," she said. "Give the man a chance. Or go to check out his friends. Maybe you'll meet someone new."

"I'll go if you go with me."

She quickly nixed the idea. She was hoping to hook up with Harvey, the CPA she had met at the previous singles party.

"Okay, I won't go to Bruce's cookout. I'm sure I'll have more fun with you."

The phone was ringing when I got home from the

after-church luncheon. It was Bethany reminding me of Bruce's invitation. She wasn't going to take no for an answer, so I caved in and went to his town house.

Bethany and Jimmy were the only familiar faces. I was outgoing when it came to my professional work, but I still hadn't overcome my introverted ways when it came to strangers. So I decided to have a beer to help me overcome my shyness.

I clung to Bethany's side for the first half hour before she used her pregnancy as an excuse to go home for a few minutes. She also wanted to check in on Lynn Ann and see how the new babysitter was doing. She and Jimmy left saying they'd be back soon. I downed another beer or two, or maybe three, as I waited for them, but they never returned.

* * *

A knock on the bedroom door jolted me awake. I could hardly open my eyes, much less move. The door opened slightly, and I heard Bruce's voice.

"Hate to wake you so early, but I'm sure you need to get to work."

It was Monday morning, and I was still at Bruce's house. *What the heck happened last night?*

The bedroom door was still ajar as Bruce stood in the hallway waiting for a response.

"Oh, darn it! I'm going to be late."

He chuckled and closed the door.

My head hurt and the room spun. I rushed to the bathroom and turned on the sink faucet so Bruce wouldn't hear me barf my guts out as I hugged the commode. It took at least a half roll of toilet paper to clean up my mess. A glance in the mirror led to panic. My frizzy hair and bloodshot eyes looked like something out of *The Exorcist*. No wonder I was spewing green stuff.

My anxiety heightened when I remembered my poor Jill was locked up in the apartment and probably wondering where her mommy was. And by now, she had most likely peed and pooped everywhere.

Thank goodness my clothes are still on. Hopefully, I hadn't done anything really, really stupid. I found a comb in the vanity drawer and did the best I could with my hair, squirted some toothpaste on my finger, and brushed and swished to get rid of the horrible beer-vomit taste in my mouth.

I felt like a cheap floozy slithering out of the No Tell Motel as I walked down the hall to the kitchen.

Bruce smiled. "Would you like some coffee?"

Why was he smiling? I hoped I hadn't given him anything to smile about. Oh my, what had I done?

My mouth was cotton-dry and I could barely speak. "No thank you" was all I could utter. The smell of bacon frying made me queasy.

He stood at the kitchen counter beating some eggs in a bowl. "Want some breakfast?"

I wanted to grab my purse and get the heck out of there and never see him again. "No thank you."

I felt the need to apologize, although I wasn't sure what I was apologizing for. Bruce must have read my mind.

"Nothing to worry about. You had one beer too many and kinda fell asleep. Didn't think it was safe for you to drive, so I let you sleep it off."

At least I learned Bruce was a gentleman and knew

how to be diplomatic. He was probably thinking that I had four or five beers too many and passed out like a drunken sailor.

I graciously made my exit and headed home to get dressed for what turned out to be a miserable workday. I knew what my boss thought of employees who called in sick on Mondays, so that wasn't an option.

Sylvia was eager to get me alone. "Inquiring minds want to know. And from the way you look, it must have been some party."

She was a little disappointed by my story. I had no romantic turn of events to report.

Dealing with Sylvia was easy. Next, I would have to endure the third degree from Bethany. No doubt Jimmy would let her know I "spent the night" at Bruce's house. I decided that when the time came, I would tell her the whole screwed-up evening was all her fault for deserting me, and that I had nothing further to say about it.

When she invited me to stop by her house three days later, I was expecting the third degree. Instead, I got the crushing news that she had had a miscarriage Sunday night. I knew she must have been heartbroken, and I wanted to comfort her, but after telling me the news, she wiped her tears and headed to the kitchen to get us something to drink.

"I don't want to ever talk about this again. I want to pretend that it never happened."

"Would you like me to tell the girls?"

"Okay. But tell them I don't want to talk about it. Ever."

I honored her wishes. It was never mentioned again.

She never asked me what happened after she left the

party. I was expecting Bruce to tell Jimmy and Jimmy to tell Bethany, but as far as I know, Bruce never told anyone else about it. I guess there wasn't much to tell. However, I was still embarrassed and hoped I would never have to see him again.

19

P*lease don't mention Bruce. Please don't mention Bruce.* That's all I thought when Bethany would call. I was relieved that a few months went by without his name being uttered. When Bethany invited me over for a Friday night cookout, I didn't have the nerve to ask if he would be there.

Bethany was my best friend, and I knew she still had to be dealing with her miscarriage, so I showed up Friday night hoping this wasn't going to be another of her fix-up attempts. But it was.

It was a party for six with Bethany and Jimmy, another couple, and Bruce and me. I had met the other couple once before at Bethany's house. The husband and Jimmy worked together at the truck dealership. She was a mousy, frail-looking, stay-at-home housewife who didn't have much to say. I envisioned her as one of those Stepford wives, a robot created by her husband.

Jimmy's good cooking made the evening worthwhile. That man knew how to barbecue.

No beer for me. I had sworn off Schlitz after the humiliating experience at Bruce's house.

I was not enjoying myself. I didn't care much for the other couple and was uncomfortable around Bruce. But I was relieved to see my dear friend Bethany smiling and socializing again.

The evening ended early. Jimmy had floor duty the next morning, and Bruce said he was going fishing.

"Bethany tells me you're quite the fisherman," Bruce said when he was leaving.

I stuttered a bit, then uttered, "Not really. It's just something I enjoyed as a kid."

"She's being modest," Bethany said. "Don't forget about our great fishing adventures."

"Wanna join me for some bay fishing tomorrow?" Bruce asked.

Bethany interjected that Bruce had a nice new boat and it would be a fun trip.

I didn't want to go with him, but I didn't want to embarrass him, so I said yes. I also saw it as an opportunity to redeem myself and show him there was more to me than being a cheap drunk.

It was well after midnight before I fell asleep. Instead of counting sheep, I counted the disastrous ways this fishing trip might end. By saying yes, did that mean Bruce might ask me out on a real date? Would I trip and fall overboard? *Maybe, if I'm lucky, this fishing trip will go so badly that he never wants to see me again.*

* * *

I kept hitting the snooze button, and the next thing I knew it was 4:45 a.m. I made a mad dash to get ready by

5:30 a.m. I hid my messy hair under a ball cap and drank one cup of coffee after another trying to wake up.

Bruce was right on time.

"My, don't you look bright-eyed and bushy-tailed," he said when I opened my apartment door.

"Good morning. Not so sure how bushy-tailed I am."

Bruce was a genuinely pleasant person. I might have liked him more if I didn't believe he was being pushed off on me. I wondered if he thought the same about me —that I was being shoved off on him.

He had packed sandwiches for the trip, iced down some sodas, and seemed to have the day well planned.

The forty-five-minute drive to the bay was an endurance test. It was hard to carry on a conversation because we didn't seem to have much in common. I tried to entertain him with some Bethany and Jackie stories. Those drew a few comments.

By the time we reached the boat dock, I regretted all the coffee I had drunk on an empty stomach. I had caffeine jitters and a queasy tummy. And I really, really had to pee.

I hated to admit to Bruce that I needed to visit the ladies' room before getting on the boat, but I wasn't sure how much longer I could hold it. Then came the horrible realization that I wouldn't be able to go once we were out on the water.

"Ladies' room?"

He pointed to the right. "Well, see that little shed over by the bait shop? That's for ladies too."

One look at the small wooden shack, and I knew I was doomed. I opened the door and discovered it was a slight step up from an outhouse. It looked fairly clean, and I *really, really, really* had to pee, so there was no turning back.

There was no porcelain toilet, only a commode seat on top of a wooden box that had a big hole in it. I had loads of public restroom phobias, and sitting on community toilets was one of them. Thank goodness there was plenty of toilet paper. I lined the seat with tons of it before I sat down. Knowing Bruce was waiting for me, I moved quickly.

Bruce was standing in the boat and waiting for me at the end of the dock. I strutted down the creaky boat ramp as though I was a top model and it was a fashion runway. Despite having no romantic interest in Bruce, I had a ridiculous need to impress him.

I passed several fishermen in boats. Some said hello and waved at me, which bolstered my self-confidence.

Keep your cool, Jackie. Strut your stuff. Shoulders back, stomach in. Don't trip!

I turned, smiled, and waved back at one group of men.

As I neared the end of the ramp, a big smile spread over Bruce's face. *Hmm, he must be glad I'm finally out of the outhouse, or he must genuinely like me.* I hesitated but kept walking. *Maybe I have overdone the charm.*

I hadn't seen a man beam like that since Angela and Mike's wedding. When Mike watched Angela walk down the aisle, he had such a huge, loving smile. The kind of beaming grin a man had when he was deeply, passionately in love and gazing at the woman of his dreams. Bruce had that same look.

Oh no. This was not a good thing, because I didn't have any romantic interest in Bruce. This could become an embarrassing and awkward situation. The closer I got to the boat, the more he grinned.

"Uh," Bruce said with a huge smile. "You've got toilet paper flying out your britches."

* * *

Toilet paper flying out of my britches was one of those comeuppance moments in my life—those times when I thought I was cool, only to find out I wasn't. Like back in the early seventies when I had worked for *HighLife* and had been assigned to cover a charity event honoring my idol Rod McKuen.

A women's club had brought him to town for a fundraising concert and welcomed him at a big society party the night before the concert. It was held at a mansion in River Oaks, one of Houston's ritziest residential communities. Besides meeting my favorite poet/songwriter, I also had the opportunity to rub shoulders with some of the city's biggest movers and shakers. Maybe one of those society matrons would introduce me to her rich son.

What to wear? What to wear? I scanned my closet and realized I had one decent choice—my yellow crepe gaucho pants and matching jacket. Off to the dry cleaners, then the hairdresser. I had to look my best.

As soon as I entered the fancy foyer of that lavish home, I regressed to my country bumpkin roots. I was out of place and didn't belong there.

Mr. McKuen was not the high society type, so he didn't arrive until late in the evening. Meanwhile, my staff photographer was taking photos while I walked around introducing myself and getting names and quotes for my story. I sensed those society women's cold, judging eyes staring at me.

Keep your cool, Jackie. You look fantastic, and you're as important as anyone else here.

I tried to be calm and confident, but they continued to throw piercing daggers my way. After about thirty minutes, the hostess came up to me and said, "Sweetie, do you know that your laundry ticket is pinned to the back of your jacket?"

* * *

My fishing trip with Bruce went from bad to worse. I got seasick and "tossed my coffee" on his glossy new boat—right as he was reeling in a huge fish. It was the big one that got away when he had to turn his attention to keeping me from falling off the boat.

I leaned over the side as far as I could, not wanting to upchuck on his fishing gear any more than I already had. A larger boat passed by, and I almost fell overboard from the wake it caused. *Wake* was fishing lingo I learned from Bruce that meant a big fat wave, something we didn't have in Granny's pond.

My dad used to say there was nothing more painful for a man than losing a fish right by the side of the boat. I was relieved Bruce handled it so graciously.

"Let's cut bait and get you back home," he said.

His tone was sweet and considerate. But I knew he must be thinking he wanted to cut our losses before I did any more damage to his boat.

"I'm feeling much better," I assured him. "Let's keep fishing."

Bruce proved to be an easygoing person, so the rest

of the trip was tolerable. I caught a sixteen-inch trout, and he hauled in a nice-sized redfish that was bigger than the one that had gotten away.

The trip home was awkward. Bruce was the quiet type, and I was too tired to conjure up any more Bethany and Jackie tales. The frequent pregnant pauses gave me plenty of time to reflect on the misadventures of the day.

As long as I lived, I would never forget Bruce telling me I had toilet paper flying out my britches. And then I pictured myself barfing over the side of the boat. *At least I didn't wet my pants.*

I was relieved when we reached my apartment. I was anxious to jump out of the truck and head for the shower. Bruce was the gentlemanly type, so I fidgeted in the seat while he walked around to open the door.

I tried to swing my feet around to gracefully step out, but my left foot wouldn't move. My sneaker was mysteriously stuck to the floor of Bruce's truck. I pulled my foot out of my shoe, embarrassed that he would see my size tens. He yanked my sneaker to dislodge it, and, in doing so, a big chunk of carpeting ripped from the floor of the truck.

Apparently, somewhere along the way, I'd stepped on a treble hook, one of those three-hooks-fused-together types. Two of the hooks were embedded in the rubber sole of my shoe, and the third one was hooked to the floor of the truck.

I tried to contain my laughter and hold it down to a quiet snicker.

"What's so funny?"

"This is a fitting end to a crazy day. I'll bet you'll never ask me to go fishing again."

* * *

That screwy fishing trip turned out to be the beginning of a comfortable romance. The next weekend we went to dinner and a movie. As the weeks passed, we got into a monthly fishing routine. Between fishing trips, we enjoyed movies, hung out with Bethany and Jimmy, and sometimes stayed in to cook and watch television. Fortunately, I was a typical Texas gal who loved her Texas football, baseball, and basketball teams, so we watched a lot of sports.

Conversations slowly became more meaningful as we talked about our families and childhood experiences. I grew more and more at ease around Bruce and could be myself without being judged. And I had stopped judging him. In my eyes, he had evolved from being a grease monkey to a successful business owner. I appreciated his country-boy mannerisms, although I wished he liked other music besides country and western. He was such a gentleman, always opening doors for me, and would occasionally bring me flowers.

Bruce grew up in a small town about forty miles from Houston. His dad owned a horse-breeding ranch, so I knew where to find manure if I ever needed it again. His mom was a homemaker who sold Tupperware and taught Sunday School at a Methodist church.

He spoke highly of them and often remarked about his great parents and his happy childhood. I was apprehensive about meeting them. It was a big step in our relationship, and I was unsure about making it. *Is he Mr. Right or Mr. Right Now?*

Knowing he was the youngest of three brothers, I

feared his mom might treat me like I wasn't good enough for her baby boy.

"Don't be nervous," Bruce said as we walked up the sidewalk to his parents' front door. "My mom will love you."

Too late. My palms were beginning to sweat and my heart was racing. I grabbed his hand for reassurance.

Before Bruce could ring the doorbell, his mom opened the door.

"You must be Jackie," she said, hugging me. I immediately felt at ease as she invited us into the den. "Have a seat while I get the tea. Sweet or unsweet?"

"Sweet, please," I answered.

Barbara had the quintessential qualities of an impeccable stay-at-home TV mom from the 1950s—short, perfectly coifed dark blond hair and a nicely starched button-up blouse with matching gathered skirt. She topped off her ensemble with a single-strand pearl choker and matching pearl button earrings. She also had the manners of a well-bred finishing school graduate.

When Bruce's dad stepped into the den, I thought he was Ben Cartwright coming in from the Ponderosa. Frank was about six feet tall with a hefty, masculine build and silvery platinum hair. He wore cowboy boots with denim jeans, a dark long-sleeved shirt, and a leather vest. A man's man for sure.

"Very pleased to finally meet you, Jackie," he said, gently shaking my hand. "I have heard some nice things about you from my son."

After greeting me, he walked over to Barbara and gave her a kiss on the cheek. Frank towered over Barbara, and his cowboy attire clashed with her pearls and prim-and-proper appearance. They were genuinely gracious people.

Next, I had to take Bruce home to meet Mom and Carl. It was Bruce's turn to be nervous.

"Don't worry," I said as we walked to Mom's front door. "She'll love you."

And she did, especially since he brought her flowers. She was impressed with his old-fashioned manners and how well he treated me. *Yes, ma'am. No, ma'am. Please, ma'am. Thank you, ma'am.* These were words that won her heart.

"He's a keeper," she said when we were alone in the kitchen.

I was glad Carl wasn't home that day. No telling what he might have done to embarrass me.

Then came our sixth fishing trip. Bruce was reeling in a nice-sized fish, and my job was to catch it in the net. A button on my fishing shirt got caught in the net. By the time I untangled myself, Bruce's big catch had spit the hook and swum away.

"I'm really, really, really sorry for not getting the net under the fish in time. It looked like such a great catch."

"No big deal," he chuckled. "As far as I'm concerned, you're my greatest catch."

His sweet comment caught me by surprise. Yes, he did occasionally bring me flowers, but when it came to verbal expressions, Bruce wasn't the romantic type. As I stood there somewhat dumbfounded, he baited his hook.

He nonchalantly turned to me and asked, "So, wanna get married?"

My jaw must have dropped to my knees. I was stunned and speechless. *He hasn't even said I love you, and now he's proposing to me. What the heck? And he's not even on his knee.*

Bruce was the complete opposite of Andrew the banker. Maybe someone like Bruce was what I needed in my life. Someone who was kind to me and treated me like a queen. Someone who loved my dog and accepted me the way I was. Someone who would be faithful and not cheat on me like John had.

Bruce was a good, decent man, the kind that was hard to come by. He was dependable, hardworking, honest, and loyal. In many ways, he reminded me of Angela's widower, Mike, the-salt-of-the-earth guy who had treated my dear friend like royalty. I still clearly remembered how I felt about Mike as I watched him recite his wedding vows. *If I ever find a man like Mike, I'm going to marry him.*

It wasn't the kind of proposal a woman dreams of, but it was fitting for Bruce.

He finished baiting his hook and gave me a so-what's-your-answer look.

"Okay," I said, which seemed an appropriate answer for his somewhat lackluster proposal.

Marrying Bruce seemed like the logical thing to do. Jackie Ann Jackson. I could live with that name. Besides, it wasn't much of a transition from Jackie Ann Johnson, and my initials would stay the same. I wondered if I would have married him if his last name had been Dieterman. Or Helfinstine. Or Waldaberger. Or Hornblower.

I had turned thirty-two, and he was pushing thirty-four. The alarms on our biological clocks were going off, and we didn't want to push the snooze button. Two months later I was standing at the altar of the First Methodist Church that Bruce's parents attended.

Secretly, I wanted to be married in my church with Sylvia at my side, but I wanted to please his family, especially his mom. Barbara and Frank also offered to host our wedding reception at the ranch. My marriage would be off to a bad start if I turned down their gracious offer, and the ranch did provide a lovely setting for a reception.

We kept the wedding simple, with Bethany and Jimmy as our sole attendants. Barbara took care of most of the arrangements. Despite the short planning period, the church was beautifully decorated with white roses, exactly what I wanted. Best of all, I didn't have to stress out to plan a wedding. Mom and Barbara did all the stressing for me.

I repeated all the traditional vows, except I stumbled a bit on "till death do us part." As much as I loved Bruce, I wondered if it was possible for a couple to love each other forever. What I wanted to say was "as long as we both shall love."

We bought a four-bedroom home in Bethany and Jimmy's southwest Houston neighborhood. Sadly, as our marriage was taking off, theirs was crumbling. Perhaps it was the miscarriage or something else that was tearing them apart. Bethany wasn't willing to discuss it and still acted as if the miscarriage never happened. Whatever it was, they were on-again, off-again for the next few years.

My first four years of marriage were amazing. I was

living the storybook life I had dreamed of. A month before our first anniversary, our daughter was born. I couldn't help myself—I wanted to name her Jillian and didn't dare tell Bruce that's what I named my dog before I shortened it to Jill.

Bruce had wanted us to choose a name that would honor our mothers and suggested Barbara Ann. The mere mention of it left me with a music loop of the Beach Boys singing that name over and over and over and over in my head. It was maddening.

I was eight months pregnant at the time and trying to control my mood swings. "Children's names should be unique and fit them. I've always wished my parents would have spent more time thinking of a name for me so I wouldn't grow up being just Jackie."

"Get over it already. Jackie suits you perfectly. If you'd been named Jacqueline, you would've probably insisted on being called Jackie."

I laughed.

"What's so funny?"

"You sound like my aunt Millie. She once stopped my complaining by asking me what I would have wanted to be called instead of Jackie. I couldn't come up with an answer."

When I held my daughter for the first time, I knew Jillian was the right name for her. I rationalized that I wasn't naming her after my dog. I was giving her the same name as the precious little girl who gave me my dog. That little girl named Jillian had been so beautiful, with light curly brown hair, adoring big blue eyes, and the sweetest smile. Even with her eyes still shut and little hair, I knew my baby girl was going to grow up with the same adorable features. I was just glad she wasn't born with big floppy ears and a bushy tail.

Bruce was so in love with me at that moment, he would have said yes to any name I suggested. If I had said, "Let's name her Malvolia," he would have said, "Yes, dear, that's a perfect name."

I don't know where I came up with Jolene for a middle name. Maybe Dolly Parton was whispering in my ear. But I liked the way it sounded—Jillian Jolene Jackson. Yes, that had a nice ring to it. A beautiful name for such a beautiful baby. It would also give her other options as she grew up, like Jill, JJ, or Jilli. I was always thinking ahead and always trying to justify my actions.

"I don't want you to go back to work when your maternity leave is over," Bruce said while we sat in the den adoring our newborn. "We can afford to get by without you working, and I think *Metro* can survive without you."

My maternity leave was almost up, and I'd been contemplating not returning to work. "I've been thinking the same thing. I can give Mr. Sanders two weeks' notice and offer to work from home until he finds a replacement."

Mr. Sanders did allow me to work from home during the three weeks it took him to find a replacement, and he asked me to work in the office for two days to train my replacement. He also offered me some freelance work, which I gladly accepted.

And so, I settled into my life as a stay-at-home mom.

Two years after Jillian was born, we had a son we named Henry. We had seven possible names picked out, none of which were Henry.

"He looks like a Henry," Bruce said, holding our

newborn in my hospital room. "How about Henry Harrison Jackson?"

I was so exhausted from childbirth I would have agreed to Rumpelstiltskin Remington or Pinocchio Parsnip. Three days later when I looked at his birth certificate, I wondered if we should have put more thought into his name.

At least my baby boy didn't have a *J* name. Frank and Barbara had named their sons Bryan, Bradley, and Bruce. Jackie and Jillian in the same household was bad enough—plus a dog named Jill. The experience made me more appreciative of my own name. No telling what my parents experienced naming me.

My focus in life became my children, and I drifted away from my church activities. Bruce had joined me for a service when we began dating, but he thought it was a lot of hooey and never went back. I wasn't sure what he meant. Perhaps it was the meditation and modern interpretations of the Bible he didn't like.

Unlike me, Bruce was brought up in a religious environment. With a Sunday School teacher for a mom, he faithfully attended church as a youngster. I had come to believe there was truth in all religions and agreed to raise our children Methodist.

Sometimes when Bruce and Jimmy went hunting or fishing, Mom would take care of the kids so I could sneak off to attend church services with Sylvia. One day, the lesson was on "finding your spiritual path." There was a time when I had thought I was on the right path, the one Rick predicted. Now, I wondered if I had gotten lost along the way. Or stumbled and fallen off it.

In between thinking about what my kids were doing

and what I would fix for dinner, I carefully listened to Rev. Randall's words.

"Your spiritual path is a journey to finding enlightenment, which is your connection to God," he said. "There is no one specific path. We each have our own pathway and experience enlightenment in different ways."

Sylvia and I enjoyed lunch at a nearby bistro after church and discussed our interpretation of the lesson. That was the day I decided to reveal my deep, dark secret: thinking I had an encounter with my guardian angel.

Her big wide-eyed look said she was excited. "That is the most amazing story I have ever heard!"

"So you think it might have really happened? I wasn't hallucinating?"

"I genuinely believe in guardian angels. I wish I could meet mine. You are so lucky."

I put down my fork and looked at her. "I still have times when I think it was a hallucination. And so many questions. Like why a woman would have a man as a guardian angel."

Sylvia grinned and shook her head. "You're over-thinking it."

"Don't make fun of me," I said, "but I was in a car accident the year before my conversation with Rick."

"The same wreck where Rick appeared as a fireman?"

"Yes, that one. At the time, the doctor said I had a mild concussion and sent me on my merry way. After my encounter with Rick, I was convinced I suffered a brain injury or developed a tumor because of the accident. I scheduled a follow-up appointment and asked for a CAT scan. The doctor asked why I needed one. No way I could say, 'because I'm hallucinating a guardian angel,' so I lied a little bit about other symptoms. He ordered a CAT scan, but they didn't find anything."

She looked at me. "So your head was empty?"

I laughed. "Yes, it was empty. Bruce once told me I needed to have my head examined. I said, 'I already did and they didn't find anything.' 'That figures,' he said."

For some reason, Sylvia found the comment hilarious and had us both cackling. It took a few minutes for us to continue our serious discussion.

"Rick mentioned words like 'spiritual awakening' and 'a spiritual path to enlightenment,' but I worry I've lost my way," I said. "I don't come to church much anymore, and I don't seem to be making any big contributions to the world."

"You're living a wholesome Christian life, aren't you?"

I nodded. "Yes."

"And you're raising your children in a Christian environment. So, every day, in some small way, you are making contributions. Besides, it's a continuing journey. Relax and enjoy the long ride."

The waitress interrupted to ask if we cared for dessert. We declined.

"Sometimes I don't feel as though I'm where I'm supposed to be, spiritually speaking," I continued.

"The Bible teaches that we are where God wants us to be," Sylvia said. "You are where you need to be at this point in your life. And remember, you don't have to be sitting in a church pew to worship God."

She always knew the right thing to say.

Church had taught me that God is omnipresent. He

was everywhere, and I didn't have to be in a church to worship him or talk to him.

Rick was right when he had said my grandfather had a profound influence on me. One of the things I remembered most from my childhood was Grandpa Will, my mom's dad, and his beautiful garden. Especially his sweet peas. He once told me his garden was his church and that's where he spoke to God. He was a spiritual person, although he wasn't a churchgoer.

"God is all around us," he'd said as he gazed at his garden. "I may have planted the seeds, but it's God's wonder that makes them grow."

There were times when I'd questioned God's actuality. Remembering how deeply my grandpa had believed in him helped me accept the possibility of his existence.

Grandpa's favorite song had been the hymn "In the Garden." I was about twelve years old when he died. I still remember the warm sensation that went through me when the soloist sang the song at his funeral.

And He walks with me and He talks with me,
And He tells me I am His own.
And the joy we share as we tarry there,
None other has ever known.

20

Apparently, I learned nothing from Karen Hornblower. I never completely stopped howling at the moon, and, to some degree, I still chased after impossible fantasies instead of living in the now. I expected to have a perfect life with my perfect husband. But five years into my marriage, I became painfully aware that there was no such thing as a perfect life or a perfect marriage. And certainly not a perfect man.

When the kids survived their toddler years, I spent more time with my freelance writing for *Metro*. Mom gladly kept them when I needed to take pictures or interview someone. I loved my children more than anything on earth, but sometimes I needed a break from motherhood.

I also needed a break from marriage. *So much for marital bliss.* Bliss was a state of mind, and my mind was slowly changing. Bruce and I started arguing, mostly about how to raise our children. He thought I was too strict as a mother, and I thought he was way too lax as a father.

Our child-rearing philosophies collided like two Mack trucks in a head-on collision. I was the unstoppable force. He was the immovable object. There were times I knew Bruce was right, and I tried to soften my stance.

"You are too much of a worrywart," Bruce said when we sat in the backyard watching our children play. "Let the kids be kids."

A few moments later, Henry grabbed some dirt out of a flowerpot and shoved it in his mouth. I rushed to stop him.

"If you keep babying them, they'll never toughen up," Bruce said after I wiped the dirt off Henry's mouth. "Eating dirt is part of being a kid. It's good for them."

I glared at him. "Good for them? No telling what's in that dirt. Are you trying to poison our children?"

When Henry turned four, I enrolled the kids in swimming classes. Bruce argued it was a waste of money.

"Throw them in the water and let them swim or drown. That's how I learned to swim."

We argued the most about Henry. When he was four and a half, Bruce took him on a fishing trip. I thought he was too young to go, but I lost the argument. Henry didn't enjoy the experience and wanted to come home to his mommy.

"You've turned him into a momma's boy," Bruce argued when they returned from the trip.

"He's not a momma's boy. Give him time. He's just not ready."

The day Henry celebrated his fifth birthday, Bruce called him Hank. He thought it was a much more macho name, as if a new nickname would make him a tougher little boy. I put my foot down. And not gently. I waited until the kids were asleep and we were in our bedroom. Bruce was sitting on the bed taking off his boots. He looked up as I stood and glared at him.

"Don't ever call him Hank again." I stomped my foot. "His name is Henry. You even named him that. He is not a Hank."

Bruce gave me a stern look. "Lower your voice. I don't appreciate you yelling at me."

"Then don't give me something to yell about."

"This is a side of you I've never seen before, and I don't like it." Bruce picked up his pillow and headed to the den. It was the first time he slept on the sofa, but it wouldn't be his last.

A night apart gave us time to cool off, and by the next morning, we were apologizing to each other. It was the first big fight in our seven years of marriage, and it scared both of us. For the next month, we worked at being more considerate of each other's concerns. Bruce also made me promise to be less of a worrywart. I said I would try, knowing darn well that would be next to impossible for me.

* * *

I dreaded Jillian's first day of school. I brushed her golden-brown tresses over and over, trying to get her ponytail perfect. I remembered the intimate times when Mom brushed my hair, so I cherished those special moments with Jillian. That morning, I didn't want to stop brushing. I wasn't ready for my little girl to be going to school.

I became a blubbering basket case after I dropped her off. I feared something terrible might happen. She could break a leg during recess. Or choke to death on cafeteria food. Or get kidnapped. I expected the school to call and ask me to pick her up because she was crying for her mother.

She didn't get hurt, she loved her school lunch, and no one kidnapped her. She didn't even miss me.

Two years later, when it came time for Henry to start school, I dropped him off and left on my merry way. Finally, free time for myself. About ten o'clock, the principal called to tell me my son was crying nonstop for his mother. Oh my. Bruce was right. I had raised a momma's boy. I decided it was time for some tough love, so I let him stay at school and cry. He eventually quit bawling and survived the day. By the next morning, he was eager to go back to class.

With the kids at school, I was bored and unfulfilled. I also missed Sylvia and my other work friends, so I started working part-time out of the *Metro* office instead of at home. Sylvia had married Harvey, the CPA she met at church, so I didn't see her very often. Lunching with her on weekdays was a treat which got me out of my stay-at-home rut.

When the assistant real estate editor left, I jumped at the chance to take his job. I accepted the position without consulting Bruce. That created a big argument. I knew it would, so I waited until the kids were asleep to tell him.

Okay, so it would have been best to ask Bruce first, but I knew he would say no. He had such a macho mentality. A woman's place was in the home, and the man was the breadwinner. The boss. The ruler. The king of the castle.

I had the plan all worked out. Mom was more than

happy to pick up the kids from school and take them to our house until I got home. There were also some after-school programs available.

I didn't think Bruce would argue with those options. But he did. And then it happened. He raised his voice and called me a vile, disgusting name. I was shocked that he used the f-word.

Yes, my mild-mannered husband used the f-word. I despised that offensive term and couldn't believe he said it.

He called me a feminist!

I don't know why I thought that was such a dirty name. I was going into the workplace during the height of the women's movement, yet I never thought of myself as one of *them*.

Bras were too expensive to burn, and I was too cheap to destroy such a precious commodity. Besides, my B cup wouldn't have made much of a statement.

* * *

It had been frustrating when I had started job hunting after college. Inequality for women was blatantly obvious. The Help Wanted ads were divided into *Help Wanted– Male* and *Help Wanted–Female* sections. Most of the writing jobs I'd sought were opened only to men. I'd struggled to get a job based on my skills and not my gender.

Women weren't even allowed to wear pants in most offices. I remember when pantsuits became acceptable, and companies had strict policies as to what was considered an appropriate combination of jacket, blouse, and pants.

The *Help Wanted—Male/Female* practice ended long before I tried to land my job at *Metro*. But even then, my future boss, Mr. Sanders, made it clear he would prefer to hire a man for the job because the position required working almost exclusively with men. Men who built homes. Men who built apartment buildings. Men who built commercial buildings. Men who owned building supply companies. Few women were running those companies.

Yes, in those days, men seemed to rule the world. But I didn't let that stop me, especially when Mr. Sanders dared to tell me he was skeptical of hiring single women because they "tend to get married, have babies, and leave the job." I simply made a good argument for why I was better suited for the position. In some small way, I guess I did my part to fight for equal work rights for women, but I never marched in demonstrations or carried signs.

* * *

But a feminist? Why would Bruce call me a feminist? Because I wanted to have it all? A career? Marriage? Family?

Maybe I was a feminist and never knew it. But Bruce's use of the word let me know he still had a caveman mentality and thought a woman's place was in the home. At least he didn't want to keep me barefoot and pregnant.

His mom represented his ideal of the perfect wife and mother. I truly admired her and wished I was more like her. However, I wasn't the type to be happy at home raising kids, selling Tupperware, and teaching Sunday School.

21

The music was soft and low, Zen-like and meditative. A faint aroma of lavender incense filled the dimly lit room. I was beginning to relax but still nervous. It had been hard for me to admit I needed help. I tended to think I was strong and capable of solving my own problems. However, my unhappiness had been eating at my insides, and I feared my despair would soon be visible on the outside.

It was the waiting room of Rev. Phyllis Watson, a psychologist and the church's associate minister. Sylvia raved about how much she had helped her and Harvey with premarital counseling. I was there for marital counseling. Life with Bruce had gotten testy after I returned to work full-time. After nine years of marriage, I was dangling at the end of a short, frayed rope, and all I could see below me was a big, dark, abysmal hole.

Arriving ten minutes early gave me time to calm my nerves before our four o'clock appointment. It was a minute before four when she entered the waiting room and invited me into her office. I brought along my trusted tape recorder to ensure I didn't forget details of what we discussed.

Phyllis was fortyish with dark auburn hair and a sincere smile. She had moved to Houston from Wales and had an interesting accent that sounded somewhat British.

After obligatory pleasantries and offering me a glass of water, she cut to the chase and asked me why I was seeking her guidance.

I pushed the record button and began talking. "I want to save my marriage. Or at least make it tolerable."

She listened attentively to my petty gripes about Bruce. I guess she was letting me blow off some steam. I was still reeling from a big fight we'd had the night before.

I wiggled around in my chair. "He was furious because I took Jillian—she's our daughter—to Neiman Marcus for back-to-school clothes. He said it was financially irresponsible and plain stupid. Told me to quit trying to keep up with the Joneses."

Phyllis wrote something on her notepad before looking up at me. "Is money an issue in your marriage?"

I took a deep breath. "No, Bruce is a good provider and I earn a good living. Anyway, I was mad, Bruce was mad, and I made matters worse by saying, 'It's my money and I'll spend it how I want to.'"

I told Phyllis how bad I felt after I said it. I'd immediately apologized to Bruce and shared my childhood hang-ups about my hand-me-downs. Most of my clothes were cast-offs from Aunt Millie's daughter. I wanted my daughter to have better things than I had and to have more self-confidence.

Phyllis put her pen down and leaned back in her chair. "Were you able to resolve the issue?"

"He cooled down a bit, but I knew he was still mad. So, I promised I wouldn't shop at Neiman's with Jillian. I didn't promise not to go to Lord and Taylor."

Phyllis gave me a you-are-beyond-help look. At least that's how I interpreted it. "Are there other sources of conflict in your marriage?" she asked as she leaned forward and picked up her pen.

"I'm a planner and like to think ahead. Bruce takes things day by day."

I paused, thinking I had said enough. From the way Phyllis looked at me, I could tell she wanted me to continue.

"One argument was about setting up college funds for the kids. He got all macho. Said we don't even know if our kids will want to go to college. If they decide to go, he'd figure a way to send them. I didn't agree and opened a savings account and started putting some money away. I know my kids, and I know they'll want to go to college. Unfortunately, he sorted through the mail one day before I did. He flipped out when he saw the bank statement."

The more I talked, the more animated I became, moving my arms around and squirming in my chair. "Oh, and then there's the issue of family vacations. I can never get him to help me plan one. Everything is last minute. One year I wanted to take our kids to Disneyland, get to see some of America. Bruce vacationed there as a child, and I thought he'd like the idea. But, no, not Bruce. 'I don't see why we have to drive across the country to a silly amusement park when we've got Astroworld in our own backyard.' When we do take a trip together, it's usually pretty short and we never leave the state."

Phyllis was a good listener and let me do most of the talking. When I paused after my Disneyland tirade, she asked, "Do you enjoy the family trips, despite the brevity?"

"I think you're trying to make a point. Yes, it is more important that we do things as a family instead of driving across the country. We do have fun. Mostly, we go camping in the Hill Country. But I'd still like for my kids to see more of the world than just Texas."

I stopped to catch my breath. I was sure my blood pressure was reaching stroke level as I recalled the many bones of contention between Bruce and me.

"Last week, he accused me of being an uptight fussbudget who always has to have things exactly right. He told me I need to lighten up." I paused, thinking that was enough of an explanation.

"Fussbudget?" Phyllis asked.

"That's his folksy way of telling me I'm too much of a perfectionist."

"Are you?"

"I don't see anything wrong with wanting things to be done right—the best way possible."

"Did he give you examples of when you were being a —what was that word? A fussbudget?"

"Plenty! During that particular disagreement, he said I made too big of a deal out of the pecan pie I made to take to his mother's house. I thought the crust was overcooked and wanted to make another pie. He said there was nothing wrong with the one I made, and he wasn't going to let me waste time making another pie.

"Then he started in on the Christmas card picture issue. He says I drive the whole family batty trying to make things too perfect. He said this year he wasn't going to put up with having to dress exactly right and go to a photography studio. We were going to sit around the tree and let his friend Jimmy come over and take a picture. He was tired of me always having to do things the hard way."

She put down her pen and tilted her head. "Have you considered that Bruce may have a point?"

Bruce may have a point? Lady, you are getting on my nerves. I'm paying you to listen to me, not make me defend myself. I held my tongue and gave some thought to her question. "Maybe he does have a point. I can be a little picky about things."

Phyllis smiled. "A fussbudget?"

I chuckled. "I'll try to lighten up and be less of a fussbudget."

"Would you care for some more water?" she asked.

We took a brief pause to refill our glasses before moving on with the session.

"I would like for you to think back to the time when you looked at Bruce and knew he was the man you wanted to spend the rest of your life with. Think about what attracted you to him in the beginning."

I was stumped. I easily remembered when I knew John was the man I wanted to marry. I recalled the deep love I had for him and how much I wanted him to propose. I could even remember a time when I looked at Andrew and felt with all my heart that I wanted to marry him. But I couldn't recall any of those moments with Bruce.

I cleared my throat and sipped on my water. "I don't

know. I can't think of a time. Well, I guess, maybe when he proposed."

Phyllis clasped her hands together and leaned back in her chair. "Until that moment, you never thought about marrying him?"

"No, not really. The thought might have crossed my mind. My best friend Bethany brought it up several times. Mostly because she married his best friend and thought it would be great if I married Bruce. I kept telling her he wasn't what I wanted in a husband."

"Why not?"

"Well, first, there never was much chemistry between us. You know that head-over-heels-in-love kind of feeling. Where your toes curl when he kisses you. He was kind of a Mr. Right Now, but not Mr. Right. Okay to hang out with. It was a comfortable relationship, but not somebody I wanted to marry. He didn't fit my criteria."

She leaned forward. "Your criteria?"

I paused, contemplating my answer. "For one thing, I wanted a college-educated husband. Bruce attended a junior college. I wanted someone more outgoing and sociable. Someone who enjoyed dancing and my kind of music. Bruce wasn't John."

"Who is John?"

Whoops! Where did that come from? I shocked myself when I said his name. Now I had to explain that situation to Phyllis. I gave her an abridged version of my John story while she wrote notes on her pad. A few tears trickled down my cheeks as I spoke.

She handed me a tissue. "You considered John your ideal man, and no one else has lived up to that standard?"

"I guess. Until now, I hadn't thought of it that way."

"You said you were in college when you met him. How old were you?

"Twenty."

Phyllis leaned back. "Do you think you have matured since that first love?"

"Well, sure."

As we talked, she helped me recognize that I was still holding on to an ideal that I developed when I was much younger. Maybe I hadn't matured much since my first love.

She stopped briefly to look at the notes she had jotted on her pad. "So, John came back to you, you went out, and then you ended the relationship?"

"That's the way I like to tell the story. It sounds better than saying we both cried a lot. Who wants to tell their friends you made a burly grown man cry? I desperately wanted to take him back. I just couldn't bring myself to do it."

"Why not?"

"I never got over the hurt. I just . . . . It's hard to explain. Our breakup was devastating, and I was so humiliated. We were—well, we were pretty much one of the hottest couples on campus. When he unexpectedly dumped me and married someone else, we became the hottest gossip on campus. It was so embarrassing. The hardest part was telling my mother. She adored him almost as much as I did."

I had to stop to grab another tissue.

"You could not bring yourself to take him back?" Phyllis asked after a brief pause.

"To be truthful—and I guess you want me to be—I did consider it about a month after our last date. I wasn't trying to keep tabs on him, but our mutual friend Donna would update me when we talked. When I didn't take him back, Donna said he decided to move back in with his ex-wife for the sake of their son. So they began living a platonic life under the same roof."

I stopped to catch my breath. "I took it as a sign that I should leave well enough alone. It was hard because I had loved him so much. I envisioned a perfect life with him—until he betrayed me. He was the total package. Everything I wanted in a man. But I certainly didn't want to be someone's second wife."

We got back to talking about Bruce. I told her about our short romance and unexpected proposal. The more I talked, the more I wondered why I'd married him.

"It seemed like the right decision at the time. Besides, all my friends were married and having children. And . . . uh, and . . . Oh no—I just remembered . . ." I stopped to replay something in my head.

She looked up from her notepad. "What did you remember?"

"What my aunt Millie said to me. She's my mom's younger sister. They were on the outs for a couple of years. The last time we visited her, she went on and on about her grandkids, and my cousin's happy marriage.

"I was so hurt when she looked at me and said—and she said it *very* judgmentally—'So, Jackie, you never did marry, did you?' Such a slap in the face. I felt like the world's oldest spinster, as though no one would ever marry me. A couple of months later when Bruce proposed— Oh my gosh, did I marry Bruce because I thought he was my last hope?"

Phyllis didn't answer. She handed me another tissue and let me keep talking.

"I did. I married a man I really didn't love. I

thought I loved him. Or maybe I thought I would learn to love him. I think I love him. I want to love him. I love his family, that's for sure. I certainly don't want my kids to have a broken home. Oh God, what is wrong with me?"

I rambled a while longer as she listened. I guessed that's what therapists did.

"What is your spiritual connection to Bruce?" she asked after a brief pause.

"What do you mean?

"Do the two of you share the same spiritual values?"

I looked at the ceiling, trying to think of an answer. "I'm not sure. We don't talk about it."

Her eyes squinted and she tilted her head. "Never?"

"No. Not really. We did once, sort of, when we decided our kids would be brought up in the Methodist church. Bruce had a good religious upbringing—his mom is a Methodist Sunday School teacher. We make sure our kids go to Sunday School. I take them. Bruce considers Sunday his day off from everything. When the kids spend the weekend with his folks, Barbara—that's his mom—takes them to church with her. That's when I try to come to church here."

She straightened her head. "Have you invited Bruce to attend church with you?"

"He came once when we first started dating. He didn't like the experience, so now I come when he's fishing or hunting."

"What did he not like?"

"Too metaphysical, I guess. He thought the service was a lot of 'hooey.' Didn't like the meditation. Just wasn't like the Methodist services he was used to. So I don't discuss it with him."

As we talked, I recognized another strike against my marriage. No spiritual connection.

Phyllis looked down at her notepad, paused, and glanced up at me. "Let us talk about the good things in your marriage. What makes you the happiest?"

I beamed. Finally, something good to discuss. "My children. I love my children more than life itself. I love being a mom. And Bruce is a great father."

"That sounds like an admirable quality in a husband. What are his other good attributes?"

"Well, as I said, he's a good provider. He's a decent man. A hard worker. He treats me okay."

"Merely okay?"

My tone became sarcastic. "Yeah, okay. He doesn't beat me or slap me around. He's nice. Average nice. He tolerates me. Indifferent is more like it."

"Indifferent does not sound like much of a good quality."

I calmed my voice. "Don't get me wrong. Our marriage hasn't always been this way. He treated me more like a queen when we dated and first married."

"What about the romance aspect of your marriage?" she asked.

"I guess the answer depends on how you define romance. He used to bring me flowers when we dated. But, come to think of it, he hasn't done that since our daughter was born. And he's never been one to verbally express romantic thoughts or display affection."

"Does that bother you?"

"Yes, a lot. His parents are such good role models. His dad, Frank, dotes on Barbara. Brings her flowers for no reason. Kisses her on the cheek when he enters the room. They're such lovebirds, even after all these years.

And his brothers show affection for their wives. Yet none of that rubbed off on Bruce."

We talked a little more before she moved on and asked me about our common interests.

"Our children, that's the greatest thing we have in common. We enjoy doing things with our families. We used to go fishing together, but not anymore. Oh, and sports. We both like sports. Or did. We don't watch games together like we used to. Now he watches games with his friend Jimmy and the rest of the guys. Oh, and we like to eat the same foods."

The conversation was beginning to end there. I couldn't think of any other common interests. We didn't like the same music or the same kind of movies. I liked to dance. He didn't. With my job, I had to socialize and be in the public eye. He disliked the social scene. I loved to entertain. He hated having company over unless it was guys only. Apparently, opposites did attract, but they eventually drove each other nuts or lost interest in the relationship.

Phyllis sat quietly, waiting for me to continue, but I had nothing else to say. "What about mutual friends?" she asked.

"Well, that's what got us together to begin with. Our best friends Bethany and Jimmy introduced us. Bethany was my maid of honor. Jimmy was Bruce's best man. They were on-again, off-again for a few years, then went through a nasty, bitter divorce. We tried not to take sides. But—" I paused before Phyllis motioned me to continue.

"But?"

"Bruce can't stand Bethany anymore. First, he blames her for the divorce. Deep down, I blame her too. Jimmy's a great guy and Bethany just didn't appreciate him.

Anyway, to make matters worse, a year after the divorce, Bethany married some old rich snob none of us could tolerate. Bruce said 'good riddance' the day she moved out of the neighborhood, which really upset me. But he was happy that Jimmy moved back into their old house."

I stopped to catch my breath and take a sip of water. Phyllis waited for me to continue.

"I get angry with Bruce when he bad-mouths Bethany, which is frequently. Her second marriage lasted about a year before she dumped the pretentious creep. Now, when she comes by to visit, Bruce leaves the house without bothering to say hello. This puts a stress on our marriage *and* my friendship with Bethany."

I sensed the hostility rising in my voice, so I stopped talking.

"Have you tried discussing your marital concerns with Bruce?" she asked after a brief pause.

"A hundred times at least. He says when I see alligators, he sees lizards. Tells me I get my bowels in an uproar over the simplest little things."

Lack of communication. Another strike. Our time was coming to an end, so we tabled further discussion of alligators versus lizards.

"I hope I have been of help."

I stopped the tape recorder. "You have."

Phyllis flipped open her schedule book. "I'd like to see you again, but the next time, please bring Bruce."

"A snowball would have a better chance in hell. And I don't even want him to know I've been here. So good luck ever getting us together for counseling. He'd never go for it."

Phyllis gave me some good tips for ways to better

communicate with Bruce. I said I would try her suggestions because I wanted to save my marriage. Divorce was not an option.

She also helped me recognize mistakes I was making. Such as asking him "what's wrong?" because he'd continue saying "nothing" and we'd never get anywhere.

There was no one else I could talk to, so I was grateful for my session with Phyllis. Bethany was reeling from her terrible breakup and would probably tell me to "divorce the damn man." Sylvia was a good listener, but she and Harvey were so happy. I didn't want to bother her with my problems.

On the drive home, I remembered reading a magazine article several years back that said to never date a man you wouldn't marry. Something along the lines that you might end up married to that person, so unless a man is everything you want in a husband, don't date him to begin with. I finally understood the point the writer was trying to make.

Sylvia and Harvey had an enviable relationship. They had a strong spiritual connection and knew how to communicate with each other. They also had a lot in common. And they did things the right way—they went to premarital counseling and discussed important subjects *before* they married.

Talk about doing things ass-backward. Bruce and I jumped into marriage and rushed into having children. Now, we needed to start from the beginning and learn to communicate and develop common interests.

22

Variety is the spice of life, so spice up your love life!

I was in the grocery line when the magazine headline caught my attention. Maybe spicing things up with Bruce would improve our marriage. I bought six women's magazines and read one article after another, trying to get some useful tips. Some of the ideas would have put me in the hospital or landed me in jail. Much of the focus seemed to be on food.

Cook dinner topless. So many ways this could go wrong, including third-degree burns. And with kids in the house, it would never work.

Use a rolling pin to— What? I could never try that, and what a waste of a good rolling pin. I'd have to throw it away because I would never be able to use it again. And after reading the article, I would never be able to look at my rolling pin without bursting into laughter.

There were endless ways to use food.

Slip a donut around his— Oh good heavens!

Besides all the empty calories, I'd have ants in my bed before I could take the first bite.

DRIZZLE SOME CHOCOLATE SYRUP, HONEY, BUTTER, OR ICE CREAM— Definitely too sticky. But I loved whipped cream, so that might work. And there was a low-fat version to consider.

SPRAY PEPPERMINT ON YOUR BREASTS. THE SCENT WILL DRIVE YOUR MAN WILD! Maybe for most men. For Bruce, I'd need to dab beer on my boobs or find something with the scent of barbecue sauce or motor oil.

TRY A SEXY LAP DANCE TO TURN YOUR GUY ON. Not the way I danced. Most likely, I would trip and fall onto his lap and send us both to the chiropractor.

STRIPTEASE—THE BEST WAY TO TEASE YOUR MAN. An even worse idea than a lap dance. With my moves, it would look more like a comedy routine and have the reverse effect.

SINGING TO YOUR MAN DURING SEX IS A REAL TURN-ON. Not with my voice!

WHETHER IT'S RAVEL'S *BOLÉRO* OR AN AL GREEN LOVE SONG, MUSIC IS A REAL MOOD-SETTER. Those would be a real turnoff for Bruce, but Johnny Cash singing "Ring of Fire" might work.

GREET HIM AT THE DOOR WITH NOTHING ON BUT A SMILE. With my luck, he'd bring Jimmy home that day.

Until now, the most risqué thing I had tried was attempting to tie a cherry stem with my tongue—which was supposed to be a seductive way to show you are a good kisser. The first thing I learned from the experience was to not try it after a few cocktails. Of course, if not for the cocktails, I would have never tried it to begin with. More importantly, take the darn cherry off the stem first.

Fortunately, the bartender had known the Heimlich maneuver.

When Bruce and I were first married, I'd tried the I'm-not-wearing-any-underwear trick. We'd been dining at our neighborhood steak house, which had a modicum of ambiance—low lights, a candle on the table, and soft music that was often drowned out by the noise coming from the restaurant bar. I had planned to wait until we were ready to leave, then whisper it in his ear. Just thinking about it had made me want to laugh, so I'd spent most of the evening trying to not lose my composure.

When the time came, I'd leaned over and used my sexiest voice. "I'm wearing underwear. No, wait, I meant to say, 'I'm *not* wearing any underwear.'"

I couldn't stop howling, nor could Bruce. Fortunately, I had been wearing underwear or I might have left the restaurant with a trail of pee running down my legs.

* * *

I decided to start slowly and work my way up to spicier things. One Friday evening I planned something special for Bruce when he got home—the kind of thing I used to do before we had kids. When he walked in, I held a cold beer in one hand and wrapped my other hand gently around his neck as I tiptoed to kiss him. His favorites— chicken-fried steak, green beans, and mashed potatoes— were on the menu.

"What are you buttering me up for?" he asked.

I moved my hand from his neck and handed him the beer. "Nothing. I'm just trying to be a better wife."

He stepped back. "What brought this on? Did you wreck the car?"

"No," I replied calmly. "Relax and take a load off. You've worked hard all week, and I want to show you how much I appreciate you."

He took a swig of beer. "If this is about taking the kids to Disneyland, the answer is still no."

"Relax and enjoy the fact that your caring wife is trying to show her appreciation and wants to spoil you."

He barely acknowledged my loving gesture before heading for the den. "Hey, kids, I'm home."

At least he thanked me for the nice dinner. By the time I got the kitchen cleaned and put the kids to bed, he was already sound asleep. The whipped cream would have to wait.

The next weekend, Barbara picked up the kids Saturday morning for a sleepover. Bruce was working at the shop until noonish, so I put my plan in motion. I got dolled up, put on my sexy new red nightie, and waited patiently for him to come home. A romantic afternoon would hopefully spice up our blah marriage.

He finally showed up around one o'clock. I was poised and ready when he opened the back door.

"Good golly, woman. Where are your clothes?"

I moved toward him, wrapped my arms around his neck, and attempted to kiss him. As he pulled away from me, the smell of burger and onions almost knocked me over.

He headed down the hallway. "I don't know what you're up to, but I don't have time for this. Gotta go shower."

"I can shower with you," I said, following him.

He stopped, turned, and gave me his you've-got-to-be-kidding look before heading to the bedroom.

"What's the rush?"

"Gotta get ready to go out to the hunting lease with Jimmy. We wanna be ready for tomorrow."

I bit my tongue. He'd made no previous mention of going hunting. Apparently, I had lost my sex appeal—if I ever had any to begin with.

I didn't give up. For the next couple of months, I tried my best to rejuvenate my marriage. I focused on the good aspects of my life and worked to open communication with Bruce. The next time he stopped the conversation with "why do you always get your bowels in an uproar?" I decided to try a new approach.

As he stood to leave the den, I walked over, gave him a hug, and looked him in the eye. "Bruce, what you see as lizards are things that are important to me. When you tell me not to get my bowels in an uproar, I wonder if you think I overreact to everything or if you don't want to discuss things with me."

"The problem is you always get your britches in a bunch over every little thing. I wish you would learn to lighten up."

I wasn't making progress, so it was time to try humor. "Yes, you know how I am about my britches. They usually have toilet paper flying out of them."

"Now you get my drift." Bruce grinned and gave me a quick hug.

A hug and a good laugh momentarily eased the tension. I reconciled my frustrations by remembering he was a good father and a good man. I did my darnedest to *lighten up* and quit seeing alligators instead of lizards

—and to not make life hard on myself and those around me.

My favorite pair of capris was almost worn out, so a week later I bought new ones as a symbolic gesture. When Bruce came home, I held up the old pants. "I wore these out by always getting them in a bunch. So I bought new ones. I promise to not wear them out."

He gave me his ho-hum look. "Any excuse for new clothes."

So much for trying to be clever.

We gradually became like robots going through the motions of being a married couple. What little glimmer we had in our marriage was gone. Bruce spent more time with Jimmy. They went fishing or hunting or watched sports most weekends. I didn't complain because I was glad to have him out of the house.

As much as I wanted to make my marriage work for the sake of my children, I also wanted to be happy.

*   *   *

Put on a happy face and pretend everything is hunky-dory. I didn't want to concern my children or my mother, who genuinely believed I had the perfect marriage.

I was also concerned about Mom's health. She didn't seem well but kept telling me she was fine and simply getting old. By the time I convinced her to see a doctor, she had waited too long. She had stage 4 ovarian cancer.

"We'll get through this together," Bruce said when he hugged me one night. Our animosity for each other dissipated as we concentrated on holding our family together during a difficult time.

The next twelve months were excruciating as I watched my mother battle cancer and wither away. I didn't have time to prepare for my dad's death or Angela's, but the months of agony watching my precious mother slowly die were heartbreaking. She decided to quit the cancer treatments and try to enjoy what time she had left.

Mom was the brave type and couldn't tolerate anyone crying. And she certainly didn't want me crying over her. But pretending to be strong wasn't easy for me.

Her death in 1992 was hard on all of us. It was Jillian's and Henry's first experience with losing a family member, and my heart broke seeing them hurting. Bruce was comforting and cried with us. He loved her too.

How would I go on without her? She gave birth to me and nurtured me through childhood and those complicated teen years. She comforted me when John broke my heart, welcomed me into her arms when I split from Andrew, and hugged me tightly when Angela died. She was such a loving mother and grandmother. She was my rock. The hole she left in my heart was the size of a crater.

For a few months, Bruce and I were close again. His warm embraces and calming voice helped me through the trauma of losing my mother.

Mom's death was especially hard on Carl. My heart ached for him because he had devoted so much time to being the man of the house. I hoped he would begin living his own life.

Her death changed Carl, and not in a good way. He started drinking, something he had never done before. He had once told me he would never take up alcohol for fear he would become a hard drinker like our father.

A woman named Sabrina came into his life. I disliked

her from the instant we met. Maybe it was because I didn't want some *wanton* woman ruining my brother's life. Carl was such a mild-mannered guy. I didn't understand his attraction to her. She even smoked.

"Sabrina. The name fits her," I told Bruce one night after they left our house. "She's a witch—with a capital *B*! Good heavens, what does he see in her?"

He chuckled. "The sex is probably good."

That wasn't what I wanted to hear. I knew Mom must be rolling over in her grave.

23

I was trapped in a room and not allowed to leave, even if I wanted to go to the restroom. My head throbbed and the guards wouldn't allow me to take an aspirin. I had to sit up straight in my chair and keep my feet flat on the floor.

While other prisoners were allowed to leave when they wanted, I had to suffer in my seat and wonder why I'd put myself in this predicament. Sylvia was trapped beside me, and I wanted to punch her in the ribs and tell her it was her fault we were stuck in this hellhole.

Well, we weren't exactly prisoners, and it was a nice hotel meeting room, not a hellhole, although it was beginning to feel like one. We were there of our own free will, taking an intense weekend seminar retreat called Learning to Live through God. Several of our church friends had taken the course and encouraged us to sign up. Basically, it was spiritually based group therapy. My positive experiences with Phyllis helped me understand that therapy was not a bad thing.

It was as also a good excuse to spend the weekend

away from Bruce and the kids. Bruce balked at the idea of giving up a fishing trip but ultimately decided it would be good for him and the kids to visit Frank and Barbara. I was still dealing with Mom's death and thought a spiritual retreat would be of help.

Sylvia and I checked in at 8:00 a.m. Saturday and had to stay until 8:00 p.m. Sunday. We had to bring a pillow and were told we would have a few nap breaks. However, we wouldn't be allowed to sleep during the weekend. That should have been our first clue that we were in for an arduous challenge.

A psychologist named Bob led the training. He was a nice-looking and extremely tall Black man. My first impression was correct; he was a retired professional basketball player.

During the opening comments, Bob told us what to expect of the program. Next, he asked for volunteers to join the Elite Team. Without hesitation and with no idea of what we were volunteering for, Sylvia and I waved our hands and jumped up on stage with the other volunteers.

"Ladies and gentlemen, this is our Living for Life Elite Team," Bob said. "Let's give them a big round of applause."

I loved being applauded and was proud of myself for being on the Elite Team. I wasn't so proud when I learned what we had volunteered for. While others were allowed to leave the room at any point, we could only leave during designated breaks. Too bad if we needed a bathroom break or wanted to stretch our legs. We had to stay seated, shoulders back, no slumping, feet flat on the floor during presentations. If we had a headache, too bad. Aspirin was not allowed. Nor caffeine. We could, however, leave the Elite Team at any time.

"Let's see how many of you can remain on the team until we dismiss Sunday night," Bob said to the twenty-one of us suckers on the stage.

After the first five hours, our Elite Team dwindled, but Sylvia and I remained committed. We weren't going to give up. The intensity of the training was grueling enough, but the limitations placed on us made it even more challenging.

We each had a notebook that we filled in as the seminar progressed. Our first task was to write a letter to God telling him what we wanted out of life. It was for our eyes only. My letter was full of crossed-out words, especially the word *perfect*. My unrealistic need for perfection was becoming evident, so I adjusted my expectations. Scratch *perfect* mother. I would strive to be a *devoted* mother. And so on.

The first session was on self-expression, where group leaders guided us in learning to express our thoughts and emotions through words and to examine the actions and the choices we made in life. My intense introspection led to an excruciating headache. I wanted to quit the Elite Team, but my pride wouldn't allow it. Always a glutton for punishment, I was determined to suffer until the end. I had to be among the last few standing so the crowd could shower me with applause and Bob could give me an award. A big trophy, perhaps?

Other sessions for the first day included self-esteem, spirituality, and relationships. Each activity became more intense and more gut-wrenching. I wanted to head to the restroom and take a break. Bob said it was easy to leave the room when you didn't want to "face the music" and deal with tough issues—a reason the Elite Team had to stay put until designated breaks.

Keep your cool, Jackie. You can do this.

When we broke into small groups or were asked to work with a partner, we had to choose someone we didn't already know, which meant Sylvia and I were separated for most of the seminar.

As sleep deprivation set in, my defenses lowered. The things I had said and written shocked me. I had never recognized how many hang-ups I had about my father. Somehow, I'd buried the memory of him coming home drunk late one night with some woman. Carl had been asleep, but the commotion had awakened me, and I'd watched through the bedroom window. Mom had gone outside and argued with the woman. The woman had driven off in Dad's car, and Dad had fallen asleep in the front yard.

To me the child, he had been sleeping. Now, the adult me recognized he had been passed out drunk. Mom had come in crying. I didn't remember what happened after that and hadn't even thought of it again.

My chest tightened. *Are suppressed memories a real thing? Have I been hypnotized? Why did I take this stupid seminar?* The gremlins in my head were hard at work.

"You're shaking," Bob said softly, placing his hand on my shoulder. "Close your eyes." I followed his instructions. "Now relax and breathe in . . . breathe out. From the diaphragm. Breathe in . . . breathe out. Keep going. You're doing fine."

His touch calmed me. As I harmonized my breathing, I recalled other instances when my parents fought over Dad's drinking. I also remembered that my way of coping was to crawl out my bedroom window and hope Peter Pan would come to my rescue.

Evidently, that incident and a few others had led me to believe my mother was a weak person for putting up with so much from my dad. I had to be a much stronger woman than my mother. My father had been a flawed man, and I wouldn't settle for any man who wasn't perfect.

I was reluctant to accept that I had these repressed hostilities, yet this was the garbage that came out of my head and onto the pages of my notebook.

"If you experience a sense of anger, use your pillow as a punching bag," Bob said.

I grabbed my pillow and hit it repeatedly. Years of pent-up and unrecognized anger slowly dissipated.

One of our other tasks was to write a thank-you note to God. The exercise helped me appreciate my life. Despite my dad's drinking, I'd had a good childhood, obtained a college degree, and found a meaningful career. Plus, a family I adored and amazing, longtime friendships. Yes, God had blessed me with a good life.

One of the last exercises was to write our epitaph. When I reread mine a week later, I laughed. It didn't sound like anything I would have ever written.

She gave willingly to others, and because of her support for the earth and this universe, the entire universe was a better place in space.

Gave willingly? A better place in space? I blamed sleep deprivation for my silly epitaph. A more fitting one would be,

She could shovel horse manure with the best of them, and she stumbled through life with a laundry ticket on her back and toilet paper flying out her britches.

Once eager to get away from my family for a couple of days, I grew anxious to see them again. I was also ready to strengthen my marriage by applying some of the relationship principles I learned during the retreat. Several of them mirrored suggestions Phyllis had made. If I heard something often enough, maybe it would finally sink in.

Bob asked us to set at least five goals for creating better relationships. Mine centered on being more understanding of Bruce's work and family pressures and expressing my respect for him. Along with devoting more time to my marriage, being more patient, and improving communication.

When the seminar wound down, I was relieved and worn out mentally, emotionally, and physically. The long hours of intense, excruciating introspection were incredibly cathartic. Taking a hard look at my life left me with a new sense of being. If I was a perfect being in God's eyes, I should strive to do my best and not put so much pressure on myself.

During one of the group exercises, I recognized that my constant need for perfection was self-imposed. Others in the group related how much pressure a parent or a spouse put on them. I couldn't recall a single instance in my life when someone told me I needed to be perfect. *What is perfect, anyway?* It was okay to have flaws. I needed to be happy with myself. Just be Jackie. Just Jackie.

Harvey had a work conflict on Saturday, so he hadn't

attended with us. Sylvia and I were glad we had the foresight to ask him to drop us off and pick us up. Neither of us would have had the energy to drive. We barely had the strength to crawl up to the stage to accept our accolades for being among the four remaining members of the Elite Team.

Then came one of those comeuppance moments.

As Bob brought us up on stage, the group applauded us. I swelled with pride. Tall and handsome Bob turned and looked at us. "You like to make life hard on yourselves, so we gave you one last opportunity to do so."

Oh my. Bruce was right. I was a fussbudget who did things the hard way. Lesson learned. Instead of making life hard on myself, I sought simpler ways to complete the tasks at hand. I tuned out the negative voices in my head, quit trying to be perfect, got the job done, and moved on.

24

Six months after Mom's death, my life was on a downhill spiral. The affability Bruce and I had shared during Mom's illness had gradually turned to aloofness. And old habits die hard. I found myself mentally formulating a new master plan, one that didn't involve being perfect at anything. I wanted to be a divorced woman and a halfway decent mother. Okay, so I still wanted to be the perfect mother. Unfortunately, that was becoming increasingly more difficult.

Jillian was eleven but thought she was seventeen. "Why can't I wear makeup?" she yelled at me when I caught her applying cosmetics from my vanity drawer. I wanted to laugh because she looked like a clown, but that wouldn't have been good parenting.

I put my hands on my hips and stopped short of saying those horrible clichéd words—*because I said so!* Instead, I tried a more motherly approach. "You're a little bit too young. Maybe in two more years."

"You're mean. I don't like you anymore," Jillian said, stomping out of my bedroom.

It could have been worse. At that age, Bethany's daughter, Lynn Ann, was yelling, "I hate you, Mom!"

Nine-year-old Henry was still his sweet, well-behaved self, but was more demanding of my time and affection. While we were eating dinner one evening, he asked, "Why don't you quit working so we can come home after school and not have to go to Daddy's office?"

Bruce laid down his fork. "That's a good question."

"Yeah, Mom, why?" Jillian said. Her tone was exasperating.

My chest caved in as crushing thoughts of failure, despair, and anguish engulfed me. My family was chastising me, and the shame was overwhelming. It was a hard question to answer. I knew the answer, but I couldn't say it. *Because I'll need to support us once I'm out of this lousy marriage.*

"Well?" Bruce asked.

I cleared my throat and took a deep breath. "I will give it some thought." *What a lie. I have no intention of giving up my job.*

At this point, I was mentally scratching through the words *perfect mom.* I would settle for being a halfway decent mother.

Things kept getting worse. I was still coming to terms with Mom's death when my dog, Jill, died. She lived a good, long life, and I had sixteen amazing years of her unconditional love. She had been through so many experiences with me—the best and worst times of my life. I took her death much harder than I expected and would create excuses to leave the house so I could sit in a parking lot and cry.

Upon Sylvia's suggestion, I scheduled a grief counseling conference with Phyllis, which was extremely beneficial. Phyllis helped me recognize that, although I was genuinely grieving for my dog, it was easier for me to mourn an animal than, perhaps, a person in my life I hadn't grieved for.

I had shed countless tears for Angela and my mother, yet I had never genuinely grieved for my father. He was a loving parent, despite his flaws, and often told me how much he loved me. Yes, he was a good dad, and I had loved him very much. At that instant, I realized how much I missed him.

Fortunately, Phyllis had a fresh box of tissues. By the time I left her office, the box was almost empty and I was more at peace.

* * *

Sylvia was the one person I could easily confide in, and having lunch with her on weekdays helped me do a better job of managing my life. Although Bethany and I were the best of friends, compassion wasn't one of her strong points.

When I looked at Bruce, I cringed. I didn't want to be near him or even look at him. But I also didn't want our children's lives to be screwed up. No matter how much I pretended to be happy, I worried my children would sense the tension between Bruce and me. If they hadn't already.

I convinced myself I would be a better mother to Jillian and Henry if I no longer lived in an unhappy marriage. I was on the verge of asking Bruce for a divorce when, once again, my world collapsed.

We were sound asleep when the phone rang. Bruce answered and said it was a police officer wanting to talk to me.

Carl had been in a car accident and was in critical condition.

Bruce and I arrived at the hospital in time for me to hold Carl, kiss him on the forehead, and tell him I loved him. His body was motionless. The only assurance I had that he was still alive was the heart monitor slowly pulsing up and down. And then that horrifying sound I would never forget, the ominous noise of the heart monitor flatlining. My precious baby brother was dead. My heart broke into so many pieces I thought nothing or no one could ever put it back together.

His girlfriend, Sabrina, had been driving the car when they crashed. And yes, she was drunk, and so was Carl. I prayed he didn't know what had happened. He was unconscious when they brought him to the hospital. Not that it was any consolation. I was glad no one else died or was injured.

The darkest part of my heart wished Sabrina had died too. But maybe it was good that she lived, so she would have to spend the rest of her life remembering she was responsible for killing my sweet, wonderful brother. He'd deserved to have a much longer and better life.

I wished Angela and Rick were there to help Carl "cross over." That Mom and Dad were there to greet him. I even pictured my sweet dog, Jill, jumping up and down and licking his face. If only I could really believe this, maybe I would survive the crushing heartache.

Instead, I found myself thinking there was no justice in this world. Carl was too young to die. He was one of the best people I had ever known—kind, loving, and the greatest brother and son imaginable.

Sylvia helped me through my darkest days and became my moral compass. I was angry at the world and had a hard time accepting Carl was gone. The one thing that kept me going was knowing how much Jillian and Henry needed me.

"I held him in my arms and watched him die," I told Sylvia one day as we ate lunch. "I don't think I can ever get over that trauma."

Mom had died peacefully in her sleep, so I had never seen anyone die before. Watching Carl die was the most excruciating pain I had ever experienced.

"How could God do this to me?" I blurted out.

Those words sounded so crass when I heard myself say them.

I wiped my eyes with my knuckle. "I'm so sorry I said that. I don't really mean it."

Sylvia touched my hand. "I know you don't. Be grateful God gave you such a precious gift. Would you have rather he died alone or died knowing you were there with him?"

Her words helped me come to grips with what had happened. Yes, there was some comfort in knowing I was there to hold him while he took his last breath. But the experience still haunted me.

The judge went easy on Sabrina and sentenced her to eighteen months in prison for manslaughter. I thought she deserved a life sentence for taking my brother away from me. I was trying not to be angry, but I couldn't help myself.

She called two days before her sentencing. "Jackie, please find it in your heart to forgive me. I am so deeply sorry for what happened. I wish—"

"You're a horrible person. I can never forgive you."

After I slammed down the phone, immense guilt flooded my veins, but I did not call her back.

Sylvia convinced me to visit Sabrina in prison, but I was unsure if I could stand to look at her. Another month passed before I got the courage. Sabrina cried when she saw me and told me how much she missed Carl and how much she genuinely loved him.

Let go of your anger. Sabrina loved Carl and she is hurting too. It's time for forgiveness. We cried together, and I wanted to hug her, but I had to remain across the table from her in the visitor's room. I told her I forgave her—Carl would have wanted me to.

That was the last time I saw her. I hoped she would leave jail a better person and find some peace in her life.

When I walked out of the building, I spotted a shiny penny glistening on the ground. A penny from heaven, just when I needed it. As I picked it up and clutched it in my hand, my resentment dissipated. I knew it was time to let go of my anger and move toward acceptance.

I had to accept that Carl was gone. My dad was gone. My mom was gone. Even my sweet dog, Jill, was gone. Yet, like Angela, they would always be in my heart.

25

Bruce came into the house as Bethany and I headed out the door for a Saturday lunch with the college gang. The kids were spending the weekend with Frank and Barbara, and I was looking forward to some gal time. It was six months after Carl's death, and Bruce and I were back to our bickering.

He didn't even look up when he passed us. "Have fun with your hoity-toity friends," he said in the most hateful, sarcastic tone I had ever heard come out of his mouth.

"Hoity-toity?" Bethany chuckled as we walked to her car. "I've been called a lot of things, but never hoity-toity."

Had I become a pretentious shrew in Bruce's mind? I never thought of myself or my friends as being snobbish or elitist. For me, that nasty comment was the last straw. I already had enough final straws to make a bale of hay, but this was the breaking point. That was the day I quit trying to get along with him. *Maybe it's time to visit a lawyer!*

Bruce and I had grown further and further apart, and he was coming home later and later. It wasn't unusual for him to work late at the shop on weekdays. Although he didn't mind letting his assistant manager open up, Bruce wanted to be the one to lock up in the evening.

But now something was different when he came home. He seemed energized instead of tired, and he was paying more attention to his appearance. *Is he cheating on me? Oh, if only he is, I'll have a great excuse for divorcing him.*

I still hadn't visited a lawyer but knew that Texas was a no-fault divorce state. I would prefer making it Bruce's fault! If he were unfaithful, or at least flirting with someone, it would have to be with his accounting clerk, Beverly. I needed to catch them in the act!

Entrapment. Yes, somehow, I needed to give him enough rope to hang himself, or at least a long enough leash so he could spend more time with her.

Back in our early post-college days, Bethany and I had envisioned ourselves as great detectives when we had landed a part-time gig working for a local private investigations company. It wasn't the type of work that spy novels were made of, but we found it exhilarating.

My first assignment had been to pose as a shopper at a furniture store to catch a clerk who was suspected of stealing money. I gave her the cash for the purchase and she'd given me a phony receipt and pocketed the money. The rest of our limited assignments had been similar.

Apparently, we'd been hired because Bethany had met the owner at a party, and he'd seemed to have a thing for her. He was a dumpy, balding older man, and Bethany had had no interest in him. After three weekends of work, he'd asked her out. When she'd declined, he'd conveniently run out of assignments for us.

Bethany was happy to help me catch Bruce cheating, so we hatched a plan. With the two of us working on a great plan, what could go wrong?

We found the perfect opportunity the next weekend. Lynn Ann was staying with Jimmy. Jillian was going to a Saturday night slumber party, and Henry had a Scouting weekend event.

"Since the kids are busy for the weekend, Bethany and I are going to drive up to Dallas tomorrow to visit Kate and Tom," I told Bruce. "We won't be back until late Sunday."

"Sure. Whatever," he said before he sipped his morning coffee.

Bethany picked me up Saturday morning, and we headed to a car rental agency. Her yellow Cadillac Escalade was easy to spot, especially with the name of her real estate company plastered on the sides. I needed to rent the least conspicuous car on the lot for our covert operation.

She brought wigs and big sunglasses for us to wear. And binoculars, a transistor radio, a cooler of sodas, sandwiches, and lots of snacks. We were prepared for our stakeout.

Unless he had a hunting or fishing trip planned, Bruce usually worked Saturday mornings, even though his assistant manager handled weekend business. He left the house early that morning, saying he had a lot of paperwork to get done.

It was almost ten o'clock before we began our spy mission. Bruce's car was at the shop, so we parked at a nearby building where we had a clear view of the front door. I didn't know what kind of car Beverly drove, so I didn't know if she was there too.

The shop closed at three Saturday afternoons, so we were going to watch the place until Bruce left.

Our bladders weren't designed for stakeouts, and we should have never downed those sodas. I was afraid we might miss something if we took a bathroom break, yet we reached a point where we had to make a mad dash to the nearest service station.

We returned in time to see Beverly drive up and enter the building. I stared through the binoculars to get a good look at her. I had gotten a glimpse of her one day when I delivered something for Bruce and had paid little attention to her. At the time, I had no reason to think she might someday try to steal my husband.

She was young, petite, and mousy-looking, with curly red hair. Yes, she looked like Little Orphan Annie. Only older and a little prettier. And she dressed better.

They came out about thirty minutes later. Bruce had his hand on her shoulder as he walked her to her car, and she gave him a hug before she got in.

"I knew it. I knew it. I knew it. The lousy good-for-nothing is cheating on me!"

Bethany grabbed the binoculars to get a look. "Isn't that what you wanted?"

"Well, yes, I want to get rid of him, but it still ticks me off that he's interested in another woman."

"If he is cheating on you, I've got a great idea for getting even with him."

"If it involves horse manure, I don't want to hear it."

"Never mind," Bethany said, handing the binoculars back to me.

That brief exchange lightened the mood. It was

warming up outside, and we were growing bored sitting in the car. Still, I was determined to see where Bruce went when he left work. Fortunately, we didn't have to wait long. He left about thirty minutes later and drove home.

We drove to Bethany's house to regroup and map out our next move. She was still between husbands, meaning she was on the search for Husband #3. Although her second marriage ended badly, she got a nice house out of it.

After a couple of hours, we drove back by my house. Bruce's truck was still there, so we rode around for about ten minutes before checking again. This time, his truck was gone.

We drove to Jimmy's house. Bruce's truck wasn't there.

My best option was to drop off the rental car, get in Bethany's car, and go to her house for a few hours. We'd go back to my house around ten o'clock. If Bruce was still gone, I'd go in the house, crawl into bed, turn off the lights, and wait for him to come home.

When, or if, Bruce came home, I'd tell him I wasn't feeling well, and we'd driven back to Houston. Or I'd come up with a better lie.

By midnight, my heart was racing, and my imagination was running wild. *Is Bruce really cheating on me and spending the night with Beverly? Maybe he was in an accident. Is he in love with Beverly? Will he leave me for her? Bruce and Beverly—their names sound better together than Bruce and Jackie. What if he marries her and our kids love her more than me? Maybe he was in a bad accident and is in the hospital. Maybe I have really screwed up my marriage and will live to regret it.*

The words to an old country song popped into my head. Something about not knowing what you've got until you lose it.

I should have been happy my marriage might be breaking up. After all, that was what I wanted. Still, I wasn't prepared for the thought of Bruce wanting another woman—and another woman wanting him. And what would our divorce do to Frank and Barbara? Divorcing Bruce would be divorcing them too.

It took a while for me to fall asleep. When I woke up the next morning, Bruce was still gone. Part of me was excited that maybe I was catching him cheating on me and now I had a good excuse for a divorce. Another part of me was a little heartbroken to think that he was being unfaithful. In my wildest dreams, I never imagined Bruce as the kind of man who would cheat on his wife.

I puttered around the house and tried to keep myself occupied. I expected Jillian to be home before noon, so surely Bruce would be back before then.

Around eleven, Bruce's truck pulled into the driveway. My heart was beating so fast, I thought it would explode. I sat in my recliner and waited for him to come in.

"What are you doing home?" Bruce asked when he walked into the den. Guilt was written all over his face. Or maybe he was surprised to see me. I was convinced it was guilt.

"We had air conditioning problems outside of Dallas. By the time we got to Kate's house, we had terrible headaches. When it cooled off, we drove back home so we wouldn't have to deal with the— Never mind why I'm home. Where have you been all night?"

Bruce stood there like a stoic cigar store Indian—

motionless and speechless. His face was flushed, and I was sure I saw smoke coming out of his ears.

"Where were you? Because unless you were in the hospital or spent the night in jail—"

"I was out, okay. And it's none of your damn business where I was. Why the hell do you care anyway?"

Bruce never cursed, not that *damn* and *hell* were strong words. But they were for Bruce. He stormed off to the bedroom, so I nonchalantly sat in my chair, waiting for him to cool off. After about five minutes, he walked out with a suitcase and some shirts still on the hangers.

"I'm leaving," was all he said before heading to the back door.

I followed him for a few steps, stopped, and yelled, "Bruce LeRoy Jackson, if you leave now, don't bother coming back."

He turned and gave me a go-to-hell look.

When he slammed the door on his way out, I knew he'd finally had his fill of me. He even left skid marks as he peeled out of the driveway.

I was stunned. Instead of being happy, I was jarred to the core. My entire body trembled. I'd barely had time to get over my shock when Jillian came home from her sleepover.

"Why was Daddy speeding off? And why are you home? Did something happen?"

Words escaped me. I tried to stay composed but felt a tear trickling down my face. It was hard to hold back my emotions.

Jillian hugged me and attempted to console me. I didn't dare tell her what happened because she idolized her father.

"We had an argument and he left," I said, pulling away from her.

"When will he be back?"

"I don't know. I guess he'll be back when he gets back. I need to lie down for a few minutes." I didn't want Jillian to see me cry.

The tears flowed when I lay down on my bed. I wasn't sure why I was crying because I wanted Bruce out of my life, and it looked like I was getting my wish. Grim thoughts crept through my mind. *Is my marriage really over? Will my children turn against me and decide to live with their father? Will Bruce disgrace me by leaving me for another woman?*

It was too much to think about, and a bad headache was forming. I needed to compose myself before Henry came home and to do my best to not upset the children.

* * *

Bruce didn't come back that day or the next. Jillian called him at work wanting to know when he was coming home. He said he wasn't sure.

I tried to be dignified and calm when explaining the situation to Jillian and Henry. There was no way I would say something like, "Your father is a lying, cheating scoundrel who is leaving me for a younger woman." And I still wasn't sure that he had cheated on me. But if he was having an affair, it would have to be with Beverly.

Our children adored their father, and I would not shatter their image of him. Bruce was a decent man and a good father. We had never been particularly suited for each other and were making each other miserable.

"We're having some grown-up problems," I explained. "Dad needs some time to himself. Please know that we both love you very much, no matter what happens."

A week later, I came home from work to discover Bruce had moved all of his things out of the house. His fishing gear was gone too. That's when I knew my marriage was over.

Bruce moved in with Beverly and filed for divorce six weeks later. At first, the kids were angry with their father. They blamed him for breaking up our family, and they hated Beverly. Frank and Barbara were devastated and mad at Bruce. I told them how much I loved them and wanted them to be with their grandkids as much as possible.

If I'd been a cruel, heartless witch, I would have done my best to turn friends and family against Bruce. Instead, I took the high road and didn't play the victim card. Deep down, I knew some of my actions helped trigger his infidelity. I genuinely wanted Bruce to be happy, and I wanted him to have a good relationship with Jillian and Henry.

"Your dad and I have been unhappy for a long time," I explained to them. "Don't blame him for wanting to be happy. He's still your father, and he loves you with all his heart. He needs your love and understanding."

When Bruce's birthday rolled around a few months later, I made sure the kids had gifts for him and helped Jillian bake a cake. They visited with him for fifteen minutes while I waited in the car. I also had them deliver a card from me, one I hoped he would open and read when he was alone. It was hard to come up with the right words, so I kept it sweet and simple.

Dear Bruce,

Best wishes for a happy birthday. The best gift I can give you is my wish for your happiness. You are a good man, and I hope you will find genuine happiness with Beverly.

You are an outstanding father, and Jillian and Henry need you more than ever. I can't imagine how hard our divorce has been on them. Let's please work together to give them the love and support they deserve.

You will always have a special place in my heart.

Best wishes,
Jackie

26

Beeeep! *Beeeep! Beeeep!* The piercing fire alarm was going off and smoke was filling the hallway. My eyes burned as I ran through the thick haze. Where there was smoke, I knew there must be fire.

Oh no! My house is on fire! I was thankful the kids were with Bruce, and I didn't have to worry about them being in danger.

As I picked up the phone to call the fire department, I got a big whiff of burned cookies.

Oh, bullcorn! I forgot to set the timer on the oven and I got distracted. My cookies for Henry's Scouting bake sale were burned to a crisp, but at least the house *wasn't* on fire. I opened the windows and the back door to air out the smoke. The alarm finally quit blaring. No need to call the fire department. Instead, I called a nearby bakery and asked how long it would take to bake a batch of chocolate chip cookies.

"We have some already made," the woman said.

"I know, but I need some that don't look bakery perfect. Can you make some that aren't exactly—well, aren't perfectly round? You know, like the ones a mom would make?"

She laughed and asked if these were for my kid's bake sale. "You're not the first mom we've had to save."

With that problem solved, I started making the cherry cobbler Henry had also volunteered me for. I was struggling to be a good mom and wanted to do anything my kids asked of me.

The old me would have struggled to make it from scratch. The new me cheated with a ready-made pie crust. Lesson learned—don't make life hard on myself.

I opened the can of cherries and somehow managed to drop it. Cherries rolled everywhere, and sticky juice covered the floor. This was a disaster. I didn't have time to go to the store for more cherries, so I scooped up the cherries, rinsed them, and put them in the pie. No one would know about this but me, and I would make sure I bought my own pie.

House on fire. Burned cookies. Spilled cherries. Just a typical day in my life as a single mother. I was on my own and no longer had Mom to help me take care of the kids. And for a while, Bruce wouldn't take them because he wasn't comfortable bringing them to Beverly's apartment. I guessed that was why he'd rushed into marrying her and buying a home. He was an old-fashioned guy, and "living in sin" with someone was not his style. That's probably why he'd rushed into marrying me.

Perhaps my marriage didn't turn out the way I'd wanted, but my children sure did!

Jillian matured into a lovely teenager. She looked a lot like me, only much prettier, and inherited my natural curls, although her hair was not as frizzy as mine.

Thankfully, she inherited her grandma Barbara's good genes and had a perfect figure.

I loved when she came into a room with hairbrush in hand. "Mom, would you please brush my hair?" She was old enough to do it herself, yet she still wanted me to do it. Those were some of our best memories.

Except for the burr haircut, Henry looked a lot like Bruce but had such a different personality. He was an avid reader and always made the honor roll. Kindness and affection came naturally to Henry.

I was fortunate to have two fantastic, trustworthy children, so I didn't mind leaving them home alone for short periods when they were older. That gave me time for fun with my college friends—my wonderful extended family.

The older we got, the more we liked to reminisce about the *good ole days*. When I thought about some of the dumb, harebrained things I did when I was younger, I prayed my kids would have better sense than I did. Thank goodness my mom never learned about some of my shenanigans.

Those reminiscences were great to fall back on because the life of a single mom was less than exciting. In fact, it was downright challenging. It was all I could do to keep up with parent-teacher meetings, help with homework, drive the kids to Scouting and other functions, wipe their noses, mend their clothes, feed them, do the laundry, clean the house, pay the bills. Oh yes, and work full-time.

So much for women having it all. But I was determined to make it work. My children were worth the effort, and they meant the world to me.

27

S lime dripped off my head. Slime dripped on my clothes. Slime was all over me. Ooey-gooey, stinky, disgusting slime. The huge crowd behind me had me pinned in with no way to move out of harm's way.

How did I get myself into this mess? The same way I got into most of my messes. Bethany!

It all started one Saturday morning when she came knocking at my back door.

"We need an adventure," Bethany said, rushing past me and waving a brochure, not even giving me a chance to say hello or invite her in.

"I found us a fabulous trip for next month. A four-day chartered trip to the tropical, relaxing Bahamas. Surely you can get Bruce to look after the kids for a long weekend or send them to their grandma and grandpa."

The price was right, and it sounded like a fun idea. Weekends were Bruce's time to spend with the kids, and I had vacation days I needed to use or lose.

Yes, I needed an adventure. *Bahamas, here we come!*

We were booked on a chartered plane full of passengers from the Houston area, all headed to the same exciting destination. As the plane took off, I was like a giddy teenager embarking on her first big trip.

Once the plane was in the air, travelers visited up and down the aisles. Bethany scoped out the men but didn't spot anyone to her liking. Romance was the last thing I was looking for, so I thumbed through a travel magazine and didn't bother to look around.

A couple of hours into the trip, our tour guide spoke over the intercom to inform us that our hotel was having plumbing problems. Our reservations were at a resort on the west end of the island that was supposed to be self-contained with all the amenities we would need. The price was right, so we had been satisfied with the group accommodations.

"We need six volunteers to stay elsewhere," she told us.

Without giving it a second thought, Bethany and I waved our hands fiercely like two schoolgirls wanting the teacher to call on us.

No telling where we'd end up, but we had come for an adventure.

Fortunately, we were taken to Freeport, the part of the island we couldn't afford. We were given a room at a swanky hotel next to the casinos, much better than what we'd paid for.

It was a quick trip and we had to make the best of it. Friday was spent en route, unpacking, and drinking and gambling in the casino. We mostly watched other people gamble and took advantage of the free drinks.

Saturday morning, we rented a car to drive around the island and soak up some local color. We picked up a map, which wasn't necessary because there was only one major road.

"What's at the end of the island?" I asked the desk clerk.

"There is a nice settlement, a cay if you will, that is lovely," she answered in a British accent. "I do believe the annual conch cracking festival is commencing."

We didn't understand what she meant by a cay, but a lovely settlement with a conch cracking festival caught our attention. Yes, this sounded like a great way to soak up some local color.

Lush, tropical vegetation and vibrant flowers lined the island road. We kept the windows rolled down and breathed in the fresh island air. But the Bahamas-style driving was hazardous. I had to remember to stay on the left side of the road instead of the right side. And we were in an American-made compact designed for driving American-style.

We arrived at a big gathering of tents and tables that lined the grounds of a schoolyard.

Our attention was drawn to a tall maypole where brightly dressed schoolgirls were weaving in and out while they went around the pole. Their pigtails whipped in the air as they bobbed around.

"This isn't May," Bethany said. "So why are they dancing around a maypole?"

"I don't know. Maybe it's an island tradition."

Watching them dance as young boys cheered them on made me think of my precious Jillian and Henry. I was already homesick and missing my children.

"Get ready. The conch cracking festival is about to commence," an announcer said over the loudspeaker.

Fishermen brought in live conchs from the ocean,

and the man or woman who cracked open the most shells and removed the most meat during the allotted time would win.

Both of us had brought along our new 35mm cameras and had the straps draped round our necks. We were overdressed in our stylish tops and capris. We concluded we should have worn jeans and T-shirts.

A crowd was forming near the contest area, and we wanted to be near the front to take action photos. I was already composing a sensational travel story in my head and eager to capture the event on film.

"Excuse us, excuse us," Bethany said as we elbowed our way through the crowd. "We're reporters from *Time* magazine, so we need to be up close to take pictures."

Reporters from *Time* magazine? I didn't know what possessed Bethany to come up with that publication, but it seemed to work, as people let us through. We made our way to the front of the crowd in time for the contest to begin. With cameras ready, we were set to take some amazing photos.

The contestants cracked open the mollusk shells and pulled out the meat before throwing it into buckets.

Our "great shots" were blurred by the slime coming out of the shells. Goop was dripping off the top of our heads, slithering down our arms and legs, and covering our camera lenses. It was disgusting. I hoped it wouldn't ruin my camera or my new outfit.

We tried to move back from our front row spot, but by now there were throngs of people surrounding us, and there was no way out. We were stuck there until the contest was over. Stuck there with slime pelting us in the face. Gunk dripping through our hair. Oozing through our fingers and slithering into our sandals and through our toes. I had not seen that much ooey-gooey stuff since the movie *The Blob.*

Bethany and I looked at each other in disgust, not speaking for fear of getting a mouthful of the yucky stuff. We couldn't get out of there fast enough when the event broke up. We bought conch shells and other souvenirs before making a hasty retreat to the car.

"This was terrible," Bethany complained. "I'm going to report them to the tourism bureau."

"Why?"

She opened the car door. "Look at us. Our clothes are ruined. We'll never get this horrible stuff out of our hair."

"Remember, you were the one who falsified our credentials. Real *Time* magazine reporters would have known how to handle the situation."

She combed more gunk out of her hair while I drove. "I guess you're right."

"How did we get ourselves into this mess? I blame you."

Bethany kept combing her hair. "It will be worth it if we got some award-winning photos. If nothing else, we have a funny story to tell when we get home."

We were exhausted when we reached our hotel room. For once, I beat Bethany to the bathroom and showered first.

"I've got a great idea," Bethany said after she came out of the shower, towel-drying her hair.

I cringed, afraid to ask what she had in mind.

"Remember the waterfall at the hotel swimming pool? Let's put on our swimsuits and head over there."

"What's the plan?" I asked as I blindly followed her to the swimming pool.

"It's something I'll have to demonstrate when we get there."

A few minutes later, we were standing under the waterfall that flowed into the hotel swimming pool. Yes, there we stood, reenacting that famous scene from *South Pacific*, scrubbing our heads, and singing at the top of our lungs—"I'm gonna wash that man right outa my hair!"

The singing and scrubbing experience reminded me of the time I howled at the moon. I pictured myself washing Bruce out of my hair, along with every boyfriend, boss, or other man I wanted to forget. *Begone!*

We only knew one verse, which we sang over and over again. The women around the pool applauded us and the men gave us dirty looks.

The trip was a good attitude adjustment. It also made me realize that being a single mom to two wonderful children was all the thrill I needed. If I ever got the travel bug again, I'd take my kids.

No dancing in the aisles or partying happened on the flight home. The passengers were too pooped to party, and most dozed off. We had a different pilot on the return flight: Captain Zoom Zoom, who regaled us with some of his inane stories.

"In a few minutes, we will fly near the Bermuda Triangle. But don't worry, I've never lost a plane."

"The Bermuda Triangle? What did he say about the Bermuda Triangle?" Bethany asked as she came out of her snooze.

"He said we will fly near the Bermuda Triangle. But don't worry. He said he's never lost a plane."

"Oh criminy, I hope we don't disappear," Bethany whispered, twirling her hair. "What if we are sucked into the Bermuda Triangle and never seen again?"

As usual, Bethany's imagination got the best of her. And, for a fleeting moment, I had an unsettling flash-back to a presentation Karen Hornblower had given on her expedition to the Triangle. I remembered something about it being a time warp and something else about a cyclops. Somehow, she'd convinced me the lost conti-nent of Atlantis existed and that the Triangle disappear-ances and UFO sightings were real.

"I'm sure we must have taken the same route when we flew in and nothing happened," I assured Bethany, even though I had some doubts of my own.

"Oh, well, it probably doesn't matter," she said. "If the Bermuda Triangle doesn't get us, we'll probably die in a couple of months anyway."

"Huh?"

"You know, Y2K, the new millennium. I'm sure when the clock strikes twelve this New Year's Eve, the tech-nology apocalypse will begin, and no telling what will happen to us."

Bethany and her worst-case scenarios. I'm going to think pleasant thoughts of seeing my children in a few hours.

A few minutes later, the FASTEN SEATBELTS sign flashed as the warning alert dinged. The crew hurried to their stations and buckled up, so I figured there was some turbulence ahead.

When the plane took a sudden nosedive, Bethany and I grabbed each other's hands.

"Don't worry, Bethany, the captain said he's never lost a plane."

"Whoops, there's a first time for everything," Captain Zoom Zoom chuckled over the intercom. Seconds later, the plane pulled up and leveled off.

He may have found it funny, but it took ten years off my life.

The rest of the travelers seemed to get a kick out of it, but not Bethany.

"Not funny! I am going to report this to the pilots' association. Or whatever agency I can complain to when we get home."

She calmed down when the flight attendants served free Bahama Mama rum drinks. The rest of the trip home remained uneventful.

This adventure was fun, but it would be my last one for quite a while. Or would it?

28

The kidnappers wrapped my body in a blanket and threw me into the ocean. I couldn't move my arms or legs. All I could do was scream for help and kick my bound legs back and forth, hoping I would float to the top.

Screaming was useless underwater and resulted in me getting a mouth full of seaweed. Maybe someone would see the bubbles I was creating as I tried to yell for help.

Why would someone kidnap me? I was a middle-class, middle-aged, fifty-one-year-old working mom with two teenage children. I guessed no one would pay the ransom, so they tossed me in the treacherous ocean waters to drown.

After a lot of kicking and moving in the water, I floated to the top and screamed for help as loudly as possible. I was engulfed in total darkness.

I think I passed out for a moment and floated on the water. I awoke to a blinding light and a woman hovering over me. She wore a hospital gown, and her hair was covered with a surgical cap.

"Mrs. Jackson, are you okay?"

"Oh thank goodness, I've been rescued," I answered.

Although my body was still wrapped in a blanket, I was glad to be alive and out of the ocean.

"You must have fallen asleep and had a bad dream," she whispered. "You've still got five minutes to go. Do you want me to turn the light back off?"

My eyes began focusing and my brain fog was lifting. I read the embroidery on her surgical gown: SERENITY SPA AND SALON. Oh, she was Joy, the aesthetician who had brought me anything but joy when she exfoliated my skin, plastered me with seaweed, and wrapped me in plastic.

The next five minutes seemed like five hours, but I would not let myself doze off again. I laid there like a mummy—a dummy mummy.

Joy took about ten minutes to unwrap the plastic and wash off the seaweed. Next, she lathered me in lotion. That part was heavenly and made the experience worthwhile.

Why did I let Gina talk me into this?

"It will be good for you," she'd said. "It's done wonders for me, ridding my body of toxins. I promise you'll feel much better, and it will do wonders for your skin."

The only wonders it did were for the Serenity bandits, who relieved me of a big wad of money.

Compared to what Sylvia talked me into a week later, the seaweed wrap was a walk in the park. *Of course, when I walk in a park, I trip, fall, and have other mishaps.*

Sylvia was getting "treatments" and taking classes from André, a "holistic medicine practitioner." She was convinced he was turning her into the healthiest person on the planet. She took yoga at André's studio and followed a macrobiotic diet. So, I had one friend who was getting wrapped in seaweed and another who was eating it.

I knew yoga would be good for me, so Sylvia didn't have to twist my arm to get me to take André's class. It was something we could do together, and we could go straight from work to his studio.

André was a nicely built Frenchman who was about five-seven. He had a neatly trimmed, dark beard that bordered his boyish face, and he always dressed in karate-looking garb. We wondered why he didn't wear yoga pants.

"Maybe he doesn't want to show his bulges," Sylvia giggled.

"Hey, we're supposed to be cleansing our minds, not dirtying them."

André had a charming accent, and I loved how he bowed and said "namaste" at the end of the class. It was easy to be sucked into some of the packages his center provided. For all we knew, he may have been a snake oil salesman from Poughkeepsie with a fake accent. Since he was a good yoga instructor, we saw no need to question his qualifications.

Sylvia immersed herself in the services at André's center. There was one she insisted I try.

"It will be good for you," she said.

Where had I heard that before?

I couldn't believe I let her talk me into getting a colonic. Yes, I paid someone a lot of money to give me a giant enema.

Between the seaweed wrap and the colonic, I was sure there wasn't a single toxin left in my body. And heaven help the person who tried to tell me I was full of crap. I didn't have any of that left in me either.

Namaste, my ass!

* * *

Ring! Ring! Ring! The sound of the doorbell sent me into full panic mode. Too late to change outfits for the third time, and my hair was beyond hope. A bun on the top would have to do. Age fifty-three and my first date as a divorced woman. I had the jitters—my mind was racing, I was on edge, and my hands shook so much I could barely apply makeup.

Bethany's third marriage had ended after ten tumultuous months. Mr. Moneybags wasn't as rich as he purported, and six months into their marriage, his house of cards came tumbling down. The foreclosure on their pricey home was part of the rubble. Luckily, she'd held onto her second home as an investment and moved back in when the renter's one-year lease was up.

After a couple of months of regrouping, Bethany was on the prowl for her next victim. She included me in the hunt and had lined me up to go clubbing with her latest flame's brother. I'm sure my jaw dropped when I opened the door. There stood Kyle, an attractive young man who looked about twenty years younger than me and could have easily been my son. Apparently, Bethany did a great job of lying about her age—and mine.

The strobe lights in the nightclub gave me a nasty headache. The music was too loud, the drinks were too strong, and the smell of cigarettes triggered a coughing fit. I was too old for this scene.

Kyle was a smooth talker, and after a couple of drinks and a few dances, he fed me the most ridiculous line I had ever heard.

"Jackie, you're the kind of woman I'd like to take home to meet my mother."

I looked at him somewhat tenderly and said, "Son, I'm old enough to be your mother."

And that was the end of my clubbing with Kyle.

Between work and taking an active part in my children's lives, dating hadn't been a consideration. But when the kids got older and were off at college, I became a little lonely. The travel club had gone out of business, and my opportunities for meeting men were limited. So, I allowed my friends to fix me up.

After Paula divorced, she joined a wine club and invited me to one of the tastings. We met two nice, clean-cut men who asked us out on a double date. They fancied themselves as wine aficionados, and all they talked about was wine and their trips to Napa Valley. I didn't like wine. It gave me a headache. But I was forced to drink it because these grape geeks kept ordering it.

At least the wine dulled my senses enough to tolerate my date, who had as much personality as a crate full of wine corks. Actually, a crate of wine corks would have more personality.

At the end of the evening, he asked me to join him the following weekend for a wine tasting party. I politely said I had plans with my children. That was the last I saw of him.

Then there were Sylvia and Harvey's endless attempts at introducing me to Harvey's CPA friends.

Because Harvey proved to be a good match for Sylvia, it seemed logical that he would have a friend who would be a good match for me. Or so I thought. His friends were nice enough, but they might as well have had NERD tattooed on their foreheads. None of them liked to fish, watch sports, or dance. Just not my type. And I was still asking myself, "What *is* my type?"

Finally, someone dateable came along. His name was Gregory, and I met him at one of the builders' association's premeeting mixers. I looked forward to the meetings and my visits with him. He managed a supply company, looked nice, and didn't wear a wedding ring. He was about five-ten—a good height for me—and had a full head of thick brown hair. His nice tan led me to believe he enjoyed the outdoors. His best feature was his fun sense of humor. I was rusty at flirting but did my best to hint that I was available.

It took three months of mixers before Gregory made a move. He asked me if I was available that Saturday night. Of course, I eagerly said yes. He got my address and phone number and told me he would pick me up around six so we could dine out first.

"I hope you like opera," he said with a smile. I thought the comment was part of his fun sense of humor.

"Sure, I love opera," I said halfheartedly.

"We'll be seeing *La Bohème*. It's one of my favorites. Have you ever seen it performed?"

"No, I haven't."

"Then you're in for a remarkable experience."

Yikes. He was serious. And now I was trapped into going to an opera.

He took me to the opera on our first date. And we

went to the opera on our second date. There was no third date.

Gina talked me into trying online dating. I met two pleasant, intelligent, professional men. But both were desperately seeking their next wife—desperately seeking a woman to take care of them. Taking care of a man was the last thing I was desperately seeking. I was beginning to understand what my mom had meant when I'd asked her if she thought about remarrying.

She'd said, "I don't want to ever pick up another pair of men's dirty underwear or socks. I have enough trouble picking up after myself."

Next, there was Terrance, the suave, well-groomed artist I met at church. The relationship got off to a good start until our fourth date when he began coming on strong. His sweet words and affection had flattered me, but I feared our relationship was moving way too quickly. He also kept hinting he would like for me to help him promote his art shows. I pretended not to take the hints.

"You appear to have an exceptionally busy life," Terrance said one night after an art show. "I think you need a househusband."

I threw my head back. "A househusband?"

"Yes, someone like me. I will stay home all day and paint, do some house chores, have dinner ready when you get home. Meanwhile, you can enjoy your career."

In other words, I would support him while he played the starving artist role. He was handsome, but not *that* handsome. So long, farewell.

Next came nice-looking Noah, whom I met at an after-church luncheon. He was about five-eleven, had a medium complexion, and a fine-looking head of jet-black hair that was shoulder-length and disheveled. His beard was scruffy, too, but he pulled off the unkempt look in a sexy way. A *very* sexy way. He had the all-American-badass look going for him. I had to introduce myself.

Imagine my surprise when he spoke with a sort-of-British accent. No, he wasn't an American; he was a South African.

We seemed to hit it off and agreed to sit with each other at a church concert taking place that Wednesday. Sylvia and Harvey sat with us—safety in numbers. Afterward, our foursome went out for drinks and had a delightful evening. Finally, I was getting somewhere.

"He seems to be taken with you," Sylvia said the next day at work. "Go for it, gal. He's the whole package."

"Seems like," I said as I turned on my computer.

"He's yummy, has great manners, and goes to our church. And did you notice that Rolex watch? What more could you ask for?"

"For all we know, he's an ax murderer who hangs out at churches to pick his prey."

Sylvia shook her head. "I don't get that vibe from him. He seems sincere."

"Hmm," I said, "a sincere ax murderer."

After attending two more church functions together, Noah took me on a real Saturday night date—dinner and the movies. I gawked when I opened my front door and saw him standing there in jeans, a long-sleeved white western shirt with pearl snap buttons, and a fancy gold-and-silver belt buckle. I hadn't seen him dressed that casually before, and it was a good look on him. The man would have looked good in a tow sack.

He gawked back at me with his sweet, seductive smile. "Look at us. We are twins."

It took me a moment to realize he meant our attire—me in a white ruffled blouse and denim skirt, him in a white shirt and jeans. A "we belong together" sensation crept through me. Yes, I could envision myself with this hunk of a man for a long time to come.

"You are stunning in that frilly blouse," he said in his charming accent. "Is frilly the correct word?"

"Oh, thank you," I gushed. "Frilly is good. And you are handsome in your western attire."

"When in Texas, dress like Texans," he said. *Why do these stereotypes haunt us?*

I stepped out of the front door with my purse and keys in hand and quickly locked the front door behind me. He wasn't holding an ax, but I didn't want to take any chances. "I'm ready to go."

As we walked down the sidewalk, I saw a bright red sports car in the driveway, unlike the sedan he had previously driven. "Is that a new car?"

"A new lease vehicle. I wanted something sportier than the automobile I had."

"What make is it?"

"It is a 2004 Corvette," he answered, opening the car door for me.

And now came the fun—getting into a sports car with a skirt on. *Why didn't I wear slacks?*

The date went smoothly, although I kept looking at him and wondering why some woman hadn't snatched him up. He had previously told me he married in his twenties, but it didn't work out. After his divorce, he said he became wed to his work in his family's jewelry business. Still mistrustful, I wondered if that was code for working in the blood diamond industry.

He kissed me on the cheek like a perfect gentleman when he walked me to my door. He seemed too good to be true, and men my age rarely wanted a woman my age. I was smitten, but still not smitten enough to invite him in.

"I enjoyed this pleasant evening," he said after the gentle peck on my cheek.

Yes, it was a pleasant May evening, despite the usual Houston humidity. But I understood he meant the date. My fifty-four-year-old body quivered like it was a December cold spell, but my insides were boiling over as I looked at Noah's handsome face.

"Let us do this again next weekend," he said.

"Would love to, but my daughter is graduating from college next Saturday and—" I stopped for a second. I should have taken more seconds before opening my big mouth. "We're having a party for her after the ceremony. I would love it if you could come."

A gentle grin sprawled across his face. "That sounds lovely."

"Come in, and I'll give you an invitation with a map on it." I unlocked my front door.

Oh no. I had invited in a potential killer into my house. He didn't have an ax on him, so maybe he would strangle me with his fancy western belt. Those were fleeting thoughts because my brain was wrapped around my real motive for inviting him.

Bruce and Beverly's eight-year marriage had ended four months prior, and Bruce would be coming to the party solo. My petty ego wanted to flaunt a handsome man in his face. I also relished the opportunity to dangle

Noah in front of friends and family and show that I might have gotten older, but I was still desirable!

As soon as I had handed Noah the invitation, it occurred to me I would also be parading him in front of Frank and Barbara. They were in their mideighties and hadn't been getting around very well. Barbara had grown frail and needed a wheelchair. She had told me the previous month that she hoped Bruce and I would reconcile, and I knew it would disappoint her to see me with another man.

Maybe I can wiggle my way out of this before it's too late. "As you can see by the map, it's being held in Clear Lake, so I'll understand if you don't want to drive that far."

He shrugged his shoulders. "It is not that far. I so genuinely appreciate your invitation."

His accent and charm made my heart flutter. I justified that I was inviting him because I wanted to be with him and introduce him to my family, not show him off.

He closely read the invitation. "Casual, and begins at five thirty. Sounds lovely."

"Well, I guess I'll be seeing you next Saturday," I said. "Or maybe at church tomorrow."

"Would you care to have lunch with me after church?" he asked.

"I would love that." I was in a swoon while we walked to the door. My eyelashes were fluttering as much as my heart.

As soon as he departed, my inner voice screamed at me.

Jackie, what the hell are you thinking? Bruce is at a low point in his life and kind enough to pay for half of Jillian's party. This is no time to be childish and spiteful. Plus, it's your daughter's big day. And you want to stir up the family pot by inviting this stranger to an intimate gathering?

Too late. I had already screwed up. Hopefully, Noah would decide not to come, or I could rescind the invitation. Yes, I would uninvite him.

As we ate lunch after church on Sunday, I looked for a graceful way to retract the invitation. However, I feared I might hurt his feelings and left the invitation open.

The big day arrived, and Noah still planned to attend. I made life easy on myself and had booked the party at an event center that took care of all the decorations and catering. My biggest task—show up looking glamorous and ten years younger.

I was such a proud momma at Jillian's graduation that afternoon. Her love of fishing with her dad had led to a love of the ocean waters and a degree in marine biology from Texas A&M Galveston. Her boyfriend had graduated the previous semester with the same degree and had a job with the state's parks and wildlife division. She had also applied with the state and would soon learn if they hired her.

"I think we might have to plan a wedding pretty soon," Bruce said while we were sitting in the auditorium waiting for Jillian's name to be called.

"Why? Do you know something I don't?"

"Just a hunch."

Bruce was being unusually congenial, causing me to feel more guilty for inviting Noah to the party. I had no desire for a reconciliation with Bruce, but I needed to be civil and understanding. After all, he was the father of my children, and I would need him to help me pay for Henry's graduation party in a couple of years. Not to mention a wedding, if that were to happen!

Two hours later, we were gathered for Jillian's party. I secretly hoped Noah wouldn't show up, but he did. All eyes turned to him when he walked through the door.

I rushed to welcome him. "So glad you could come." I gave him the once-over. "You are very dashing in that sports coat and—" I paused. "Your hair, you cut it."

He grinned. "I wanted to make a good impression on your family."

Oh heavens, this gorgeous man really wants me. He even shaved. I had loved his disheveled-bad-boy look, but he was even more handsome with short hair and a clean-shaven face.

Meanwhile, Henry was doing an excellent job of playing host, allowing me to turn my attention to Noah.

Barbara's face tightened when I introduced her to Noah. It was the face she made when she was disappointed, adding to my guilt.

Bethany acted way too happy to meet him. She slithered up to him like a giant boa constrictor ready to squeeze its prey and held her hand out. "Hi, I'm Bethany, the best friend," she said in a flirty voice, tossing her hair over her shoulder.

Noah grasped her hand. "Such a divine pleasure to make your acquaintance," he responded in his alluring voice.

Bethany turned to me. "Where have you been hiding this hunky man?"

Henry saved me from the embarrassing situation when he announced the dinner buffet was open. Bethany followed us to the line and sat next to me as we ate.

"Details. I want details," she whispered. "And if you don't want him, I'll take him."

I shushed her. "We'll talk later."

"You have a beautiful family," Noah said to me as we ate our seafood meal. "I so appreciate you inviting me. It makes me feel special."

I felt my face lighting up. "You are special."

"I would very much like to stay longer, but I don't want to impose on your family gathering and take you away from your obligations. Would it offend you if I left early?"

What a relief! "You aren't imposing, but I'm sure it is a little uncomfortable being around all these strangers. I understand."

"Will I see you at church tomorrow?" he asked.

I nodded. "Certainly."

"Would you care to join me for lunch afterward?" His voice was intoxicating.

"I would love that."

"Very well." He grabbed my hand and kissed it.

I hoped Bruce was watching. He had never kissed my hand.

My inner voice yelled at me. *Jackie, this is no time to be spiteful. Show some class and act your age!*

Noah's impeccable manners were on full display as he said goodbye to Jillian and other guests.

"It was such a divine pleasure to meet you," he told Jillian. "Your beauty is much like that of your mother's. I wish you well in the new phase of your life."

We both gushed like giddy schoolgirls. Jillian was warming up to him, which was good because earlier she had criticized me for inviting him. I knew she had her heart set on getting Bruce and me back together, but I told her it wasn't meant to be.

With Noah gone, I headed to Frank and Barbara. She seemed so fragile sitting in her wheelchair.

"So, tell me about Noah," she said. "Is it serious?"

"Oh, heavens no. We are just good church friends."

"So, why did you invite him? Must be serious."

Barbara had me cornered, and there was no graceful way out. Fortunately, Bruce's brother Bryan interrupted our conversation. With Frank and Barbara no longer able to drive, he had become their chauffeur.

By the time I got home that night, I was exhausted. How would I get up in time for church the next morning? But the thought of having lunch with Noah became a motivating factor.

We sat together at church and later lunched at an exquisite eatery—he knew how to spend money. We sat in a quiet booth in the back corner and were enjoying a friendly conversation. Then he grew quiet and tenderly looked at me. "May I have your hand?" he asked, reaching across the table.

Right hand or left hand? Jackie, it doesn't matter, just stick out a hand.

He clasped my hand. "I have no family left in South Africa and I immensely love your country," he said with his sensuous accent. "I am giving consideration to selling my Cape Town properties and remaining in America."

I smiled, excited that he would be staying around for a while. "That's wonderful."

"I'm very rich," he said, as if I hadn't already guessed from his fancy sports car, Rolex, and lack of a job. "I would like to make a proposal to you?"

Huh? Did we have a language barrier? Maybe he meant proposition.

"I will give you twenty thousand dollars if you will marry me so that I can stay in your beautiful country."

My shoulders flinched and my head reared back. I moved my hand away and shifted into my what-the-heck look.

"It appears that I have offended you," he said softly. "This is merely a business arrangement so I can stay in America."

"I'm shocked *and* offended."

He leaned forward. "Then I will give you forty thousand dollars to marry me."

There were no words. I rolled my eyes and shook my head.

"Do not worry. This will be strictly business, and no sex will be expected. I am gay."

And with that, I picked up my purse and headed for the exit. *If anyone asks what happened to Noah, I'll tell them the truth—he wanted to get married and I didn't.*

No more dating men from church!

Meanwhile, Bethany had joined the Martini Magnates, a group of professionals that met for happy hour at various clubs. She was partying and dating regularly and kept pushing me to "get with the program." I attended two events but didn't find the social scene as satisfying as she did. Nor did I understand how she could be involved in two or three relationships at a time. She said she had finally found the key to a successful relationship.

"Just find someone you can tolerate."

Merely enduring someone didn't seem like a good

foundation for a relationship. I still hadn't found someone I could tolerate for very long.

At my age, I wasn't looking for a hot romance, and I didn't need a man to complete my life. My wonderful friends were the best company for dinner and movies. I was an independent woman who was capable of taking care of herself. Car trouble? Call AAA. House repairs? I had mastered unclogging toilets and fixing leaky faucets and was good with a hammer.

As my coworker Marjorie put it, who needs a man when you own *The Practical Handyman's Encyclopedia?*

One marriage was enough for me.

* * *

After Bruce's divorce, our kids did their best to get us back together. For their sake, we decided to be civil and friendly at family events. Between work, my children's lives, and fun with friends, I had plenty of things to keep me busy.

Jillian married a year after she graduated from college. Henry received his business degree the following year and got engaged three months later. The next year, Jillian gave birth to the most precious boy ever born, at least in my grandmother eyes.

Henry became an account manager for a banking firm and married an adorable elementary school teacher. She was perfect for him—intelligent, considerate, and fun-loving. When they had first started dating, I'd given him "the talk." The one about the importance of being romantic. Knowing my sweet Henry, it would have come naturally to him anyway.

Jillian gave birth to another son six months after

Henry's wedding. Wedding showers, baby showers, and other family celebrations kept me occupied for a few years.

The good times were mixed with some difficult ones. Barbara developed pneumonia and passed away in 2009. Six months later, Frank died, mostly of a broken heart because he was lost without Barbara. I was glad they lived long enough to see Bruce and me being friends. Barbara had always been hopeful we would get back together and remarry.

The years flew by. Henry's wife gave birth to a boy and a girl, giving me four grandchildren to dote on. Our college gang enjoyed cruising the Caribbean out of Galveston, and Bethany and I took a few short road trips around Texas. I was always busy!

Before I knew it, I was old enough for Medicare. My next adventure in life—retirement!

29

New Year's Day 2019 seemed like the perfect time to restart our lives. Bruce and I were married in a small home wedding attended by family and close friends. It rained right before the wedding, and I wondered if it was a sign that I was doing the wrong thing.

The rain was followed by the most beautiful rainbow I had ever seen. When I stepped outside to gaze at the magnificent colors that arched across the sky, I found a shiny penny sparkling in the driveway. It was as if the universe and my special angel Angela were telling me I was making the right decision.

Sylvia had been ordained online so she could officiate. She wanted to use contemporary vows and was trying to keep me from saying the "obeying" part. I just needed the basics to be there. I needed to hear myself say those important words:

to have and to hold from this day forward, for better, for worse, for richer, for poorer, in sickness and in health, to love and to cherish, till death do us part.

Our revived relationship wasn't romantic. It was a deep friendship between two people who had a history together, both good and bad. Two people who also shared two fantastic children.

I had great respect and appreciation for Bruce as a father, grandfather, businessman, and friend. Being grandparents created a bond that was far stronger than the one we'd had as parents. Instead of arguing about how to raise our children, we were busy spoiling our grandchildren.

* * *

Over the years, Bruce had expanded his automotive repair business. In 2017, Bruce enticed Henry to work for him as vice president of the company. Henry didn't share his dad's love of cars, but he relished the business aspect. As his dad, Bruce had an ulterior motive: He hoped Henry would take over the business when he retired. I joined them part-time to handle the marketing.

It made me happy to watch them working together. After our divorce, Henry had shown his true colors as a momma's boy and preferred being with me over Bruce. I was glad they eventually connected and found some common interests.

Henry kept busy the first year by computerizing the business and bringing the place into the twenty-first century. The business was expanding, thanks to my marketing efforts, and I enjoyed working with my son. It also made Bruce happy to have us there.

With Henry running the place, Bruce and I would sneak off for a few hours at a time. We began doing that two months before we remarried.

Henry never questioned our regular departures. He grinned at us like we were a couple of young lovers who wanted to sneak off for some alone time. We laughed that our son probably thought we were off for a "nooner." Ha! At our age, a nooner was more like lunch and a nap.

On the outside, we were happy, but on the inside, we were hiding a sad secret. Our frequent getaways were to see lawyers and doctors. Bruce had lung cancer. He became a smoker when he served in Vietnam and didn't quit till his midtwenties.

As we were leaving Jillian's house one Sunday several weeks earlier, Bruce had asked to follow me home. He had some important business to discuss with me in private.

Bruce had grasped for words as he tried to tell me what was going on in his life. I later learned Jimmy had convinced him to tell me about his cancer diagnosis.

A big "hunting trip" a few months back had been a cover story for Bruce's surgery and the beginning of his cancer treatment. I thought he should be up front with the kids, but he didn't want to worry them until it was absolutely necessary. He kept apologizing to me for putting the burden on my shoulders.

"That's what friends are for," I said.

I hated lying to our children; still, I had to respect Bruce's wishes. Surgery couldn't get all the cancer, so he was hoping treatments would buy him more time. We were fortunate to be living near one of the nation's top cancer centers, and there were new options to consider.

Bruce wanted me to have power of attorney for him, and he informed me I was still listed as his executor on his will, even after our divorce.

"I realize I'm asking a lot, but I think of you as my most trusted friend. I know you will make all the right decisions for our children."

It was stressful going over the drafts of the legal work his lawyer had drawn up, especially when I got to the medical power of attorney. I pictured myself rushing to the hospital with Bruce. The nurse would ask, "Are you family?"

I would reply, "No, but I have his medical power of attorney."

Then she would say, "I need to see it."

And I would say, "I don't have it with me. It's at home."

To which she would reply, "Well, too bad, I can't let you in his room." By the time I got back to the hospital, Bruce would probably be dead.

There had to be a better alternative. And there was: marriage. This time, I proposed to Bruce.

"This would be much easier if we were married," I told him. "So, wanna get married?"

My proposal to him was as unromantic as his proposal to me many years back on his boat.

"Appreciate the offer," he said. "Don't want to marry you and make you a widow a few months later."

"What's the worst thing that could happen?" I asked. "Oh yes, you might get cured and be stuck with me for the rest of your life."

Bruce smiled. "There are a lot worse things than spending the rest of my life with you. Okay, let's get married."

I tried to keep him motivated and hoped for a miraculous cure or at least a treatment that would extend his life.

We announced our engagement at Christmas, which was the best present we could give our children. We had gotten our marriage license a few days ahead of the holidays and planned to marry on New Year's Day.

Our friends and family were elated for us, and our kids were particularly ecstatic. Then there was Bethany. She wasn't the least bit thrilled about my pending nuptials. She thought it was too sudden and that I hadn't thought things through.

I had thought it through. This time I was going into marriage with my eyes wide open. I cared deeply for Bruce. He was the father of my children and had become my best friend. I just wasn't in love with him. I was approaching seventy and still wasn't sure what it meant to truly be in love with someone. But the special sparkle I had always wanted to have for a man wasn't there with Bruce.

But this time it didn't matter. I was too old to howl at the moon, both literally and figuratively. Or be exasperated by blind dates. Or go on madcap adventures. I was content with my decision to marry him.

Our world seemed perfect. Bruce treated me like a queen, and I couldn't do enough for him. His burr became so thin, he went for the shaved Telly Savalas–Bruce Willis look. It wasn't difficult to adjust to his lack of hair. He'd never had much anyway. His beer gut was gone, and he was losing weight. He joked that eating my cooking and giving up beer was causing him to slim down.

I wasn't going to give up on Bruce. I researched

available cancer treatments as well as alternative medicines. However, his medical treatments were taking their toll and he was often too tired to go to work. The time had come to tell our children.

First, we told Henry. We waited until the end of the workday one Friday. After the doors were locked, Bruce asked Henry to visit with us in the customer waiting lounge before he left. The devastated look on Henry's face was heartbreaking when Bruce told him of the diagnosis.

"I like my doctor's attitude," Bruce told him. "He says I'm not dying from cancer. I'm living with it. We'll get through this together, but I'll need help."

"Tell me what you need from me," Henry said, standing from his chair.

"Well, you'd better sit back down," Bruce said. "I need for you to take over the business for a while."

Henry remained standing. "I'll do my best, Dad."

"We'll talk more about this next week," Bruce said. "The business is yours if you want it, and if not, we can sell it."

When Henry came to work on Monday, he had his answer. "Dad, I'm up for the job. I wish I knew as much as you do about cars, but I know how to run a business."

We had nine good months together as a family before Bruce's health declined. When the cancer started to spread, it moved quickly. I rarely left his side and set up hospice care in our home. Our master bedroom became a hospital room, with him in his medical bed and me sleeping in a bed next to him.

I had been down this dreadful road with my mother, and it was heartbreaking for me and the kids to see Bruce withering away. When the hospice nurse was on duty, I would go into the guest room, shut myself up in the closet, curl up on the floor like a child, and cry. Despite the morphine, he was in pain.

I regretted the years we were apart and blamed myself for the failure of our marriage. I temporarily forgot how unhappy I was when we divorced and that he had cheated on me. All I remembered were the good times, as though we never had those many tough times.

I had never spoken to Bruce about my Rick experience or my beliefs about angels or life after death. As he lay there semiconscious, I talked to him about it. I was unsure if he heard me or comprehended what I was saying. I prayed that my words would be of comfort. I also prayed that Rick or some other guardian angel would be there to help him cross over.

The end came much too quickly. Bruce died on the third of November, a week shy of his birthday. He would have turned seventy-two.

Facing Thanksgiving and Christmas without Bruce was tough. I operated on autopilot until the day after Christmas. Then I decided it was okay to cry, curse, throw things, be self-indulgent, or do whatever it took to relieve the stress of the past few months.

Whatever it took—even if that meant eating a liquored-up fruitcake, running away from home, and being detained by the police. Yes, the Lord does work in mysterious ways. My New Year's Eve misadventure did the trick. And having lunch with Bethany on New Year's Day also helped pull me out of my doldrums. I was beginning to feel like myself again.

30

*C*rack! *Crash! Kaboom!*

The resounding clangs of lightning and thunder wake me from a deep sleep. I sit up in my recliner and take a few moments to focus. The sky sounds like the sonic booms of dozens of jets flying overhead and breaking the sound barrier. The house shakes. So do I as I pull my blanket around my shoulders.

I have no idea what day it is or how long I've been asleep. The illuminated clock on the cable box reads 8:12. The drapes are closed, and the den is dark. Is it night, or is the blackness caused by the storm? A shred of light peeks through the small opening in the drapes as a bolt of lightning strikes nearby.

The sky hushes after a few minutes. Then the pouring rain begins to pound the ground. I open the drapes and see the faintness of daylight. Morning has come. Time to get up and greet the day. The den remains cluttered with photo albums and memorabilia. A chill goes down my spine, and for an instant, I think I see Rick and Angela sitting on the sofa. Did they visit me earlier, or was it a dream? I blink. When I open my eyes, they are gone.

The startling sound of the phone ringing jolts me. It's Jillian asking how I am doing.

"I'm okay. I got a good night's sleep, or maybe two. What day is this?"

"It's January 2. How long have you been asleep?"

I'm relieved I hadn't been in a coma for several days —just one night of exceptionally sound sleep. By the time we get off the phone, the rain is slowing and the sky is clearing.

Obviously, I've spent the past umpteen hours reliving my life. My trip down memory lane was like watching a TV marathon of *This Is Your Life, Jackie Jackson*. My mouth is as dry as cotton, although there are empty soda cans and water glasses on the end table. I must have talked to myself all night. Or maybe I was visiting with Rick and Angela, and my not-so-imaginary friend George.

My back hurts from sitting in that darn chair for so long. Yet despite the discomfort, I am at peace for the first time in months. Reliving my past reminds me of what a fantastic life I have, and I am grateful for each experience, good and not-so-good.

Should I go back to sleep or make a strong cup of coffee and try to stay awake? The coffee wins out, and I savor the aroma and taste of my heaven in a cup.

The back patio beckons me to enjoy the slowing rain. My backyard and rose-filled garden used to bring me lots of comfort. Now the plants are dying from lack of care.

Looking at my rose bushes triggers a memory from

last night. Yes, Angela did visit. I clearly remember the conversation.

"Even a rose has thorns," she said as we discussed recent life events. Maybe I dreamed she said it, or maybe I heard the expression elsewhere. But I'm convinced she visited me last night.

I smile, although there is nothing cheerful about my neglected garden. I doubt I will ever have the energy or desire to replant it. Hopefully, the rain will revive it.

I close my eyes and remember what my backyard used to look like. Then I imagine Grandpa Will's beautiful garden and how it was where he talked to God. I hold the beautiful memory of his garden in my mind as I breathe in the glorious smell of the morning rain. Remembering a particular family photograph taken in his garden gives me such a warm, uplifting sensation.

A few months ago, a speaker at church encouraged us to hold special photographs in our mind. He said to visualize these picture memories because fires, floods, and other catastrophes can destroy the print. But if you can see that picture in your mind, you will be able to hold on to that memory forever.

The rain slows to a light drizzle. I wish it wouldn't stop because it is so soothing. There's something about rain that seems to cleanse the soul and heal the heart. I can feel my heart beginning to mend.

Here I am in my senior years and finally becoming a grown-up. I wasted too much of my life seeking perfection, or at least my definition of perfection. I've decided it is okay to be imperfect because we live in an imperfect world. Sylvia often reminds me that God loves us the way we are. His love is unconditional, and he never stops loving us while we're on our journey to goodness. We simply need to love ourselves the way we are.

Although my life didn't turn out the way I often wanted it to, it turned out the way it was supposed to. Maybe everything does happen for a reason, and maybe God does know what's best for us.

There's no proof I have a guardian angel or that Angela sends me pennies from heaven. It's more rational to think people accidentally drop pennies all the time. Most are old and dull and hard to see, so I only notice the shiny new ones. But I'm happy to go on believing they are pennies sent from heaven and dropped by a special angel.

I quit questioning God's existence a long time ago. One's faith doesn't need scientific proof. Sensing his presence brings joy to my heart, and that's what counts. I also believe God lives within us.

At long last, I'm comfortable with the person I have become, and I'm content with my life. Bruce and I had some months of happiness and the closure we both needed. Still, I realize deep down, if he had miraculously recovered, it wouldn't have been long before we were getting on each other's nerves. I had no illusions of a happily ever after when we remarried.

As the sky clears, I see the makings of a rainbow. It's hard to see rainbows when you live in the city, so a mere glimpse of one is exciting. This one doesn't compare to the amazing colors that filled the sky when Bruce and I remarried, but it is still a rainbow. And to me, it symbolizes a promise of hope and good things to come. It's a new year, a new day, and many happy tomorrows are coming my way.

I walk inside and begin putting away the photo

albums. I open Jillian's wedding book and remember her walking into the den on her big day, hairbrush in hand.

"Mom, will you brush my hair and help me put it up?" she'd asked.

"Sure," I answered as she took her usual seat at the dining table. I tried to quiet my sniffles and stopped to wipe my nose on the back of my hand.

"Mom, are you crying?

"No, it's just allergies," I answered. "Okay, so I'm a proud momma today. I'll get the crying out of the way before the wedding."

A few minutes are spent thumbing through my travels-with-Bethany album. We had some fun adventures, and I'm sure there will be a few more to come.

A stack of sympathy cards seems to beckon me to read them. There is one envelope I am reluctant to open. It's from John, my college heartbreak. Donna updates me on him from time to time, so I know he quit living with the ex-wife years ago when his son entered high school. He never remarried, and, as far as Donna knows, he doesn't date much.

Donna's husband, Max, had a heart attack and passed away two weeks after Bruce died. Several of our college friends attended the reception following the burial, including John. It was hard to avoid him. As we were exchanging brief pleasantries, Susanna walked up and gave me a big hug.

"This must be so hard on you, so soon after losing Bruce." She turned to John and said, "Did you know Jackie recently lost her husband?"

She couldn't have been more obvious.

"No. I'm so sorry to hear that," he said.

A little pitter-patter started up in my heart—not

acceptable behavior for a grieving widow. All it took was one look into his sweet puppy-dog eyes, and I was suddenly back on campus and ready to pounce on him. It was time for me to graciously leave before embarrassing myself.

I shake my head, scattering the memories. Too much water under that bridge. Or maybe it's a bridge I need to cross again. Tomorrow is a better day to open his card. Maybe I'll call him after a customary time of mourning.

As I clear the coffee table, my notebook from the Learning to Live through God seminar falls out of one of the scrapbooks. I grin as I read the convoluted epitaph I wrote while sleep-deprived, and then the one I modified a week later. Maybe it's time for another revision.

She wasn't perfect, but she did her best as she howled at the moon with toilet paper flying out her britches.
She was just Jackie.

THE END

GINA'S RUM AND BRANDY FRUITCAKE

PRE-PREP: Chop fruit, place in a container, and pour dark rum over it (use spiced rum for more flavor). Cover and store in the refrigerator at least one day in advance. The longer, the better!

Ingredients

- 1 box spice cake mix
- 1 small package instant lemon pudding mix
- 1/4 cup apricot brandy
- 2/3 cup apricot nectar
- 1/2 cup vegetable oil
- 4 large eggs
- 1/2 cup coarsely chopped candied red cherries
- 1/2 cup coarsely chopped candied green cherries
- 1 cup coarsely chopped dried pineapple, dates, or cranberries (pineapples add color)
- 1 cup coarsely chopped pecans or walnuts

Instructions

1. Combine cake mix, pudding mix, apricot brandy, apricot nectar, and vegetable oil in a large bowl. Beat on medium speed until batter is smooth. Add one egg at a time and beat after each addition. Drain excess rum from chopped fruit and fold in (the fruit, not the rum). Fold in nuts.

2. Generously coat a loaf pan* with baking spray with flour. (*Depending on size of the loaf pan, you might have enough batter for two cakes or one cake and a mini cake. Refer to baking time on cake mix box to estimate cooking time for smaller cakes)

3. Pour in batter.

4. Bake at 350°F for 50 to 55 minutes, or until cake tests done. (*If you screw up and add too much brandy or forget to drain the rum from the soaked fruit, it may take longer to bake. This has been known to happen.*)

5. Cool for 15 minutes in the pan, then remove it to a rack.

While cake is still a little warm, brush or spoon it with brandy. How much brandy to use depends on your taste and how much brandy you have left after sampling it.

Fruit cake tastes best when wrapped and stored in the refrigerator for at least 24 hours. The longer it's stored, the better it will taste.

WARNING: DON'T BAKE AND DRIVE

ACKNOWLEDGMENTS

Thank you to my friends and family who, for many years, kept encouraging me to write a book. Sorry it took so long, but I finally did it.

Connie Fennel Lewis, you were my first writing partner back in the sixth grade. We were high school journalism buddies and worked side by side our freshman year in college to edit the institution's publications. As adults, we fulfilled our childhood writing dreams as feature writers, journalists, and editors. Thank you, Connie, for your friendship and support throughout the grueling process of writing this book. I sincerely appreciate the hours you spent reviewing differing versions of my manuscript and the feedback you provided. There were times I wanted to give up, but your encouragement kept me going.

Jacqueline Carmichael, you are such an inspiration and a dear friend. If not for you, I may have never started writing this novel. You motivated me from the first draft through the finished manuscript and continue to support me.

My first few drafts were a mess. Then I discovered Richelle Braswell of RBCE—book editor extraordinaire! Richelle, you are marvelous to work with and I learned so much from you. I couldn't have hoped for a better book editor.

My sincerest appreciation to the focus group

members who read various drafts of the manuscript and provided invaluable feedback. You will remain anonymous, but you know who you are.

To Chris Cox, the wonderful man who has put up with me for the past sixteen years—your patience and cheerleading got me through this writing process. Thank you for making my toes curl and for telling me when I have toilet paper flying out of my britches!

Jenny Cummings wrote her first book at age twelve. The mystery story never made it to print because she and her coauthor, a close friend, couldn't agree on whose name would appear first in the byline. It took several decades, retirement, and a pandemic before Jenny got back to writing fiction. (Her childhood coauthor remains a close friend.)

She received dozens of state and national advertising and marketing awards during her career, including a prestigious Communicator of the Year honor for her promotion of higher education. Jenny has a bachelor's in journalism from Sam Houston State University and a master's in speech communication from The University of Texas–Pan American (now UT Rio Grande Valley). She lives in South Texas.

www.ingramcontent.com/pod-product-compliance
Lightning Source LLC
Chambersburg PA
CBHW060339310726
48976CB00003B/650